PATCHWORK

D0808451

CAROLYN BANKS

AVON
PUBLISHERS OF BARD, CAMELOT, DISCUS AND FLARE BOOKS

This is a work of fiction. The characters, incidents, and dialogues are products of the author's imagination and are not to be construed as real. Any resemblance to actual events or persons, living or dead, is entirely coincidental.

AVON BOOKS
A division of
The Hearst Corporation
1790 Broadway
New York, New York 10019

The Crown edition contains the following Library of Congress Cataloging in Publication Data:

Banks, Carolyn.
  Patchwork.

  I. Title.
PS3552.A485P3   1986   813'.54   85-28807

First Avon Printing: May 1987

This novel is dedicated to

my husband,

Robert R. Rafferty

RACHEL ENTERED THE NEW TEXAS PAWNSHOP
and looked at the guns along the wall and in the big
glass display case. Guns of every shape and size; snub-
nosed guns that looked like pieces of sculpture, long-
barreled pistols that reminded her of cowboys and the
open range. Had any of these guns actually been used to
kill someone? That's what they were for, wasn't it? To
kill?

Protection, the clerk approaching her suggested. Then
his eyes narrowed, as if he'd sensed the questions she'd
been asking, the thoughts about killing, thoughts that
seemed almost normal under the circumstances. Yes,
Rachel repeated, protection.

But she wanted to ask the man just how far the con-
cept of protection could go. If she sought Drew out and
shot him before he got the idea of coming after her,
would that be protection? Or would that be murder?
Would that make her just as bad as he was?

He's already coming after you, was her thought.
Don't kid yourself.

The clerk continued showing her weapons. "Now this
little .32"—he wrapped her hand around it—"should
suit you just fine." It felt so perfectly shaped to her palm
that when Rachel stared down at it, her hand began to
shake.

"I know, I know," the clerk said. "Guns make you
nervous, am I right? Women always get nervous. Seems
like the prettier they are, the more nervous they get." He
paused and licked his lips. "Where do you live, anyway?"

Rachel blinked. He was an old man whose belly

1

strained against the lower buttons of his shirt. Was he coming on to her? Would he dare?

He was still talking, still trying to pinpoint where it was she lived. North Austin or South? " 'Course, no matter where you live these days, there's crime."

If she bought the gun, she'd have to give the man her address, wouldn't she? And then he'd know how to find her. Then he'd either come himself or, for money, maybe, he'd tell Drew.

You're crazy, crazy, she told herself. *He doesn't know Drew. This is probably his idea of flattery, not a come-on.*

She looked around the shop. A beer-faced woman whose hair looked as if she washed it only occasionally dusted merchandise in the aisle nearest the door. The man's wife, probably. No wonder he'd be drawn to Rachel, her ash-blonde hair, sleek as a cap; the clean, flowery smell of White Shoulders wafting around her.

All the more reason to get out of here, get out of here. You don't belong. You stand out like a sore thumb here.

Rachel laid the gun down carefully against the cold glass countertop. For a moment she feared that it would stick to her hand. Then she shook her head, no, and began to ease away from the clerk and his continuing questions.

"Hey," he protested, "what? Did I offend you or something?"

Unfair, unfair. It was supposed to be easy to buy a gun in Texas. You were supposed to be able to just plop your money down and carry it away.

She all but ran to her car. She could barely manage to find the right key, and the minute she did, she wrenched the door open, tumbled in, and pushed the button that locked the door. Then she straightened her dress, trying to look casual, but all the while, she watched the pawnshop door. Good. The clerk had the sense to stay inside. His wife, too. Good.

But then she felt another bolt of fear. Was he calling the police? Telling them he'd found a suspicious character? She'd better leave now, before he noted her license-plate number. She put the car in gear and began to drive. She hadn't even thought about where.

No point going to another pawnshop. It would be the same, she reasoned, wherever weapons were sold. Weapons were for seedy people, and Rachel was—or looked—too nice to want one. Unless, of course, she bought one of those tiny pearl-handled numbers that rich, well-tailored women bought in movies. Would a gun like that be able to do the job? She imagined the small, neat hole such a gun might make, as if a paper punch had been applied to a shirtfront. But beneath the shirt, there would be, yes, flesh. Flesh!

With a shiver, Rachel wrenched herself free from this line of thought. She had to concentrate on defense, not offense. She had to decide what she ought to do next. Should she go home to her apartment? Or would she have to start all over again, someplace new? She wished there was someone she could talk to, someone who could help her decide.

Not that Rachel didn't know anyone at all. She did.

There was Peyton, her partner in the soon-to-open store called Patchwork. And there was Zachary, Rachel's boyfriend, for want of a more dignified term.

But no one to whom she could tell the truth.

That was her own fault, really. When she'd come to Austin, she'd been fleeing her past. It didn't make sense to share it with the new people, the people she'd just met. That had been the point of Austin—to forget.

Until today, she'd pretty well managed to. Now her achievement was more like a curse. It meant that, with Peyton and with Zachary, it was too late to tell the truth.

What would they think of her if she did? They'd know that nearly everything she'd said about herself so far had been false. They'd turn away from her, and understandably so. It meant she couldn't tell, was trapped in the lies she'd told.

She thought herself so clever, too. She'd taken her story from a magazine article she'd just read. And it seemed so appropriate. She'd been in the convent, she'd said. An ex-nun.

It had a kind of rightness, considering the sexless life Rachel had led. But more: Who could check it out? The details in the article were plain enough, and the rest Rachel could either research or invent. Actually, like most girls growing up Catholic, at one time Rachel had wanted to be a nun.

But the story was apt in other ways, too. Telling the story to Peyton and then to Zachary seemed such an enormous confidence, sharing, that it almost guaranteed their friendship. Plus she could ask them to keep the information to themselves, not spread it around. And she could, if she wanted to, lower her eyes and say, "I'd really rather not talk about it," if an uncomfortable circumstance arose.

It hardly ever did. Because neither Peyton nor Zachary was Catholic, everyday knowledge of the religion that Rachel had once practiced sufficed. Even when Peyton had asked her about losing her faith, Rachel merely grafted the way it had actually happened onto the overlay she'd constructed.

She'd even gone to a revival of the old Audrey Hepburn film *The Nun's Story*, with Zachary, and managed to talk convincingly about how her own experiences differed from those on the screen.

Made in heaven, Rachel had thought of her tale.

As if to confirm this assessment, Rachel's needlework also seemed a logical outgrowth of the convent story. Sometimes Rachel could actually picture herself in a neat black habit, fingers nimbly turning fabric.

Now she imagined herself offering Peyton or Zachary or anyone who knew her the startling truth: that her life was in danger. That the person who sought it was her son, Drew. And that she knew all this because, the night before, he had killed her ex-husband, Rob.

You've had it now, Rachel, she told herself, unable to imagine what it might take now to convince Peyton or Zachary or both of the truth. *You've dug your grave.* When the actual words, *You've dug your grave*, sank in, Rachel felt all hope, all energy drain.

Rachel pulled onto the shoulder of the highway and tried to get hold of herself. Almost immediately a car pulled up behind her. A man got out, a perfectly respectable-looking man. He probably wanted to help. Probably wondered if she was having car trouble. Rachel released the emergency brake and lurched back into the stream of traffic, leaving the man there in the small cloud of caliche dust she'd created.

Can't tell anyone. she thought. *Not anyone.* They would think she was crazy. They might even think she was making the whole thing up. Wouldn't that be something? Making it up? She could see herself getting shrill, insisting that it was the other story, the one about the convent, she'd made up.

You've done it, Rachel. You've cooked your goose.

But she couldn't just run, either. She needed money, clothes. But even if she went home to get those, she couldn't just take off, because if she did, one of them, Peyton or Zachary, would tell the police. They, Peyton or Zachary, would think something awful had happened to her and then her face would be plastered all over the TV screen the way other missing people's faces were. And that would be worse, wouldn't it? Wouldn't Drew find her then for sure?

For the first time since she'd heard about Rob, Rachel smiled. *If this were a movie,* she thought, *I would leave and Peyton and Zachary would begin to search for me and fall in love. . . .* In real life, she knew, it was unlikely, There was a tension between them, an unease. But wasn't that the way it often happened? In movies at least.

My God, I am crazy, Rachel thought. *I'm sitting here thinking about movies when my life is at stake. What I should be doing is thinking about escape. About formulating a plan. All right. I'll formulate a plan.*

But she had seen a movie where that had happened. Where a woman disappeared and her sister started searching for her. And the boyfriend of the woman and the sister fell in—Rachel caught her breath when she realized what movie it was. It was *Psycho. Psycho!* It had been on television just the other night. Of all the movies to think about.

Escape. I have to think about escape.

She forced herself back to formulating a plan.

She could go into the shop, tell Peyton there had been a death in the family—ironic though that was—and that she had to go back home, to El Paso. Did Peyton know that Rachel's own father had died years earlier? Probably not. No, no, she was sure that Peyton didn't. So she'd tell her that her father had died and then she'd leave.

Zachary was a bigger problem, because he'd want to come with her. Maybe she should leave Zachary a note. The story ought to work. But she had to be careful, had to make sure he couldn't follow her, because he loved her, he would.

As that thought flickered through her mind, Rachel felt a sense of loss. *But I love Zachary, too,* she thought. Then she reminded herself that she had no time for it, no time for loving anyone. *Not if you want to live. Plan, Rachel, plan.*

But planning wasn't easy, Not when you had to leave all that you'd come to love behind. And not when every so often panic grabbed at you, upending every decision you'd made, every rational thought.

Stop it! Stop stop stop!

She got herself together again and went on. The car, meanwhile, seemed to be driving itself. Rachel, had anyone asked, would never have been able to detail the route she'd only just taken.

Plan!

Long-range. Okay. After a week or so, she'd call and tell Peyton that she was needed there, in El Paso, that her mother needed her, and that Peyton would just have to find someone else to manage the shop without her. Of course, Rachel, meanwhile, would be somewhere else, somewhere safe, Mexico, Canada, California. If there were mail, if there were any legal papers to be signed, she could use one of those forwarding services. And Zachary? She didn't dare call him at all. She'd just have to leave him behind, forget that he'd existed. She couldn't chance talking to him, couldn't chance that she might weaken. She could write to him, though, via the same service.

Yes, that was the way to do it. Sensibly, this time, not just careening across the countryside with everything left behind, but sensibly. With a plan.

But suppose the police were looking for her? Wouldn't they be? Rob Cassidy, after all, was her ex-husband and a semicelebrity, Of course, how would they know about her? Their marriage had been so brief, and the divorce had happened ages ago. With Rob dead, would anyone even think of her? Why should they? She was nothing to Rob. Rachel tried to think of television crime shows. She hit upon *Cagney and Lacey.* How would Cagney and Lacey find out about her? If they found out about her, they'd be sure to know about Drew.

Oh, what a mess. What a tangled mess. A couple of days ago, she'd thought her life was finally falling into shape. And about time, too! Rachel was thirty-nine years old, and getting it together at last.

Who had come first? Her lover, Zachary, then her best friend, Peyton. And after that, the promise of a business, Patchwork, which would mean financial success. Now everything was spinning apart. As if a cyclone had struck, *or*—the bitter truth crossed her mind—*Drew*.

Rachel heard something behind her, a brief siren's whir. She looked in the rearview mirror and saw a patrol car flashing its lights. She moved into the curbmost lane so that it could pass.

But it didn't pass. Instead, it, too, switched lanes and emitted another whir.

Could it be? That they'd found her after all? She pulled to the curb and watched as the trooper came toward her car. She felt herself sweating, almost as if it had begun to pour from her. She glanced down and saw that the sea-green linen cloth of her chemise was stained wet, and not just at the underarms, but across the chest as well, as if she were running already, physically running, legs pounding hard on the pavement, breath coming quick.

It occurred to her to drive away, as she'd done earlier. But that had just been a civilian, a good Samaritan who thought she needed help. A trooper would radio for help, wouldn't he? For backup? That was what Cagney and Lacey would do.

Rachel smiled. The trooper was at her window, and he smiled in return. When she rolled the window down, he asked for her license. Rachel handed him her wallet. No, he said, just the license. Rachel trembled trying to remove it from its slip. "Was I speeding?" she asked, hoping that she sounded okay.

"Naw..." He seemed hesitant. "You've just been... erratic. I've been behind you since you turned off Congress and you... well, you cut a couple of people off. You've been changing lanes. You... well, you haven't broken any laws, you've just been..."

"Erratic," Rachel finished.

"Right."

"So are you giving me a ticket?" Was there an edge in her voice or did it just seem so to her? She searched his face, found it friendly. That meant no edge.

And no ticket. He told her to keep her mind on her driving, though. Said that the highway was no place for daydreaming. Told her that Ben White Boulevard, because of its congestion, was especially bad. "Unless," he tried, "you're not feeling well?"

She made it easy for him. "I do feel a little queasy," she said.

"Well, take care." He yanked at the brim of his hat. Rachel watched him walk back to his car, start the engine, and inch ahead onto the highway. He looked back at her, tugged again at his hat, and then tipped his head to one side, as if questioning her. Did she have anything to tell him? *I should,* she thought. *I still can. I can wave at him to stop and when he comes, I can say, Listen, I need help. My son is going to kill me. I need protection.*

Instead, she watched him drive away, then did the same herself. This time she tried to concentrate on driving, on the other cars, on the stop signs and yields.

Ahead, the trooper was looking in his rearview mirror, looking for her. But that was crazy. He wouldn't be following her that way, in the lead, would he? Would he? And if he were, shouldn't she feel, not worse, but better? Shouldn't she?

There were two cars between her own and the police car. If she shook the cop, perhaps she could shake the feeling, the dread, the sense that she was being hunted, chased.

HE SAT UPRIGHT AND TRIED TO ADJUST to the light and the heat. Though it had obviously been day for a while now, he'd continued sleeping there on the bench beside the Exxon station. He rubbed his eyes, pulled the collar of his shirt toward his nose, and sniffed at it. Phew! He needed a bath, that's what he needed. He looked over at the men's room and wondered if the attendant would try to stop him. He'd practically had to break the last guy's arm. But this time the attendant wasn't anywhere in sight. A stroke of luck.

The soap dispenser was either empty or clogged. He used some coarse brown paper and plain water as best he could. He rinsed his mouth, saturated his hair. He felt a lot better when he came out. And amazingly, after the bench, his joints weren't that stiff at all.

He fished around in his pockets and came up with a quarter, a dime, and a nickel. Ten cents shy of a Coke. He sat back down and pondered this.

"Why so blue?" A silky voice out of nowhere.

He looked up to see a moonfaced girl with fine, straight hair more than a yard long. She sat down next to him and pulled the length of it across her shoulder and then her lap. Then she began stroking it with two hands alternately.

"Blue?" he said. "What makes you think I'm blue?" He felt as if a great deal of time had elapsed before any of the words would come. He thought about the expression "blue," though. It seemed very old-fashioned. The way she would have looked in some other clothes. As it was, she wore a tube top and narrow jeans over cowboy boots.

Stroke, stroke, her hair was gleaming with the oil from her palms. He felt better, much better. Especially when, after sizing him up some, she asked, "What's your name?"

"Drew." Girls liked his name, liked his looks. Always had. It was sometimes a curse, but not right now, not with having to get from wherever he was—a place called Rosenberg—to Austin, where his mother lived.

The girl didn't offer her own name in return. She just asked, "You feel like something to eat?"

He gave a little smirk, thinking how wide open she'd left things, if he'd wanted, for instance, to make a lewd remark. On purpose? Maybe. But it could be that she was just dumb, that was all. Anyway, he couldn't risk offending her right off, not when it seemed like she was sent from heaven, so he just said, "That'd be nice."

"My treat," she told him, and gestured at the field beyond the station. An oil well was pumping out there. "I saw you looking at that well," she said, as if it were some kind of explanation.

"Oh, yeah?" He hadn't known that he had been, but now that she pointed it out, it seemed to him that yes, she was right.

"You were thinking about money."

"Oh, I was, huh? And what are you, a fortune teller?" They were smiling at each other, much too genuinely, he thought. "As a matter of fact," he told her, "I hate oil wells. I think they're ugly."

"They are ugly," she agreed. "Like the front halves of praying mantises. The head and the thorax."

He laughed and repeated, "Thorax. That's pretty good." Actually, it wasn't, but at that point anything she said, dumb or not, would have sounded wonderful. He was hungry, he recognized, for far more than breakfast.

Was there time? Hell, he'd make time.

"We had a well," the girl went on. "I used to ride it. It was kind of like riding a mechanical bull. Not as jarring though, maybe. I'd climb on it and let it carry me up. I was little then. My daddy didn't know about it, but I think my momma might have seen me. I thought I saw her watching me one time."

The well didn't seem so ugly now, not with the image of the girl astride the mantis part, her long, hand-stroked hair flying straight out behind her. "I can see why she didn't stop you," he said.

She gestured toward an old two-seater Thunderbird, bright blue. The attendant was in sight now, slamming down its hood. "Come on," the girl said, tossing her hair back over her shoulder to let it swing down behind. "Let's go." But then her confidence fell. "Okay?" she asked, her clean white brow all furrowed.

What did she think he'd say? What would anybody say, any guy, anyway? Maybe she had said that leading thing of hers—did he feel like whatever it was—on purpose after all. She had picked him up, right? Offered to buy him a meal? What kind of girl did that make her? But then there was that real uncertainty, that "Okay?"

He appraised her anew. She didn't look slutty at all. So maybe it was a natural, friendly thing, her picking him up. You never could tell, and half the time it was better not to wonder.

One thing was for sure, though. This girl could, if she wanted to, find herself in a helluva lot of trouble.

"Okay," he answered. Then he got into the car and didn't say another word—though neither did she—until they were inside the little truck stop and sitting down right next to each other at a long, cup-stained Formica counter.

"How old are you?" Drew asked. He still didn't know the girl's name. Their order had come and he'd watched in amazement at the huge amount of food the girl had put away: eggs, hash browns, sausage.

"Why do you want to know?" She was putting grape jelly on a remnant of toast. It seemed to require a great deal of concentration. She didn't look up at him, but kept moving the purple mass around with her butter knife, positioning it as a master sculptor might.

"It's not the only thing I'm wondering," he admitted, watching her open her mouth to its widest.

She did look up at that. He expected some kind of protest, whether she meant it or not, but instead, she just beamed at him. As if he'd said something she'd been waiting and waiting to hear. She popped the toast and the jelly into her mouth and chewed and swallowed. All with a great big smile upon her face. And when she was done chewing she shrugged and said, "So ask me."

Jailbait, probably, Drew decided. He'd better ditch her. Maybe have her first, but ditch her for sure. But the car. The T-bird. That he'd need.

"I know what you're thinking," she said, wiping each of her fingers separately with the thin paper napkin. Like she was pulling on fine kid gloves.

"I doubt it," Drew told her, careful to keep a note of tease in his voice.

And then they were outside again, where the air felt like someone had soaked a washcloth in hot water, wrung it out, and dropped it on his face. He said something like that and the girl said she knew just the remedy.

"Right," he muttered, thinking she meant the little air-conditioned car. But she walked right past it, saying that she knew about a stream that licked this way, back behind the truck stop.

How? he wondered. He tried to imagine her out back with a gang of truckers, but he couldn't.

"A girlfriend told me," she explained, though he hadn't voiced the question.

He thought about the creeps inside the truck stop, though. Tattooed long-hairs wearing gimme caps. If they wanted to, they could lift the little T-bird up with their bare hands. Lift it and put it in the back of one of the big rigs parked at the edge of the lot, too.

"Hey," he said, putting an arm around the girl's shoulder. "We gonna leave your car here or what?"

She looked disgusted. "Worrywart," she accused.

He repeated the word, which he'd never heard anyone use in real life. He vaguely remembered hearing it on the sitcom reruns that had been so popular at Benedict House. Worrywart, indeed.

He decided to trust her, but for the life of him, he couldn't understand why she would trust him in return. "I guess you never worry, right?"

"I worry sometimes," she said. "Just not now."

Oh, right. Because he looked boyish and sincere. The all-American boy. He'd heard that a hundred times. They said he looked like Tom Cruise mostly. "I know," he said. "I have an honest face."

She stopped and turned to look at him. He let his arm fall and stepped back. "You look like an ad," she said. "I'm not sure for what." She appraised him, his grimy Levis, his sleeves-rolled torn T-shirt reading FEAR. "Maybe," she decided, "for Guess jeans."

"I thought I was the Paco Rabane guy for sure."

"What?"

"Nothing." He'd have to buy a copy of some slick men's magazine, maybe *Gentleman's Quarterly*, and show her. It was too damn hard to explain.

The whole while they were talking back and forth this way, they were walking through scrub brush, down a little incline, too. Sure enough, at the bottom was a moving stream of water.

"There's supposed to be a dammed-up place, too," she said. "We should follow it."

"Which way?" he asked.

She answered just by looking glum. "I don't know," she admitted.

He took off his Adidas and his socks. Then he rolled his Levis as high as he could. To his amazement, the moonfaced girl removed her boots and then her own jeans. She stood there in nothing but a tube top and bikini panties, digging in her limp blue-jean pocket.

"What are you looking for?" he asked her. His voice was thick. He walked toward her, but she, he could tell, hardly seemed to notice, so intent was she on whatever it was she was after.

"Here," she said, holding two small white pills flat on her hand, as if she were offering sugar cubes to a horse.

Oh, Christ, so much for innocence. If he ate one of those he'd be here fucking his brains out for eight solid hours.

"No thanks," he said.

"It's Ecstasy." she told him.

"Come on," he said, "put those away. I'll give you ecstasy." He yanked his T-shirt off, then undid the top button of his jeans. "Sweet ecstasy," he said, pulling at the two sides of his waistband, forcing the zipper down. "Sweet ecstas-ee." He looked down at himself as he did so, thinking how like a movie it was—the girl, him getting it on this way, the whole thing.

When he looked back up, she was gaping at him, though, as if his cock were something all brand-new. She dropped the pills and began walking toward him, tugging on her panties at the very same time. She even tripped, and the whole while, she never took her eyes off his cock. It was comical, not sexy at all. It was like a skit on television, *Saturday Night Live*.

"What's so funny?" she demanded. She'd stopped coming toward him. She had a mad look on her face before she turned away from him, cheeks bright red.

"Hey," he said. "You should have seen yourself." The starch had gone right out of his cock at the sight of her, actually. "It was pretty funny. Especially when you got your legs all tangled up." He executed a pratfall, but she didn't turn around to see it.

She went down to where the water was flowing. He watched her think about trying to cross on some rocks that jutted out. Then he watched her change her mind and drop right where she stood. She sat on the dirt bank and stirred at the bottom with her feet, first one, then the other. Her hair trailed behind her, some of it spread out on the ground. It was night and day, her tripping toward him and her sitting there now. Night and day.

He looked for the Ecstasies, and when he found

them, he tucked them in his own jeans pocket. Couldn't have her drugged out, eyes rolling back in her head. Not if he was going to get to Austin.

Then it hit him. He'd abandoned the idea of ditching her, taking the car. Why was that? Was it because he hadn't fucked her yet? Or could it be that something about her got to him? The way she'd reacted to being laughed at, for instance, or the picture she made in her underwear, sitting there, that hair and all.

He went and sat beside her. Didn't touch her, though.

"I didn't really want sex," she told him.

Sure. She'd picked him up for conversation's sake, right?

She looked at him, measured his skepticism. "I didn't," she repeated. "It's like, I don't know what I want. It isn't sex and"—she glanced back at approximately the spot where the Ecstasies had dropped—"it isn't drugs either. I don't know what it is." After a silence, she added, as if he'd suggested it, "It isn't something piddly like stealing, either."

The thought came at him like a bolt: *She stole that car. I've been riding in a stolen car! I could have been picked up by the cops, and then where would I be?* He had an urge to turn on his heel and run run run just as fast as his feet could take him. He should have known better than to follow this girl back behind a restaurant out here in the middle of nowhere. She was a looney, she had to be, to have picked him up at all. That should have tipped him off. A looney in a stolen car.

Still, he wondered, if she didn't want sex and she didn't want drugs, what the fuck was it that she did want? And why was he thinking about waiting around to find out?

She tugged at his arm. Read his mind again. "It's my daddy's car," she said. "Honest. And you did say you had to get to Austin, right? Didn't you?"

It was that last couple of sentences that tipped him off, what she said as well as the whiny delivery. She needed him for something, maybe for her very first fling. He grew generous, thinking, *Well, hell. Even Jerry Hall had to start someplace.*

The moonfaced girl was looking up at him so wistfully, so make-or-break, he just couldn't bring himself to make such a smart remark. He sounded like some goddam counselor. "You running away from home?"

"No. I'm older than I look, I swear."

He grabbed a handful of her hair and yanked on it. "Well, go on, do it. Swear."

She screamed and he kept at her.

"Did you hear me? I said, 'Swear.'" He had only been teasing when he started out, only been trying to break out of this pisspoor thing he'd fallen into, sounding like a shrink and all. Now, though, he started really getting into it, getting boisterous. Next time he yanked it was pretty hard and she was almost crying. "Come on," he said anyway. 'Swear.'"

"What do you mean?" she whined at him. "Do you mean like 'shit' and 'damn' and stuff like that?"

He let go, shoved her away. She caught her balance and said, as if apologizing, "I didn't know what you meant."

"Hey, listen." He caught at a new idea. "Put your hands behind your back, okay?"

"Wait," she said, looking around for something to wipe her nose with. She had to settle for a knuckle. Then she did as he suggested, head drooped to one side.

He went behind her and attempted to tie her hands with her hair.

"Ow," she protested. "It isn't long enough for that. Come on." She was right. Oh, it reached, but when he wound it around more than once there wasn't enough left to tie. He stuck the end into her own hand and went around front to look.

The way she looked kind of took all the fun out of things. Her head was at this awful angle, and her eyes were red and her nose was sniffly. It was as if there were two sides to her, a sniffly side and a side with some spunk. When she was sniffly, she was awkward and ugly, and when the spunk came out, she had something really fine. A kind of grace and appeal. He wondered if she knew that about herself. Then he wondered if she'd end up one or the other. Then whether or not the time she'd spent with him would have anything to do with how she ended up.

He reached for her again, her shoulder this time. She pulled back and away. Her spunky side. He got hard again, thinking about how he would scuffle around with her after he got her down. She'd fight, of course, but there wasn't any way she would win. Then he thought about what it would be like if she just wimpy-like went along. No fun there, no fun at all. "What's the matter with you?" he yelled at her, as if she knew what diagnosis he had made, as if, in fact, she was responsible for it.

She came forward with her little fists flying, banged them on his chest. "I don't want you laughing at me," she said.

"I'm not," he said, his fingers closing like shackles around her wrists.

HER HEART WAS POUNDING LIKE CRAZY when she pulled into the shopping center. So far so good. She parked in front of Sun Harvest, a sort of health-food supermarket. Even though the cop car had gone on without her, she still felt like a fugitive. But why?

She had to admit that the trooper hadn't even seemed to notice when she'd turned off. She had to admit that, except for one small glance in his rearview mirror, he'd seemed to have forgotten all about her. But maybe that was part of his surveillance. He'd seemed nonchalant because he'd turned her over to another unit, some plainclothes cops. That's right, the one with the short blonde hair. Pretty, yeah, the one in the light green dress. You got her, that's the one.

That was right out of *Cagney and Lacey*, too.

But just in case it was true, she had to follow through. Had to go into that supermarket and act as if her ex-husband hadn't been murdered, hadn't been murdered at all. It was just another day.

She walked through the automated door and drew a small but immediate measure of comfort from the bedding plants on the floor. Geraniums, begonias, all in strident good health. She could smell the deep black earth they were planted in, and that made her feel better, too.

Maybe I'm wrong, she consoled herself, placing a red and a pink geranium into the kiddie seat on the metal cart.

Drew, Drew, I wheeled you this way, in my grocery cart, when you were just a little boy. You'd point at the cereal boxes you'd seen advertised on television, re-

20

member? She felt a pinch at the bridge of her nose. She always did, near tears.

Could she be wrong? Couldn't Rob's death be totally unconnected to Drew? *Not Rob's death,* she reminded herself, *Rob's murder. His murder. But still . . .*

Rob himself had told her Drew had been in touch. He seemed to be bragging. "Sent me nineteen Father's Day cards all at once," he'd laughed. "One for every year. Said he was makin' up for lost time." Rachel didn't find it funny, but beyond that, didn't know what it was she felt. Jealousy, perhaps. That Rob could have abandoned Drew when Drew was an infant and not have any price to pay. She had put in a lot more years and yet Drew hated her, wanted to hurt her, kill her. . . .

Nineteen Father's Day cards. No wonder Rachel had trembled. Now she saw so clearly that they'd been a threat. What else had Rob told her? "Kid's got a real good sense of humor. Called me 'Daddy Dearest.'" *Too late, too late, but I ought to have told Rob,* she thought, *warned him.*

"Need some help?"

Rachel started visibly, then laughed. The produce clerk laughed too, then repeated the question. Instantly, Rachel wondered if her behavior had been odd in some way. Maybe she was talking out loud, talking to herself. But the clerk didn't seem to be regarding her as a weirdo. Rachel relaxed a bit. "The sprouts," she said, pointing at them.

"Which ones? We have mung bean, alfalfa . . ."

"Bean," Rachel said. "A pound of them." She watched as the girl weighed a large, wormlike mass.

When Drew was born, nineteen years before, Rachel had never even seen a bean sprout. She doubted that anyone in Kingsville had. The health-food trend hadn't started then, but even now, she doubted that the stores in the flat little Texas town would consider bean sprouts anything but exotic. Kingsville was like that, dingy and narrow, filled with stale air, stale ideas. She had gone there with Rob, had stayed there because of Rob, had gotten pregnant there, given birth to Drew, had been abandoned there with Drew by Rob.

"All that kid ever does is cry," Rob said. It was true, and all Rachel ever did was walk him, walk him end- lessly in the hope that he'd stop. "Can't the doctor give you something to shut him up? Paregoric or some kind of dope?" That was Rob, Mr. Chemical Solution. That was one thing Kingsville had in spades, good drugs, all kinds of drugs, drugs on their way up from Mexico, Guatemala, from South America, too. Of course, you had to know the right people, the sleazebuckets who handled the stuff, but Rob did, Rob always did.

Maybe that's why he was killed. Maybe it was a drug deal gone bad, not Drew, not Drew at all.

But no. Last time she'd seen Rob he'd been more than clean, he'd been disgustingly healthy, trendily so. He'd stopped eating cooked food altogether, he'd told her, even ate potatoes raw. It was a familiar progression, hippy to yuppy, Or was Rob too old to be a yuppy?

He'd looked young enough, younger than she looked. His hair was short now, almost a military cut. His clothes had been stylish, too—wonderful fabric, gener- ously cut, right out of some elegant magazine, *Town & Country* or *Vanity Fair* or *Ultra*.

She remembered that about Rob, how, no matter what the style, he was right in step with it. Never mind that back then she had bought her clothes at the Goodwill or had worn her old ones. Worse than that, he even com- plained about springing for disposable diapers. Not that he ever changed one in his life. Never mind any of that. Rob had to be perfect but his family could just go to the dogs.

He'd liked the way Rachel had dressed in the beginning; he said so often enough. Then he stopped looking, just plumb stopped looking. He'd probably—Rachel eventually, long after it was too late, realized—met someone else. But then, then she couldn't figure it out. Nothing she put on seemed to interest him. He'd just stopped looking at her, so what the hell difference to him or to her did it make what she wore?

Rachel yanked open one of the freezer compartments and grabbed a quart of strawberry kefir, tossing it into her cart. A blast as cold as the hatred she'd stored since her marriage washed over her. She found herself thinking, not unhappily: *Rob will look terrific in his coffin.*

THE GIRL WATCHED HIM IN THE LITTLE stream, scrubbing at his armpits, his chest. "What is this thing you have with cleanliness?" She laughed, splashing crystal-clear water up toward him.

"It isn't a thing," he told her. "I just haven't had a bath for a good long time. I told you, I've been hitchhiking around."

"Maybe I should get myself dressed," she teased, "and drive around looking for soap."

He didn't seem to realize she was joking. "That's not a bad idea," he said. "Maybe they have some back at the restaurant. You—"

She splashed some more water at him, this time hard enough for it to reach and soak his pants. Then she shrieked as he came after her to get even.

They tumbled around on the ground together and then were still. "I was sort of afraid of you. For a minute there," she confessed. She reached up and pulled some dry weed out of his hair. "Once we got back here and I knew that nobody would hear me."

"You were right to be," he said. "Dead right to be. I could do anything to you. Still can."

"Oh, yeah?" She reached toward his crotch. He'd had a second erection earlier, for about twenty seconds. Since then, it had been like it was now. Flabby, like one of those rubber chickens you buy in gag shops.

He'd heard guys talk about this, especially old guys, and he'd always thought, *Hey, not me, man. Not Drew Fucking Cassidy.* Now that it had happened, it was no big deal. He'd even said to her, "Come on now. Now you can laugh at me."

She just shook her head at that one, no.

He valued that. Still, he couldn't stop tormenting her. Like pulling on the elastic of her tube top and letting it snap back.

"Ouch," she said.

"What hurts?" he asked her. "You don't have any tits, so what can hurt?"

She whipped the damn thing off, and she *didn't* have any tits. He'd seen guys with bigger ones.

"You're too fucking skinny," he said. She was, too. "You couldn't turn anyone on."

"Well, neither could you," she said, working his jeans down over his hips and then standing back and leaving them there. "If I had a wang it would be just as dead as yours is."

"A wang?" he said. "A wang? I thought a wang was a computer." She was okay, he decided. He could run around with her naked and playing around this way forever, kidlike, with no complications.

Except for one: Rachel. She was one complication he couldn't, try as he might, forget.

He hiked his pants back up and told the girl that fun time was over.

YOU SHOULD HAVE GONE TO THE EXPRESS aisle," the woman behind the register chided.

"What?" Rachel felt as though she'd been abruptly awakened.

"The express aisle. Look how little you bought." She gestured at Rachel's kefir and sprouts. Rachel had also picked up a long thin loaf of bread. "Oh, well." The woman shrugged and began totaling up Rachel's purchases.

Rachel paid by check, then carried the lightweight plastic bag to her car. The bread jutted out like a spear. She laid the bag inside, then wondered whether she dared take these things home. *Have to*, she told herself. If she didn't, the sprouts and the kefir would spoil in the car.

Why had she bought these things? She had turned into the shopping center to see if the trooper would notice she was gone and follow. Then, more or less to follow through on the subterfuge, she'd entered the Sun Harvest store. When had she begun to buy things? Had that been mere habit? Or was it her mind's attempt to negate all that had happened?

Rachel glanced at her watch. It had been three hours since she'd heard. Maybe there was some more news, maybe the killer had been caught, maybe she'd been wrong, had heard wrong.

She turned the radio on, then off again, deciding that she didn't want to be here, in public, when she listened to it. She would go home, go somewhere, listen to it then.

She'd been having her hair cut this morning when the bulletin was first read. It merited a bulletin because Rob's talk show, broadcast from Houston, was a smash all over Texas, but in Austin especially. One of the magazines had called him a one-man radio revival. People talked about his show on street corners, in offices, all over town. Whenever Rachel heard them talking she wanted to shout about what a bastard he was, how he'd left his wife, his child. How he never sent money, even long ago, when Rachel really needed it, when Drew really needed it.

Things might have been different had Rob cared. She often wondered why he'd married her at all, though she'd heard him often enough on the telephone, trying to line up auditions. "I'm young, but I'm a family man," he'd say, and, maybe because he expected points for it, he got them. She could remember when their dining-room table was scattered with tapes selling Rob's wholesome and cheery and convincing radio voice. Every time Rachel set the table, she had to push the reels aside. He didn't even ask her what she thought of his rap the way he used to in the beginning. After a while, Rachel felt he had married her only to give some kind of homey boost to his résumé. Family man! If only they knew! And Rachel would bet anything he went right on saying that long after he'd walked out on her and Drew.

No wonder Drew had that huge store of anger. She, Rachel, had quite a store of it herself. *You asked for it, Rob. You deserved it.*

THEY WERE BACK IN THE CAR NOW. THE heat of the day was starting to gather, and she had turned the air conditioner on. It was Mickey Mouse, not factory air, but it did the job. Trouble was, the box took up almost all of the available legroom and the sound from it made even listening to the radio impossible. Of course the stations were probably all just country anyway, so it was no great loss.

She still hadn't told him her name, but she had said her age. Seventeen, she'd said, but she'd gotten out of high school already. Her daddy had sent her to some fancy girl's school and she'd been able to accelerate. That was how she phrased it, "accelerate."

The unfortunate thing was that the school talk had segued into parent talk. He had had it up to here with shit about her folks and how much she owed them, how they'd given her everything she'd ever wanted and how they stood around now just waiting for her to ask for more.

Sure. He'd heard lots of kids start out this way at Benedict House. Exactly.

He figured he'd let her get away with it, but not if it went on too long. He saw a road sign saying that a town called Plum was up ahead and figured that once they crossed on over into it, too long would have come.

He'd been listening pretty attentively, saying things like "Uh-huh" and "Mmmhmm" when it seemed called for. Now he turned on the freeze and said nothing. Funny how that worked. How you could feel the right kind of silence building.

27

She was uneasy with it, just as he'd known she would be. Just as everyone at Benedict House had been. "What's your problem?" she finally asked.

"You mean *your* problem, don't you?"

"What do you mean?"

"You know what I mean."

"I don't," she said, "but, like, you could tell me."

He had to tell her, really. Couldn't take that Goody Two-shoes number she was doing anymore. Had to make her face facts, the way he'd learned to face them.

"Pull over then," he said. He didn't feature having her careen all over the highway when he did his number on her, Parents, Part One.

She sighed as disgustedly as she could, but she swung right over. Then she saw a store with a gas pump up ahead and she drove on toward it, parking away from the pump and near the door. As if she might want to run inside for help, maybe. She bit at her lower lip, staring straight ahead.

Drew leaned back and did the same, though from time to time he shot a glance her way. When he was sure that she was good and mad he said, "You'd really like to rub their noses in it, wouldn't you?"

"Who?"

He scoffed at her. "You don't know, oh, right. I'm sure you don't know."

She looked around, though now not as if she were seeking an escape route but as though afraid someone —a stranger—might overhear. "Who?" She almost whispered it, as if she knew but feared the answer.

He liked that response. He stuck his face right up next to hers and breathed it right back at her. "Them. Your parents. You'd like to rub their noses in it. You'd like to see them dead. Yeah, dead. Blood running out of their ears and their goddam noses."

He remembered one black girl in psychodrama cutting a sheet cake into tiny slivers, maybe thirty of them, though there'd been just six kids in his class. When she'd finished cutting, she'd beamed. "That was my dad, the cake. I just carved him up good. Into pieces." They'd all applauded and then someone had asked why her father wasn't devil's food.

The parent thing was easy, a given. Especially with someone like this girl, always talking about how wonderful they were, trying to convince herself. Shit, he was pretty sure they weren't wonderful at all. All this stuff, it was part of the side of her he didn't have any use for.

"Let me tell you something," he began, but she covered her ears with her hands and turned her head away. He should have dropped it just like that, because he'd proved his point, but he reached for her hands and she pulled away and then she jumped right out of the car and toward the door of the store.

He hoped she wasn't in there bawling her eyes out, but there was no way he could tell for sure. Man, his timing ate shit sometimes. He would just have to wait until she came out.

He knew he was right about her hating her folks. What she didn't know, apparently, was that everyone did in some sort of way. Everyone in his experience at least. Maybe he ought to say that to her.

She came out with a bag of stuff, but she didn't dig into it and so he didn't either. She came right up to his side. No dried-up tears, he noted.

"You want to drive?" she asked.

"Uh-uh," he said. "You do it."

TO GET TO HER APARTMENT SHE HAD TO PASS through one of Austin's bleakest suburbs—a plot of "starter" homes, which, translated, meant tiny, unimaginatively designed. The south side of town was filled with places like these, and more were being planned every day. That was one thing she and Rob had had in common: shared scorn for the ticky-tacky that most young couples seemed to yearn for. *The only thing in common,* she reminded herself.

It was odd how that seeped into Drew, almost as if by osmosis. She remembered passing through such a suburb on the outskirts of Corpus Christi with him when he was, oh, eleven or twelve. She hadn't said a word to sway him but all of a sudden he asked, "Why would anyone want to live here, Mom?" She'd been torn between saying what she knew she ought to say—that people lived where they had to, that people had different tastes—and the truth, which was that she couldn't imagine why. Finally, she'd told him that she didn't care for the houses either, but that some people must have liked them or they'd not have been built.

There was another incident like it. Perhaps she could even call it astounding in its way, She'd been looking at an atlas, a two-page map of the United States spread out before her, when Drew, maybe fifteen at the time, had come into the room. He'd sat on her side of the table so that he could look at the map too. "I could live in Florida," he told her, "or maybe up here, in Maine or New York. But never here"—he pointed to Arkansas—"or here"—Mississippi—"or . . ." Everywhere he couldn't live, Rachel knew that she couldn't either, and everywhere he could, she could, too. And yet, to the best of her recollection, she had never talked about places with Drew, had never mentioned states she liked, states she hated, states she'd visited, states she'd never wanted to see. Osmosis, yes.

But that meant anything could be passed along this way. Her hatred of Rob, for instance, the fact that she never never never had forgiven him, the fact that he had irrevocably changed her life, pinched it into something small, and walked away.

SHE'D PULLED INTO YET ANOTHER CON-venience store before he could protest, this one a Sigmor, its neon sign lit even now, in daylight. He wondered if they were aware of it inside, if one of the clerks would have hell to pay as a result.

It seemed to him that they were wasting an awful lot of time making all these stops, but he had only himself to blame for the last one. Anyway, it was her car, her gas, and she was the one behind the wheel. Also, he couldn't very well object when she told him that she had to go to the bathroom, now could he?

It was curious, though, that she'd left the keys behind. Almost as if she were tempting him to steal the car. She'd probably claim he'd raped her, too. She'd probably cheer when the Texas Rangers caught him, gunned him down.

He leaned over, yanked the keys, and bounced them up and down a couple of times in his hand. They were heavy, so heavy that they'd probably wreck the ignition switch, given enough time. There were eight keys on the chain, plus a brass tag that read, "Orient Express, Compartment 13." Orient Express. How about that.

"It's not real," she said, bending down beside the car. "My daddy had it made for me or something."

He got out of the car, jerking the door so quickly that she had to jump back to keep from being shoved by it and him. He dropped the keys from about shoulder height and she just did catch them. It pissed him off that the tag wasn't real and it pissed him off even more that she'd mentioned her dad again. He'd thought he'd settled all that parent bullshit, at least to the point where she wasn't going to talk about it anymore. Now, it seemed, he was wrong.

He stalked into the store.

She followed him, crossing her arms and rubbing at her shoulders as if the air conditioning inside the store was making her cold. Good. The bitch could freeze for all he cared.

He kept telling himself to calm down, calm down. He wasn't even sure what it was that he was mad about. That he'd tried to process her, the way they'd done at Benedict House, and had failed? He hadn't done it in-depth, hadn't really broken her down or even tried. He'd just done a sort of skim. Nothing to be mad about, really.

If anything, she was the one who'd had her balloon pricked, she was the one who ought to be mad. And she wasn't, wasn't at all. Maybe that was what was pissing him off.

Save it, he counseled himself. *Don't spend your anger here.*

"You ready?" she asked. He still didn't know what she'd picked up at the last place. Maybe that was the way she got rid of her anger—dragging him around to one store after another, slowing him down. That would really make her a bitch, one of those slow-striking tormenting kinds that marry big executives and never shout and scream but do you in just the same.

He looked up at her. Her eyes were big and round and she didn't bother with a smile this time. She wasn't one of those slow-strikers, he knew, but still he had to keep the upper hand. He couldn't let her, now that he'd decided he would keep her around, run a lot of bullshit by him.

He bought pretzels, two Pepsis, and a beef jerky. "She'll pay," he told the clerk. He had planned to stride out of the store without a backward glance, very stay-tough, but the news rack stopped him. He picked up a Houston paper. "Would this . . . ?" He paused, wondering if he was about to call attention to himself in a way that the clerk might remember.

"It's fine," the girl saved him, "just take it. Come on, I just paid for it."

"Primo," he told her.

But it was almost impossible to open the paper inside the little cockpit. He was never very good at the sort of fold and read that passengers on a train or bus, for instance, seemed so easily to master. Now he struggled with the paper almost as if it were alive, the pages resisting, refusing to turn under or to smooth.

The girl laughed. She repeatedly had to push his left hand out of her way, "Give it up," she suggested. "Or wait until we stop again."

"I'm hoping that we won't," Drew said, but he bunched the paper up as best he could and wedged it back behind the seat.

They went on in silence for a few miles, the air conditioning humming at a softer level now. "What was it you wanted to see?" she asked.

"Just the want ads."

Silence again. Then, "That's not the part you were reading."

"What?"

"You heard me." She gave him time enough to reply. When he didn't, she went on. "I'll betcha I know." Again, she waited in vain. "The murder, right? Rob Cassidy? Hey, look, it's no big deal. You can admit it."

Drew felt as though he couldn't breathe. Felt as though he had to force each word to surface. "Admit what," he said, but pointedly, a dare rather than a question.

"Oh, 'fess up. It's like the *National Enquirer*. I mean, everybody's into junk like that, but they're too embarrassed or something to admit it. Look, I heard the news this morning, too, and I thought, *Hmmm—*"

Drew interrupted her. "'Fess up? Did you say ''fess up'? I mean, who talks that way? Who in the hell ever talks that way?" He'd heard punk girls talk that way, but never anyone in plain-jane jeans and cowboy boots. "'Fess the fuck up. Scoobydoo, coocooca-choo." Meanwhile, he tried to think of something else she'd said earlier, so that he could throw that back up to her, too, but he couldn't.

"You're changing the subject," she said, but she was clearly delighted.

Drew settled back in his seat. He felt the way he used to feel a long time ago, when he could make people laugh whenever he wanted them to laugh—except his mom, of course. But he could, by making them laugh, win people over, make them like him. It was mostly a matter of being silly. Girls liked it, old people liked it. So he went around saying things like "scoobydoo" and "coocoocachoo."

With his mother, it wasn't that easy. It wasn't as though she never laughed, it was as though she couldn't ease up enough, or as though by laughing with him she would be losing something, some measure of control or power or something. He could remember times when she was mad at him and he would try to say or do something funny and he could see her trying really hard not to laugh and succeeding until not laughing became a habit with her. His mental picture of her, the one his psychodrama teacher had him make, was of Rachel with deep downturning lines at the corners of her mouth.

Even times when she wasn't mad, when he wasn't trying to win her over or anything, she wouldn't laugh. Like one time she was on her hands and knees trying to clean some dried-up crap off the kitchen floor. She was on one of her cleaning binges and she'd made him sweep while she went around with a bucket with Pinesol in it and a rag.

What happened was, he'd found a roach that had eaten the poison shit that Rachel always laid out, a dead Texas-size roach about three inches long, belly-up behind the stove.

And there was Rachel across the room on her hands and knees.

He'd had a stroke of genius, real inspiration. Everybody he told the story to cracked up. But not Rachel.

He'd lined the roach up with the broom edge, just so. And then he'd swiped the roach so that it flew across the room toward her. "It's roach hockey!" he'd shouted, as the roach slid like a puck into Rachel's knee.

She'd been wearing shorts, too.

Rachel didn't laugh. Rachel screamed and just about went straight up before she fell right over. Rachel even spilled the bucket in her crazy scramble, which, to his mind, made the whole thing even funnier. And then Rachel had rubbed at her knee with the Pinesol rag, and she'd just about turned purple coming after him, and she'd gone on and on for hours on end about how vile and disgusting he was and how vile and disgusting roaches were and how they were filthy, filthy, carrying just about every sort of disease.

As comic as it was, he was sorry he had done it, especially when she'd demanded to know if he'd touched the dead roach with his hands and how, even though he told her no, only with the broom, she'd made him stand there at the sink and scrub with the Pinesol while meanwhile she just about wore her knee out where the roach had brushed against her. It was a wonder she hadn't dipped his hands and her knee in boiling water.

Worrywart, he remembered. Yeah, that was the other word the girl had used, all right.

He wondered if he ought to tell the girl the story about Rachel and the roach. And then he wondered if maybe that story explained the thing he had about being so clean.

RACHEL PULLED IN FRONT OF ONE OF THE ticky-tacky houses and forced herself to listen to the newscast again. It didn't have the impact that it had had earlier this morning, when it had fallen out of the blue. She'd jerked forward while Roxy was finishing up the triangular sideburns Rachel had asked her to shape, even causing the scissors to graze her neck. Roxy laughed. "Easy does it. I hate losing a customer."

Rachel laughed back, but only with great effort. She

strained forward to try to hear the radio in the background.

Talk-show host Rob Cassidy . . .

Yes, murdered. They'd said murdered.

. . . in his Galveston beachhouse at about ten o'clock last night . . .

What had made her think of Drew? The business about the quilt.

. . . Cassidy's body had been wrapped in a patchwork quilt. One police spokesman said it was almost as though the killer felt sorry for him afterward, tried to tuck him in.

Rachel couldn't remember paying Roxy, couldn't remember getting to her car. All she knew was, Roxy was knocking on the car window with her knuckles, asking, "What's the matter? What's wrong?" Rachel became aware that she had sealed herself inside the car, but hadn't turned the ignition or the air conditioner on. "Hey!" Roxy was roil-faced, but kept banging. "Are you all right in there?"

Rachel stared at Roxy's knuckles pressed against the glass for what seemed a long, long time. Then she rolled the window down and, not very convincingly, nodded, yes, she was fine. After Roxy left, Rachel just sat there, watching women come and go. What would *she* do? Rachel would wonder, settling on one or another of the passersby. She'd met the eyes of a particularly hard-looking woman with dyed black hair and she'd thought, *Shoot him. Shoot him dead.*

From there, Rachel had driven to the gun shop and now she was almost home. She eased her car forward again, barely breathing until the steep rooftop of her apartment complex came into view. Something was wrong—or no—maybe not. Maybe the neighborhood was always this quiet, this empty, and she'd never noticed it before. Come to think of it, that was the case.

She remembered, for instance, a mid-week morning when her phone had gone on the blink. She'd walked around the little complex rapping on one door, then the next, then the next. She hadn't found anyone home, though there'd been a few scattered cars in the ports that fronted the building.

At the time she'd been amused to know that she had the place, including the pool and the whirlpool, all to herself by virtue of the fact that she worked at home. Now the knowledge terrified her.

And Zachary was away. She was wholly alone, wholly at Drew's mercy.

If he had any. She remembered being alone with him a few years back. She'd driven him from Kingsville proper to one of the tiny roads that ran around the town. She'd done it purposely, knowing that he'd argue with her when she mentioned the drugs and not wanting anyone to hear. Lately their arguments had been hideously loud, the sort that Rachel had always associated with tattooed men and overweight women with their hair in curlers. Drew always used profanity, knowing that she'd be cowed in the face of it. "Fuck you," he'd holler, "and fuck this shit of yours."

Rachel had begun to steel herself, had begun to fight back, push her point of view no matter what he said. "You're killing yourself, Drew. Drew, listen."

"I don't have to listen," he'd say, and he was right. He'd storm out, and what was she to do? Follow? Run through the streets in his wake? Beg him to stop filling himself with whatever was making him act this way?

So she'd lured him away, this time, taking him, she'd said, to dinner at the King's Inn. First, she'd told him, they'd have to talk. He rolled his eyes at that and let his breath whistle out through clenched teeth. But that was all. He got into the car and let her head on out of town.

She tried to make small talk, but it fell flat. He fiddled with the radio dial and found a Spanish station. He turned it loud and left it on, goading her to lower the volume or click it off. She did neither, even hummed along with some of the tinny mariachi brass. Doing it made her feel better, as if she were getting even.

He finally turned it off himself and began singing "La Cucaracha." She knew what he was up to. He was going to throw the part about the marijuana back at her, the part where the singer says he can't walk because he's been smoking marijuana. What a laugh. Marijuana was the least of her worries. He was agreeable when he was smoking marijuana. Whatever he was taking lately made him mean.

Was it PCP? She'd been hearing so much, reading so much. Is that what it was? He'd seemed okay today, and that was why she'd decided to approach him about it, try again to get him to see a counselor or something.

"Hey." He'd spied a dirt road off to the left. It was probably near the water. "Go down there."

"It's probably private property," she said. Much of the land was ranchland, especially near Laguna Madre.

"So what? It's not marked."

She turned. The road was deeply rutted, as if it had been meant for a jeep or a mule train. But the ground was dry, and so Rachel kept on. Soon they came to a sandbar, with water seeping up around it and the Laguna blue beyond. There was litter everywhere, but also birds aplenty, pelicans especially.

"Stop the car," Drew said, jumping out before she was able to do it completely. He took his shoes and socks off and tossed them onto the passenger seat. He ran out on the bar, birds flapping off as he neared them.

Rachel followed, calling out, "Watch your feet! There's glass!" Much glass. Broken bottles, even some that appeared to be pieces of fishermen's floats. And metal, wicked-looking chunks of it. Rachel spied a slip-

pery something and added an additional warning.
"There might be jellyfish!"

She was irritated. He was so careless. He never listened to her, never. He wasn't even waiting to hear what
it was she wanted to talk to him about.

"Come on," he shouted back at her, waving her to the
sandbar's edge.

"I'm fine right here," she shouted back.

She saw him bend down and scoop something up. He
took a glance back at her as he did. Now what? It had to
be something awful. A jellyfish or a moldy old crab or
something like that. She turned and began walking back
toward the car as he ran toward her, whatever it was
behind his back. She tried to keep cool, tried not to
quicken her pace, but she couldn't help herself. She
could just picture whatever it was, maggoty and slimy,
and Drew bringing it back toward her, toward her face,
Drew poking it at her right back in her face. She glanced
back, and he was gaining fast. She broke into a mad run
and hurled herself back inside the car. She rolled the
windows up and locked the doors.

Drew was laughing maniacally, making faces through
the windshield, then the window on her side. "What do
you think I have?" he was asking, and Rachel, who still
didn't know, turned away. Her eyes filled with tears,
and Drew went around the passenger side and saw that.
He stopped laughing, grew angry; through her tears Rachel could see that. He held out something, something . . .

"Stupid bitch!" he screamed at her. "Look at this! Just
look!" He held it against the window, his face contorted
behind it. It was a pale glass bottle. Rachel could see
that there was a note inside. A message in a bottle.
That's what he'd been bringing her. Not a jellyfish, nor
a dead crab, but a message.

She wanted to apologize, hug him and apologize, but

he was furious. "Bitch!" he shouted, swinging the bottle hard against the fender of the car. It shattered, and he hurled the piece in his hand away.

He ran back along the road she'd driven then, and Rachel stayed there, locked in the car. No way to make it better. No way.

She'd driven home before dark, and though she'd looked and looked and looked she hadn't seen him along the way. He was there when she got home, though, eyes blank, all that anger flattened out like something she'd run over with the car.

She'd been right to take him out there where she did. There'd been no one to hear, no one to see.

SO WHAT ARE YOU THINKING ABOUT?" the girl asked.

"What's it to you?"

"Nothing, I guess."

"Well all right then." What had he been thinking? He wasn't sure he knew. About his own mother, in response to the girl always chattering about hers. About Rachel.

"You never said why you were going to Austin," the girl tried. But to look at the bright side, it was a damn sight better than listening to her going on and on about her folks. "I can tell it's not UT."

She meant the university. He was offended by the way she'd assumed that he wouldn't be going there. "Oh, yeah? How can you tell?"

"You're just not the type."

"What type is that?" He had a sudden vision of the fucking wimp who'd taught him, or tried to teach him, seventh-grade math. "You're just not college material, Cassidy," the wimp was fond of saying. "Better join the service, Cassidy, if they'll take you."

"Oh, hey, look," the girl said, backing off. "Summer session's already started, that's how I knew. Honest."

He didn't say anything in reply. He was remembering the high school equivalency test he'd taken at Benedict House and how simple it was. Fucking simple.

"I dropped out, myself," the girl said. "I was taking this creative writing course—"

"Hey," he interrupted her, "it's still too goddam hot in here. Let's turn the a/c up." He flipped the lever to high before she could answer. Now, he figured, they could finish this trip in relative peace.

RACHEL COULD NOT BRING HERSELF TO GET out of the car and unlock her own front door.

If only Zachary were here, she thought, and then she marveled at her admission of reliance on him. But there was no denying it, she would feel safe if Zachary were there.

Not that she wasn't strong, not that she wasn't self-sufficient. It was just—what? So nice not to have to be for a change. Rachel could remember how, for years, she dared not even have a headache lest she lose the precarious hold she'd had on her life, her finances, her means of support.

Every day, every single morning, she'd awaken in a leaden state, revive herself with a cup of thick black coffee and a shower—in that order. While showering she'd plan her work day, only occasionally letting her mood or a stroke of inspiration dictate.

Money mattered all too much.

Thus it was crazy patchwork that she mostly did, crazy patchwork, more or less haphazard, only color to be considered as she snipped, arranged, and sewed. And she concentrated on the small, high-mark-up items: potholders, aprons, pillowcovers.

In the beginning she kept her evenings free for more intricate quilting, for artistry. In the beginning she even decorated an old-fashioned cotton petticoat that she'd found in an antique store with delicate trapunto.

Eventually, she had to forgo the work she loved most in order to survive. She felt like a cheat sometimes, rushing work through an assembly-line process, precut pieces all in a row, while her mail-order clients thought they were getting just the opposite, what the Patchwork ad promised: each stitch lovingly laid.

Living a lie even then. Still, it was necessary to support herself and Drew after Rob left. She'd done quite well, in fact, if money was the measure. What was more, she'd learned she could. But the best thing, as it turned out, was that she could take her work, her business, anywhere.

When she'd fled Kingsville, she'd taken a batch of samples and her purse and her precious sack of fabric scraps. Nothing more. She'd even left the petticoat behind.

But making it in Austin wasn't as easy as she'd expected it to be. She'd carried her potholders and aprons and pillows around to Austin shops but found she'd realize only a percentage of what her painstaking needlework was worth that way. And so, after a month or so, she'd taken the chance and run the ad for Patchwork yet again.

While she'd lived in Kingsville she'd run it in regional magazines: *Texas Monthly, Third Coast,* and so on. Now she placed it in national magazines, using a box number, to be sure. The response was huge, so huge she wished she'd thought of that sort of advertising a lot sooner. Back when money had been brutally scarce, for instance.

She even had a catalog printed, and in it she offered to reproduce, for what she thought a stupendous price, any quilt at all. Orders poured in, enabling her—for pay!—to return to the intricate stitchery she loved. She reproduced an overall clamshell pattern, for instance, a design which relied not on color, but on the placement of the stitches alone. Still another order asked her to re-create the Princess Feather pattern, which, to Rachel's mind, was the needlework equivalent of a fireworks display.

But the ad brought much much more. It had brought a letter from Peyton, who had become Rachel's friend and backer. And it had brought Zachary into her life.

If anyone had asked Rachel in the years after Rob had left her whether or not she planned to remarry, she'd have said yes, God, yes. But in fact, she did nothing to arrange her life so that remarriage would be likely.

Arrange my life how? she'd have argued, but, in point of fact, there were any number of things she might have done. Taken a course at the university, gone more often into Corpus or to Brownsville. To Mexico. Or, for that matter, she could have courted invitations to various receptions around town—not just the university but the hospital, the Chamber of Commerce, the naval base. Instead, Rachel retreated. Drew needed her, she told herself and anyone who might ask. She could not simply go gallivanting all over town.

And anyway, what did unmarried people—adult unmarried people—have to do in Kingsville anyway? Some went to dance at a private club in the Holiday Inn, and she tried that once with a woman who lived down the street from her. It was excruciating, embarrassing. The men were either cowboys who lived in or near the town or salesmen passing through it. They'd say things like "And what do you do, little lady?" and Rachel would hear herself say, "I sew." Hang around with boring people and you become one. That night, she recalled, was one of the few times since Rob had left that she'd missed him. At least he could talk, for God's sake.

In that way, Zachary reminded her of Rob. His way with words had, in fact, led to their meeting. Like Peyton, Zachary had written Patchwork following the receipt of a quilt he'd ordered, a replica of a modern-looking Amish piece. One of the Patchwork touches was to enclose washing instructions done on a sort of parchment with a fine italic pen with each order. But Zachary was at odds with them, writing that "despite the fact that they were charmingly done," they seemed a tad modern to him. He then offered his own method, culled, he'd told Rachel, "from a quarter century of interviews with various robust septuagenarian laundresses." Rachel wrote him back, and he wrote yet again. The next thing Rachel knew, she was standing in front of the Austin Public Library at an agreed-upon time, wondering which of the passersby he might be. And he'd fooled her. He'd been *in* the library and he'd come up behind her, saying, "You don't look at all homespun. I'm surprised."

Zachary had a small publishing firm that specialized in Texana. He continued to travel all over the state either acquiring manuscripts or distributing finished books. He had even talked to Rachel about the possibility of her compiling one on Texas needlework.

He seemed to know all there was to know about Texas history, even odd bits and snippets—what the weather was like when the Battle of San Jacinto was fought, things like that. What was more, he knew everybody—not just names but wonderful bits of gossip. Often when Rachel was with him, at dinner or at lunch, he'd be recognized and, often as not, gushed at. He was treated, Rachel thought, with deference. "Nonsense," he'd said when she'd told him. "They're closet writers, every one of them. They're hoping I'll discover them, which, of course, means publish them." Then he whispered, "Epic poets, usually." And when she looked at him, he winked. Then she did begin to notice that they always did want Zachary to "take a look" at something. That was how they phrased it. What was especially nice about this was that it enabled Rachel and Zachary to exchange a fleeting, knowing glance.

Nonetheless, it wore on Zachary, and he retreated from most social outings. He preferred, as Rachel did, a quiet evening at home.

Rachel was amazed at the contentment she felt on nights they shared. Zachary reading, deep in the plush of his chair, while she plotted, at first in her mind and then with pencil, what she would stitch. He liked to read about houses and furniture, and appreciated woodgrain as much as she did fabric. Sometimes he would call to her and she would stop and peer over his shoulder at the detail of a chest or washstand or armoire. Something about this touched her, the way the mending on old cloth touched her too.

She wished, almost from the very start, that she hadn't had to lie to Zachary. Once when she spread her bag of scraps, the memories that each piece stirred almost made her tell the truth.

If only she had. She could see herself, holding the flannel that had been Drew's pajama top, the satin that had once been her own wedding dress, the tie that had been her father's. Zachary, so attuned to history and the past, would understand.

Too late then and now, later still. Now, maybe never, maybe never at all.

She felt a physical sensation, a hollowness, like hunger, at the thought. She loved Zachary with her body, too, with her body, maybe, above all.

For the longest time, Rob had been her only lover. She hadn't known, until Zachary, what a horrible lover Rob had been.

She'd gone through a good part of her life thinking herself a woman who could do without sex, a woman who, during her marriage, wished she had done without it. She still cringed to think of Rob, who thought his erection the ready mark.

She honestly didn't think he knew he was awful. She'd certainly never said anything to him about it. She was dry dry dry, though, but Rob solved that, probably after talking to the guys at the radio station about how frigid his wife was, with a tube of KY jelly. It never occurred to Rob that she was dry because she didn't desire him at all.

The funny thing was, her mother had told her once that it would be this way, something to put up with.

One time, Rob lifted her up off the bed and did it to her as he stood up. He actually turned to watch this in the bedroom mirror, and at one point she did, too. She almost laughed out loud, it was so grotesque, her perch as well as his strain to keep her there. Why? What was this supposed to prove? She could tell from the way Rob had strutted around the house afterward that he thought this made him pretty hot stuff, but, in fact, it was the same as always, boring and repetitive. He'd set her down, in fact, as soon as she'd received what she thought of as the most revolting substance in the world, his semen.

She'd read articles since then, and she'd been incredulous to read that women resented men doing that, leaving them, apparently, in the throes of red-hot desire. Rachel felt no desire for Rob whatsoever, and so she was glad, glad, glad, when he ejaculated and left her alone.

Then came Zachary. Rachel could sometimes feel herself moistening just at the thought of his name. So different, so completely different with Zachary.

It was odd, because Rob, even recently, had looked sexy: young, stylish, muscular. Zachary, on the other hand, looked distinguished: gray, dapper, thin. She might never have gone out with Zachary, if the idea of sex had occurred to her. It was Zachary's intelligence that attracted her. Only later did the physical draw her as well.

Rachel would not have thought it would. She'd have bet money. Not only had she never once enjoyed being with Rob, but by now she'd been without a man for so long that the physical wasn't something she thought about or dreamed about or yearned for. It was a distant realm, and had nothing, but nothing, to do with her. Deep in her heart she suspected that the sexual revolution that magazines were so fond of writing about was nothing more than a hoax. She didn't even need affection, much less sex.

Then, after perhaps her sixth or seventh date with Zachary, he'd kissed her. Rachel could still remember it with a glow. It had happened near Christmas, though given Austin's sunbelt location, it was still warm enough for them to be out walking at dusk. They'd walked near Town Lake under trees that still looked green. Rachel had commented on them. "They're barren," Zachary told her. "What you see is mistletoe."

Rachel looked up, and sure enough, the bare tree limbs were wrapped around with pale green and pale white berries. "Mistletoe!" The thought of a kiss crossed her mind, and she knew, when she saw Zachary smiling at her, that it had crossed her face as well. What followed was, for Rachel, all the kisses she had missed with Rob, a sort of universal kiss, an introduction to romance itself.

All of a sudden, Rachel had realized that Rob pressed too hard. Fortunately, she didn't laugh, and Zachary held her close for a long while afterward, his cheek brushing hers, stroking her even with his nose.

But that was merely comfort.

They drew apart and continued their walk, though he held her hand. Occasionally, she would come off balance, and there would be a brush, her hip against his. They climbed the steps to a lakeside gazebo that was wrapped in wisteria vines. Zachary stood behind her and talked about how the gazebo looked when the wisteria was in bloom, how they'd have to come here then. Rachel leaned against him, glad they were alone, though not sure why she was glad.

And then she felt his hands press on her shoulders and, at the same time, behind her, the swell of his groin. Rachel didn't pull away, but quite the opposite, felt almost that she wanted to weld herself against him, even against his Rob-hard penis.

Unlike Rob, Zachary waited. It was almost a taunt, a tease. And Rachel found herself unable to keep from reaching for him with her hands, reaching in a hungry way, a way she'd never wanted to before, never had before.

When she turned and he kissed her again, she knew her lips had parted and were moist and enveloping, and the sensation was the same elsewhere, between her legs, a kind of yearning receptivity.

Rachel didn't care that they were at the gazebo, on city property, in public. She heard herself emit a moan.

She felt his hands along the seams of her skirt, and instead of protesting she helped him bunch it up.

It was Zachary, not she, who withdrew. He did it with a light remark, a remark about her convent past and all that she had missed as a result. His eyes glistened, as if he were fiercely grateful for the passion that had overtaken her. If only he knew that she, Rachel, was far more grateful than he could ever be.

Long minutes later, at Rachel's, she learned Zachary was nothing like Rob, he had hands and a mouth as well as a penis, and he used them fluidly, fervently. Rachel learned by copying him. By the time he entered her she was—in her mind at least—begging him to.

Less than a week later he'd given up his efficiency apartment and moved in with Rachel, though, old-fashioned as he was, it wasn't enough, he said. He wanted to marry her.

Rachel became afraid.

Zachary knew nothing about her real past, not even Rob's name, much less about Drew. But worse. Whenever he talked about his own past, Rachel listened with a sense of suspicion, mistrust. *She* had lied, after all, so what guarantee had she that *he* was telling her the truth?

However many times she told herself that she was being irrational, she couldn't believe the stories he told about his former wife, who still ran an antiques store in Kyle, a small town to the south of Austin.

According to Zachary, she, his first wife, hadn't liked sex at all, though Rachel couldn't, couldn't imagine that, not with Zachary. What was more, his wife had deceived him, Zachary said. She had claimed to want, as he had in the early years of their marriage, a family. Then, he said bitterly, it turned out she had all along been using a diaphragm. She was afraid to have a baby, she confessed, and while he might have understood—even forgiven—fear, he couldn't bear the lie. *The lie.*

Rachel reacted forcibly to that, but, rather than give her away, it drew Zachary to her even more solidly than before. "Ah, Rachel, Rachel," he said, tracing the furrow of her brow with his finger. And then he quoted *Othello,* which, strangely, she remembered from high school. "'She loved me for the dangers I had passed, and I loved her that she did pity them.'"

The dangers.

The thought brought Rachel back to the present, and, though she was unobserved, she was vaguely embarrassed to be sitting in her car, engine idling, in front of her own apartment, afraid afraid afraid to go inside. *Come on,* she prompted herself. *Come on.* Inside was solace: her furniture and Zachary's, her clothes and his. Her bag of scraps. If only someone in the complex were at home.

She cast yet another glance about. There was no one. Almost all carports were empty and the surface of the pool was still and flat, like glass.

Rachel could not risk it.

She could try Peyton's home, she decided, or, yes, a better idea, she could go to the shop, where Peyton was far more likely to be. Then, later, when the complex was populated once again, she'd come back here.

But what about the groceries? She really ought to put them in the fridge. Did she dare? Rachel was furious with herself, but couldn't muster the courage to go inside even to perform a task which would take seconds. On the way out of the complex she detoured to a large trash bin and deposited the kefir and the bean sprouts there.

She got onto the interstate and followed it north to the Sixth Street exit. Then she curled back under it to turn west. She liked the drive along Sixth, despite the traffic. All of Austin's trendy shops and galleries and restaurants were here, as was her own, Patchwork. Or would be. The official opening would be held in three days, with a gala party—champagne and catered munchies, courtesy of Peyton—to celebrate.

Peyton had also answered Rachel's Patchwork ad. In addition to ordering quite a lot, she'd asked a lot of questions, historical stuff about quilts in general. Rachel rarely got a chance to show off what she knew, and so she was happy to comply. Then, at one point in their correspondence, Peyton also suggested that they meet.

Peyton chose an Indian restaurant called Shalimar, in a shopping center on the north side of town. It was a shabby but colorful place, and the food, very highly seasoned, was unlike anything Rachel knew. Peyton had ordered for Rachel, and in fact, it was there, at that restaurant, that she'd first had kefir.

Rachel and Peyton were the only people in the place, other than the brown-skinned, gauze-clad waiters. Maybe that was why Peyton had laughed and said, "Oh, don't worry, you'll know me," when Rachel had asked.

How? Rachel had wondered, but she didn't press.

Rachel could remember when the Beatles had popularized things Indian, but Peyton was too young to have been a part of that. She was in her late twenties, Rachel had guessed. Peyton didn't look the way the girls who'd followed that Indian trend had looked either. In fact, if anything, Peyton looked slightly punk.

Or maybe it was just her hair, long behind, but spiked and crew-cut short in front. She made Rachel, with her short sleek blunt cut, feel suddenly quite out of fashion.

It didn't seem to matter, though, the difference in their appearance, once they started to talk. Peyton knew needlework, and had sketched some of the pieces she'd designed. She was as modern as Rachel was traditional, but, like Rachel, knew stitchery, appreciated quality.

Peyton mentioned, at the end of that first meeting, that she'd been wanting to invest in a shop that specialized in needlework. Rachel, with her detailed historical knowledge and sewing skill, might be a good person to back. Did Rachel think she might be interested?

Rachel fought hard to sound casual. Maybe, she said.

She was a little skeptical of the notion that Peyton—so young, so trendy—had money. Once she'd accepted that, she found she was even more stunned to hear that Peyton might invest some of it in her. Such a thought had never occurred to Rachel at all.

Rachel was making more than ever from her catalog sales. Nothing further had occurred to her. And, Peyton said, there was no reason why Rachel couldn't continue that end of the business on her own. The shop would give her visibility.

What, Rachel asked, if it didn't pay its way? She'd heard somewhere that new businesses weren't likely to. She didn't want to risk someone else's hard-earned money.

Peyton told her, matter-of-factly, that she hadn't had to work for what she had. The money had been her family's, she said. "All I did was outlive them," she added.

Rachel would have thought that after her own fierce struggle to survive, she'd feel an immediate animosity toward someone like that, but in fact she was almost reverent now that she was faced with it.

Peyton described herself as having "pots and pots of money," which prompted Rachel to visualize the woman surrounded by the sort of stew pots that appear in cannibal cartoons, only in those pots, not victims, but an endless and overflowing supply of solid-gold coins.

When she told Peyton this—and she thought it a measure of how much she liked Peyton that she did tell her—Peyton laughed and countered with the way she envisioned Rachel: in a simple one-room dirt-floored cabin, photographs of Rachel's ancestors all over the walls.

"Oh, Lord," Rachel said, wishing she could tell her new friend the truth. About Kingsville, about the assembly-line patchworking method she'd devised, about Rob and Drew. Instead she offered the convent story.

"Now that you've told me," Peyton said, leaning back in her chair there in the restaurant and regarding Rachel, "I can picture that, too. In fact, I can't believe I didn't guess." She went on to mention that Rachel wore little makeup, had her hair simply cut, and at that moment had on a black cotton dress that had—and needed—no adornment at all. "A sister. Well, of course!"

Rachel laughed nervously.

Rachel shared one portion of her true past with Peyton eventually: her scrap bag. One rainy afternoon she brought the bag to Peyton's and dumped its contents on a work table for Peyton to see. She didn't tell Peyton about the pieces, at Peyton's own insistence. In fact, Peyton closed her eyes with various individual pieces of fabric crumpled in her fist and attempted to divine their significance.

For the most part, she was joking. She identified one piece as altar cloth and another—from Rachel's wedding dress—as a baptismal garment. But then, clutching a scrap from an old woolen plaid shirt that had been Drew's, Peyton grew serious. "Did you teach, Rachel? Don't all nuns teach?"

Puzzled, Rachel shook her head to indicate she hadn't taught. She didn't know what she would say she had done, but as it turned out, she didn't have to.

Peyton put the scrap down with a sort of shiver. "That's really eerie," she said. "I was getting little-boy vibes."

It was all Rachel could do to keep from visibly reacting.

Later, when she was at home and alone, Rachel clutched the cloth herself and attempted to conjure the image of Drew. She even chanted his name.

In the middle of this episode, the telephone rang. It was Peyton. "Hey," she said. "I meant to ask you. Are you or are you not interested in this shop deal? In Patchwork?"

Now, she thought, admiring the storefront from the street, it was a scant three days from being reality. She turned right and then down the alley so that she could park in the lot in the rear. Even from behind, the shop looked fashionable: native Texas stone with brightly enameled ivory trim.

Rachel let herself in the rear door and walked inside. There was a faint sweet aroma. Incense, Rachel thought. A sure sign that Peyton had been on the premises. Rachel would never have expected to like the smell of incense, but the sticks that Peyton used smelled so much like vanilla that Rachel had even considered taking some home to try. She suspected, however, that Zachary would frown on the notion, just on general principle. Once she'd tried an aerosol spray—a very expensive one—and he'd complained about it.

She understood why Peyton used it, especially lately. Peyton hated cigarette smoke, and the workmen couldn't seem to get that fact through their heads. They'd hammer and saw, puffing furiously away, when only Rachel was present. When Peyton came, however, she gave them what-for. It was amusing to see her walk up to a brawny workman at least a foot taller than herself and say, "No smoking in here."

The workers would always look to Rachel for confirmation, partly because Rachel was older than Peyton, but partly, too, because Rachel was most often there. "That's right," Rachel would say. "She's the boss."

Peyton was an unlikely-looking boss, all right. Rachel thought about how she must have appeared to the workmen, who, Rachel was sure, lived terribly ordinary lives. Peyton, for instance, frequently wore anklets with shoes that, to Rachel's eye, would've looked a lot better with hose.

But then Peyton thought of Rachel as conservative. Rachel supposed that, not even by comparison, she was right. She'd owned the same Coach bag for eleven years, to think of just one example. She did bow to fashion enough to have bought flat shoes for dress-up, but could not shake the feeling, when she was wearing them, that she was underdressed. She'd returned to her old standby pumps and felt better for it.

When it came to quilts, however, Peyton and Rachel's tastes did not exactly mesh, but certainly did complement each other. A glance around the shop could tell her that. There were Peyton's panels, which included fabrics such as Lurex, right next to Rachel's own much-laundered, well-worn cottons, silks, and wools.

Then there was the shop itself, which, by and large, Peyton had designed. It had rough-hewn timbers and wrought-iron accents, a bare wood floor that was pegged rather than nailed. The back wall was stone and had been whitewashed as old basements once were. And yet there was an overall impression of lightness, probably because of the white, yes, and all of the glass that Peyton had insisted be used.

One side wall of the shop flanked the alley, and so it was easy to install windows there. The other, however, was shared with an ice cream parlor, and Peyton had had countless conversations with the owner there in order to convince him that both stores would benefit from a bit of frosted glass, high enough to maintain each party's privacy. Rachel smiled now at the result: not just a long thin light-emitting pane or row of glass block, but a fancifully executed crescent moon and star that had already been photographed by the local newspaper for use in its Sunday section on houses and buildings of note around town. But the big thing, the event she and Peyton had toasted, was not the window itself but the day Peyton had actually worn the ice cream store's owner down.

"How?" Rachel had wondered.

"By footing the bill," Peyton had said.

Indeed, Peyton had spent a fortune on the renovation of the little store. Rachel was dazzled by it. *It must be nice,* Rachel sometimes found herself thinking. Then she'd catch herself, tell herself to be grateful.

But she was! And it wasn't just money, either, though until the store began to show a profit, she would be paying Rachel a good salary, to make up for the orders Rachel had lost from catalog sales. Peyton was not just fair, but generous.

What counted even more was that Peyton had enabled Rachel to recapture the ability to have fun. She could remember riding around in Peyton's Mercedes, the soundtrack from *Flashdance* blaring from Peyton's tape deck. Rachel had laughed and laughed. She'd put her feet up on Peyton's dashboard, shoes and all. Never, in all the weary years with Rob and then later with Drew, had Rachel ever imagined herself in such a carefree situation.

But Peyton also had a serious side. She was a serious student of yoga, for one thing. Rachel had marveled to see Peyton doing her yoga routine one day, marveled at Peyton's strength and her ability to control each limb as if it were somehow a separate thing to be lifted and bent and placed here and there. Rachel had seen ballet dancers working out, but somehow Peyton's yoga was more impressive—slower, more deliberate, with more real power, perhaps, brought to bear.

She'd witnessed this the first time she'd been to Pey-

ton's cliffside home. Invited to breakfast, Rachel had
been unsure of how long the drive would take, and
found, to her chagrin, that she'd arrived a full half hour
early. She would have parked somewhere, or cruised
around the area, but unfortunately, she came upon Peyton herself, making the steep climb to her home.

"Oh, no!" Peyton shrieked. "Am I that late?"

"No." Rachel pushed the door on the passenger side
open. "I'm afraid I'm unfashionably early."

"I always walk this hill in the morning," Peyton explained, getting into the car. Though the roadway was
extraordinarily steep, Rachel noticed that Peyton wasn't
even huffing. Even more astonishing, Peyton was barefoot. The occasional chunk of caliche gravel, Rachel
knew, would have cut her own tender feet to ribbons.

The gate was open, and Rachel guided her car, which
suddenly seemed quite old and dirty, inside. She thought
the vegetation lush—almost like the vegetation in the
Rio Grande Valley. This was possible in Austin, but
only with much tending, both actual and monetary. But
there it was: myrtle and banana and bougainvillea,
masses of the latter, pink and red and fuchsia.

The house itself hung out over the cliff, supported by
cantilevers, and was exactly the opposite, spare, with an
industrial feel. Huge warehouselike windows, exposed
pipes, flat-woven flooring.

"There are five levels, but you'll see," Peyton said.

Rachel followed Peyton into the long expanse of the
living room, built on the largest of the cantilevers, Peyton said. It was monochromatic, all of it in neutral
shades of gray and beige and brown. Rachel found it
gloomy. The upholstery on the furniture—what furniture there was—was the grim sort of cloth that movers
use to protect things. Rachel would never have guessed
that her friend would have decorated in this stark, utili-

tarian way. She wondered if Peyton was leasing the place, but no, she remembered Peyton saying something about actually having it built. She could, she thought, accept anything about Peyton, anything at all.

"Since you are early, Rachel, would you mind if I did my morning exercises?" Rachel said of course not, and only then noticed that Peyton had been wearing a long-sleeved, long-legged leotard with stirrups. How thin she was!

She went behind a wet bar and came back with a cold glass filled with a syrupy thick substance. "Papaya juice," she explained, handing it to Rachel. "I have guava, too, if you'd like."

Rachel sipped and thought it far too sweet. Peyton, meanwhile, went past a glass wall at the end of the room and settled beyond, on a wide concrete deck. A mat had been spread there, a narrow-ribbed mat that looked more uncomfortable than the concrete itself.

While Rachel watched, Peyton centered herself on the mat, then bent and rose and swooped and stretched, her body as supple as a willow switch. She later told Rachel the names of some of the postures: Locust, Cobra, Leaf. "Want to try?" she asked, but Rachel could tell that Peyton knew all along that Rachel wouldn't. Watching, Rachel had felt large, ungainly, even fat. And old. Rachel had felt quite old.

But of course she was a full eleven years older than Peyton. Rachel smiled, thinking of the time she'd jokingly suggested that the shop be called Peyton's Place. Talk about generation gap! Peyton at first hadn't caught Rachel's allusion, but then said something about a television show. She even considered the suggestion seriously, saying, "I thought you'd want to use the name you've been using—Patchwork." Rachel hadn't the nerve to explain that *Peyton Place* had been *the* risqué novel in Rachel's day.

Still, here, right now, in the shop that she and her friend had created, Rachel felt calmer than she had all day, or, at least, since she'd heard the news about Rob. Something about Patchwork was soothing—the bright glass shelves and display cases, the newness, the hope that it all represented.

The spotlighted "quilt of the month" was hanging on the back wall, a Heavenly Steps that Rachel had recently completed. It went with the educational display in the window, all about the rhomboid and its use in quilt design. There was a drawing of a trellis pattern using rhomboids, and a square that showed a cross that was composed of rhomboids and triangles. That was what Rachel liked most about quilting: that it was as simple or as deep as you wanted it to be.

She noticed one jarring note—a magazine lying open on the floor. Probably one of the workmen had left it there. Rachel strode across to it, noting that it was one of those supermarket specials, a gaudy oversized color newspaper called the *Star*.

Rachel shrank back when she saw the pages it was opened to: a two-page spread on John Hinckley, the boy who had shot President Reagan. Hinckley had always troubled Rachel, always made her think, whether rationally or not, that it might just as easily have been Drew. She thought about Hinckley's parents over and over again and sometimes wished she could talk to them, ask them, was he ever like *this?* did he ever do *that?* But that was selfish, wasn't it? Their son had committed a crime, and hers had only hinted that one day he might. . . .

Oh my God, Rob. I forgot about Rob. I forgot about his corpse there in his beach house. Forgot about his screams, lost in the slap of waves on the Galveston beach. Forgot!

Just then she saw the blurred but unmistakable outline of a male form at the door. She blinked, expecting, foolishly, that it would go away. It seemed connected to the article, the Hinckley thing, and Rachel didn't know why. She had just picked the paper up when whoever it was tried the knob.

It was like a horror movie, the bright brass knob slowly turning, first this way, then that. Rachel let the newspaper fall and regretted even the slight rustle that the pages made wafting to the ground.

She stepped backward—instinctively, but, she knew, ineffectually. The sound of her footsteps seemed to boom above the sound of her heart. *Easy, easy, there's still the back door,* she told herself. *Relax, you can run.*

Whoever it was tried the knob again, then shook the door when it didn't open. Rachel, frozen with fear, listened to the scrape of wood, rattle of glass. She tried to see beyond the frosted white surface, see the form, see who it was. It was ghostly, seeing this way, when a flash the color of flesh meant an arm, a neck, a face. As if her eyes had of a sudden grown cataracts, bottle-glass lenses to keep her from knowing the truth.

The figure jolted backward, as if to prepare to heave himself into the door, which would surely give way. But then there was a pause, a gathering, and, just as suddenly as it had appeared, the figure turned and went away.

Rachel pivoted and started toward the back. She stopped herself. *No!* Whoever it had been would surely head there. Having tried the front, wasn't it likely that he'd also go around the building to try the back?

Was it Drew? Oh, was it, was it? *No time, no time, just run run run.*

But what if she chose wrong, ran headlong into the intruder? Why wouldn't instinct lead her now? Damn!

Rachel turned again, this time bounding through the showroom to fumble with the front door's deadbolt lock. With a huge effort, she all but hurled herself forward into the street.

She bumped into a shirtless male, and he caught her as if she were falling. She looked up at him slowly, painfully. Would it be Drew? She was afraid, but yet she had to know. She had to know.

It was a stranger, a student, probably, and he seemed amused. "Hey, take it easy, lady," he said, more or less rocking her firmly upright before he moved away.

"The door," Rachel said, pointing back, over her shoulder, in an attempt at explanation, but he had already gone off. Indeed, only seconds later, she could barely pick him out among the others on the street.

What time must it be? The sidewalks were starting to fill with University of Texas students, their classes done for the day. Later, when it got dark and some of Sixth Street's celebrated night spots opened, there would be a crush, but even now there were far too many people outside for Rachel to worry that no one would hear her if she was in any kind of danger.

There was nothing inherently scary about Austin, Rachel had decided, early upon her arrival in that city. Indeed, Austin, if anything, seemed filled with fitness nuts: cyclists and joggers and people walking dogs. Kingsville, whatever its statistics, struck her as the opposite.

Kingsville had been downright creepy. Once or twice Rachel had gone out very late to the all-night convenience store there. She'd felt threatened all the way. By what? She wasn't sure. Just something thick and evil that hung in the night air along with the humidity.

Rachel had cut her thumb in Kingsville and it had taken weeks upon weeks to heal. She'd gone to the doctor, but he'd assured her there was no infection. It had only been a shallow cut, but it had left a scar. The cut and whatever kept it from closing seemed a perfect metaphor for the little South Texas town that Rachel had grown to despise.

Discomfited by the memory, Rachel rubbed at the scar, now a pale, tissuelike crescent. Not knowing what else to do, she walked slowly back inside the shop. There was no sign now of the would-be intruder. Nor of Peyton, nor of . . . she mustn't lose sight of the source of her peril . . . Drew.

NO KIDDING?" SHE SQUEALED WHEN HE told her. "Your father?"

Rob Cassidy's death hadn't really fazed Drew until right then, when he was face to face with the girl's stupid reaction. There was no other word for it—glee. He wanted to slap the girl silly, but he couldn't, not if he wanted to get to Rachel, which he couldn't do if the girl just dropped him off somewhere in Austin and left him to fend for himself, maybe hitch another ride.

It occurred to him that she was probably, in the only way she could, getting even for that trip he'd laid on her about her own folks. Well, okay. That he could understand. So while she was still being callous about it, he said, "Look, cunt, I see what's going on here, okay? I see what you're doing, and fine, I get it. But enough, okay?"

Her foot got heavier and heavier on the gas pedal while she was deciding what to do. Was she going to pull this wild-eyed Texas bitch thing or was she going to be whatever the fuck she was? And would they, for Christ's sake, be alive when the answer came in? Because by the time she finished making up her mind, the little T-bird must have been doing ninety-five.

He was scared, yes, but he sure as hell wasn't going to holler at her to stop. It was her decision, as far as he was concerned. Which is not to say he wasn't relieved when she pulled over to the side.

"I'm sick of driving," she said. "You do it for a while." And without even waiting she got out, came around to his side.

A line from a song passed through his head, about the pros and cons of hitchhiking. Except that he hadn't started hitching, this girl had just kind of sniffed him out, right?

He spotted the brown paper bag with the stuff she'd bought in it. He reached back behind the seat and pulled it forward. Then he shifted to the driver's seat and peeled out, loud and on purpose.

"Hey, quit," she said. "You're gonna get us killed."

"I'm gonna get us what? Do you see me careening around the way you were doing back there?" With that he yanked the wheel from one side to the other, making the little T-bird groan and sway. "It's like dancing, isn't it?" He laughed. Then he started to hum the hitchhiking song, and she laughed too. Until he started rooting in the bag again.

She snatched it away from him. "It's makeup," she said.

"I'm sure."

"No, it is."

He stopped the car right on the roadway, grabbed it back, and looked. She'd been telling the truth. He drove on, a little disgusted, but unsure why. He tried to pull out of it. "Read me the names," he said.

"What names?"

"The names of the makeup. You know, like, Kissable Pink."

" Kissable Pink," she scoffed. But she dumped the contents on her knees and began to look at each container. "You're right," she said.

He shook his head in wonder. What did she think, that he'd made that up? Rachel used to read the names to him when he was little. That was how he knew. He remembered one he liked especially called Fire and Ice. God, it had been so long ago.

Meanwhile, the girl began to read. "There's, um, Misty Teal and, uh, Wine and Roses, and"—she had to squint to make out the tiny type—"Sunlit Sherry." She thought for a minute and then she said, "Hey, wouldn't that be a fun job? Naming makeup? I wonder who does that. Names makeup." She dropped the stuff back into the bag and stowed it. Then she leaned way down in the seat, as if she was going to drop off to sleep.

"Hey, get that map out," he told her. "I'm pretty sure this is Austin coming up."

She smoothed the map across her knees and teased him.

"Just think," she said, "our first date and already I'm going to meet your mom."

He knew that she expected him to laugh at that, but he couldn't. Even before the Austin city limits sign came into view, his insides had begun to shake. It seemed too easy. Rachel's name and even her address right there in the Austin phone book. Too easy for something that was going to be so hard.

By the time they got to the complex Rachel lived in, he must have been shaking visibly, too. The girl put her hand on his forearm and patted it, saying, "Don't you worry. It'll be all right."

He was very mixed up about the girl, very mixed up about what it would be like when she wasn't around anymore. The fact was, he liked her, liked the way they got along together, sometimes at odds but most times not.

Sisterly. He probably got that from the fact that he hadn't screwed her. It was on the one hand hard to fathom, and on the other hand easy. How could he be expected to walk around with a hard-on when he had so much on his mind? Like murder, for instance.

But the truth was he ought to be plenty pissed off at the girl, pissed off because she'd gotten him, in some sneaky underhanded way, to confide so much in her. But maybe that was normal, just part of spending time.

He remembered Rachel telling him—and, for all he knew, maybe that was part of it, too, Rachel telling him, Rachel, all husbandless and friendless in Kingsville, dumping it all into his lap—about how when he was born she'd shared a hospital room with a fat woman who ran the local bakery. She'd ended up telling this woman everything, as though they'd been best friends forever. They promised, Rachel and the woman, to see each other faithfully when they got out, too, which in Kingsville wouldn't have been too hard. Fact was, though, when they got out they avoided each other—at least Rachel avoided even going near where the bakery was. She was embarrassed by all that she had spilled, and Drew had a hunch he was going to feel exactly that way with the girl: anxious never to see her again once all of this was over.

UNEASILY, RACHEL MADE HER WAY TOWARD the rear door of the store. She opened it, involuntarily stepped backward, and caught her breath.

There was, right in her line of vision, something, an enormous fan or mask, she couldn't quite tell which. And at the very moment she saw it, she smelled it, too, a vague formaldehyde smell that clutched at her throat and threatened to gag her.

Rachel gaped at the thing, almost leathery in texture. While it repelled her, it fascinated her too. It was a creamy sort of beige that was pocked with varying shades of brown. But there was a facelike coloration, a grinning U-shaped mouth in the center of it. That and brooding little ovals for eyes. Rachel wanted to strike at it as much as shrink from it. She felt that this conflicting urge came, dark and atavistic, from some just-tapped part of her. The part that sensed danger, some sort of swirling, primal place. Rachel was almost as afraid to know that feelings such as this existed as she was to face the ugly, awful thing in front of her itself.

"Boo!" Peyton said, peering from behind the thing, stunning Rachel with a sense of how exaggeratedly she had begun to perceive events.

It was a mask after all, but a terrifying one, no doubt about it, Rachel thought. The mask was attached to a stick, like a lorgnette. Peyton lowered it and laughed. "I saw your car," she explained. "I decided I'd wait out here for you."

A remark like that would have seemed odd had the speaker been anyone but Peyton.

"Where did you get that thing?" Rachel asked, still shaken, still breathless, though trying to hide it. She could not bring herself to look at the mask more closely. At the same time, she wanted to, wished she could. Maybe get the knot of fear to dissolve.

"Like it?" Peyton threatened to raise the mask again. She had, by this time, divined Rachel's reaction, so to flaunt the mask now would be cruel. She lowered it to her side.

Rachel noticed. She looked at her friend with a sense of gratitude, if not relief.

"I bought one for you, too." And with that, Peyton swooped back out of range and emerged with yet another mask, a beautiful white mask of feathers. She looked through the eyecuts before handing it to Rachel.

"This is crazy, Peyton." Rachel laughed now, timidly raising the white mask to her face. "Utterly and completely crazy." What she felt now was a pang of envy, that Peyton was young now, in a period when masks could be worn, when masks could be found. She said this.

"Oh, baloney," Peyton protested. "And you're not too old to turn up wearing one of these either."

"Oh, sure," Rachel said. "And where would I do that?" The thought of going to a party with a mask on a stick was a funny one. The thought of Zachary accompanying her was funnier still. The mask suited Peyton, though, because she was in so many ways an exotic.

Peyton began rattling off a list of Austin events at which a mask would not seem out of place. It was a long list, too. Austin was that kind of city. While she talked, she drew Rachel out into the parking lot, closing and locking the shop's back door.

"What's it made of?" Rachel reached out to stroke the pale slick feathers of the mask.

"Don't know. Could it be egret?"

"I think egret's illegal." Even as Rachel said it, she wondered how she knew. If she did know. Maybe that was just a myth, like the one about it being illegal to pick bluebonnets, the wildflower that carpeted every field and roadside in the spring. Peyton would pick them by the armload, and Rachel would tease her about being arrested for it.

But Peyton had argued that it wasn't illegal at all. She even wrote to a local problem-solving columnist, Ellie Rucker, about it, and thus managed, in print, to prove her point.

But this time Peyton didn't bother disputing whether or not the feathers in the mask were legal or not. "You don't want it, do you?" she said.

"I didn't say that," Rachel told her.

"You practically did." Then Peyton raised the feathered mask and strode away in an exaggeratedly regal fashion.

Rachel watched as if the whole thing—first frightening her, then giving her the egret mask, and finally taking it away—were a dramatic performance. An act that had some sort of planned ending. She was disappointed, actually, when Peyton dropped both masks inside the Mercedes and asked, "So what are you doing here?"

Then Rachel remembered. She'd been afraid to go home, that's what she was doing here. "I don't know," she said lamely.

"Getting cold feet?" Peyton was referring, surely, to the shop. To the fact that Patchwork was about to open.

"No," Rachel said. Rachel looked at her friend, wishing she could find even a starting point, wishing she could begin to tell her about Rob, about Drew, about everything. But how could she? It was obvious, just looking at Peyton, that she would never understand. Never in a million years.

For one thing, Peyton had never been married, never

had children. How would she know what it was like to give your heart to someone, give your life, and have it turned into pulp in return? This must have shown on her face, because Peyton touched Rachel's arm. "You okay?" she asked.

For a moment Rachel felt as if it would all come tumbling out. That Rob was dead, that Drew was coming now to kill her, too. But she managed to keep it inside. "I have to get away," she said, and instantly wondered if Peyton would know she meant Drew.

Peyton seemed relieved. "Opening-night jitters, right? Well, listen. I've got to be somewhere in about half an hour, and I'll be gone well into the night. So why don't you go on to my place? Think of it as a vacation. Take Zachary, too."

"Zachary's away," Rachel told her.

"Better still. Really get away. Just float."

Peyton's cliffside house, with a pool that seemed suspended in midair, was the perfect place for that. Rachel thought of the solitude there, so close to the city and yet so seemingly remote. Indeed, from any of the levels at Peyton's, nothing but wild, undeveloped land was visible. It was—and once Peyton had told her she had planned it to be—a world apart. Rachel's face must have reflected her need for such tranquillity, because Peyton smiled and went again to the Mercedes and produced from somewhere within it a small ring with two keys. "One's for the gate," she said, "and the bigger one for the house."

"But how will you get in?" Rachel asked.

"Just don't lock up when you go to bed, okay?" She slid in behind the wheel and started the car's engine.

Rachel tried to tell her that was impossible, that she had to lock up, but already Peyton had the car backed into the little alleyway. Rachel stood there helpless and Peyton roared off shouting, *"Ciao!"*

You'll be safe at least temporarily, Rachel told herself, annoyed that Peyton hadn't given her a chance to protest or even to really decide. She tried to make the best of things, reminding herself that this, after all, was just the sanctuary she'd sought. She didn't *feel* safe, though she knew objectively that her circumstances were better now. Drew didn't—couldn't—know about Peyton and therefore couldn't possibly find his way to Peyton's house.

All right, so . . .

She began arranging the things she ought to do in her mind. She would go to her own apartment, gather up some clothes, and then spend the evening and the night in a state resembling peace. She would also stop by a 7-Eleven or someplace like that and get a Houston paper, read whatever else there was to read about Rob's death. And tomorrow Zachary would be home and she could . . .

What did it matter? If she fled Austin as she had Kingsville, what did Zachary's being there matter? But she wouldn't run, not again, not now, at least she felt that way here and now, with Patchwork there in front of her, and with Peyton's offer of a safe place to spend the night.

There had been nothing to leave in Kingsville, not really. Here, there was everything, her life. She didn't *want* to go.

She would tell Zachary, Rachel pledged, and maybe Peyton, too. Not right away, but one day soon. If they loved her—and they did, they did—they would understand.

But no one ever had understood. Rachel's problems with Drew, it seemed now, began right after Rob left. Though Drew hadn't even been a year old at the time, he'd sensed it, Rachel knew. If he'd cried while Rob had been there, he'd doubled, tripled, his protests in Rob's absence. And it wasn't just the crying, it was the soiling and the bed-wetting, too. The soiling went on long after it should have, went on when Drew was old enough to speak in whole sentences. Not all the time, but maybe once or twice a month. And what did the doctor say? That Drew just got more involved in play than he should. That he forgot himself. That it was nothing, and that the quickest way to end it was to ignore it.

It was hard to ignore something so awful, hard to ignore something so hard to clean. Whenever Rachel went to do the laundry and found a mound in Drew's underwear, it was all she could do to keep from waking him up and smearing it on his face.

Then one day it stopped. The bed-wetting, though, went on. For all Rachel knew, he might be bed-wetting to this day.

At first the bed-wetting seemed like nothing compared to his other, earlier problems. As time wore on, she hated it more; in fact, it seemed to Rachel not just deliberate, but also aimed at her. Even then, Drew was aiming his actions at her.

At first she tried the methods that various books and articles advised. She woke Drew up several times during the night; she withheld, or tried to withhold, liquids. But neither worked. He would be so crabby, even abusive, when she tried to get him out of bed. The clincher came when she saw him—saw him!—drinking glass after glass of water just before bedtime.

"You're doing this on purpose!" she said, grabbing a handful of his hair and shaking his head back and forth and back and forth. She wanted to slam his head against the sink, against the wall, against any hard surface, she didn't care, wanted to break his head in two.

"I forgot!" he wailed. "I forgot!"

She let go of him. "The hell you did! The hell you did!" She stalked out of the bathroom, out of the house.

She walked around and around the block thinking awful awful thoughts. She thought she'd calmed down when she came back inside, but the minute she did she was angry again. She went into Drew's bedroom and turned on the overhead light.

He grimaced and squirmed awake. She walked to his bed and when he looked up at her she said, "From this minute on I'm not washing a single sheet, a single blanket, do you understand? If you pee in that bed, you'll sleep in your pee, do you understand? I'm not putting up with you anymore, do you, do you, do you understand?"

He was crying, nodding yes, yes, that he understood. That satisfied her, and she doused the light, left the room. She waited for the guilt, the remorse, to overtake her, but it didn't, not that time. More and more she was feeling that she'd done all she could do. "Let someone else take over," she would sometimes say out loud. The silent part that followed was, *Anyone but me*.

How old was Rachel then? In her twenties. No feathered masks, no parties for Rachel. Only Drew and survival. Drew and cooking and cleaning and trying to keep from cracking up.

One time she'd gone to the university, to the child psychology department. She'd seen an article about it in the newspaper, and she'd gone in cold, hadn't even called first. She was so afraid they'd turn her down or, worse, make her wait. The relief, as she'd walked across the campus, was enormous. They'd know what to do with Drew, they'd know. They'd be able to fix things.

By this time, it was more than bed-wetting. A week before, Drew had found an injured dog and had penned it up, saying he was going to advertise for the owners. She'd felt proud of him, but then the owners, a sullen couple, had come by for the dog. Rachel couldn't understand why they were being so sour when her son had not just found the dog but gone out of his way to find the people who loved the animal. He'd also soaked the dog's foot, and rubbed some Vaseline down into what appeared to be a gash made with wire. But the man told Rachel the dog hadn't been accidentally hurt. The implication seemed to be that Drew or maybe even Rachel had done it. Rachel could still remember the way the wife had tried to restrain the man and the way the man had gone on anyway, "We think that at the very least your son stole our dog." He was never lost, that seemed for sure. In the man's mind, he was never lost at all.

Rachel thought the man was crazy, but when she looked at the wife, she knew that the woman agreed with her husband. She hadn't wanted to say anything about it, but she did agree. "I'm sure it's just a stage the boy is going through," the woman had said unconvincingly.

"But why would Drew do such a thing?" Rachel protested, getting louder as she went on. "It isn't as though there was any reward. I mean, why would he want your dog?"

The man said that he didn't know, and the woman said, "Boys will be boys," in a way that gave Rachel the willies.

Rachel had felt a kind of fury at that. "Get out of here," she'd shouted at the couple. "Get out right now!" Rachel could still remember pushing at the man's shoulders, actually propelling him physically down the hall and out the door.

She found the departmental office and explained to the clerk that she wanted to see a child psychologist. Was this about a course? No, Rachel said. What was it about, then? A child, Rachel had said. My son. What about him? the girl asked. Rachel began rooting in her bag. She'd put the article in there somewhere. She found it, smoothed it on the counter so that the girl could see. "It says here . . ." she began. The article was on the work that was being done with disturbed children. None of the psychologists had been mentioned by name.

"Just a minute," the clerk said. Then she picked up the phone and said, "Dr. Herzel? There's a woman here who says her son is disturbed . . ."

The rest of the conversation was lost for Rachel, who suddenly became the focus of everyone's gaze. Secretaries, students, even a mailman who'd been on his way out of the office.

"Is he an adolescent?" The clerk's voice burst through Rachel's embarrassment. "Is he . . . ?"

"I heard you," Rachel cut in. "I . . . I don't know."

"You don't know how old he is?"

"No, I . . ." How old was an adolescent? A teenager? Younger? "What I mean is . . ."

But the girl had hung up the phone. "I'm sorry," she said, "but Dr. Herzel is busy."

"But I . . ."

The clerk turned away. The others, the ones who were staring, did not. Rachel felt the heat of their gaze on her back as she left the room. In fact, though she didn't look back at the building to verify what she suspected, deep down inside, Rachel felt they were up there still, lining the windows, secretaries, the clerk, the mailman, Dr. Herzel, too. Staring at her, laughing, as she walked, defeated, back across the campus, mother of the disturbed, and no wonder. She could hear them saying it to each other up there, incredulous, every one: *Didn't even know how old the kid was. . . .*

Once Rachel had overheard a woman talking to another about her own son. "I'm fed up to here with him," the woman had said, and the other had agreed. Rachel listened intently, marveling at their friendship, marveling that they could admit these terrible things to each other this way. "I told him," the first woman said, "that if he wanted to go to school in the East, he'd better shape up." "Oh?" the second asked. "Where do you plan to send him?" "We thought Choate," the first woman said, "but there's no point even thinking about it until he turns those Bs into As. He's got two Bs on his card this semester!"

Rachel tuned out, two Bs being light-years away from what she had to face. Indeed, smart as he was, Drew had failed every single subject. He'd been absent, too, she'd discovered, an ungodly number of times. Where did he go all day long? What did he do? When she'd asked him about it, he'd denied that it had happened at all. "They just put that on my card," he'd said. "They hate me. They'll do anything to get my ass in trouble."

When Rachel called the principal, he'd asked her questions about her personal life. He kept stressing that Drew had several strikes against him, being from a broken home. Rachel felt like screaming, "I'm not the one who broke it, goddam it, I'm the one who stayed." Sometimes, the principal had gone on, a young, single woman, eager to have an active social life of her own, might not be available when a boy Drew's age needed her.

Rachel hung up before she'd begun to call the man names. How dare he! How dare he imply that she was out carousing while Drew languished at home, a latchkey child!

The fact was, Rachel had no social life whatsoever. She kept things afloat by selling patchwork through the mail. She had no friends of either sex, no dates, no anything. If anything, Rachel was an enforced recluse, too swept up in Drew's problems to think about a life of her own. Every now and then she surfaced to think, *If*

*only I'd walked away, done what Rob did. If only I'd
been the one.*

Occasionally she tried to apply legal screws. Even
back then, Rob Cassidy was starting to be a name. He
was a disk jockey for a time, and later a radio executive.
Never a father, though. Rachel thought then that she
could make him pay.

But it took forever. She couldn't afford a regular lawyer and had to go to the local Legal Aid. There she sat
for hours reading tattered magazines and wishing she
had brought something with her to sew while waiting to
get to see someone. The someone she saw seemed curt
and uncaring, but he filled the paperwork out and said
he'd be in touch. Three months later, when he hadn't,
Rachel called and no one in the office seemed able to
recall her or find her file. She asked for the lawyer she
had seen, but was told that he wasn't with the legal
service anymore.

The girl she'd talked to on the phone had a slight
Chicana accent and was very nice. She urged Rachel to
come back in and reapply, but somehow Rachel wasn't
able to muster the energy. Once she went so far as to
drive to the cottagelike building in which Legal Aid was
housed, but she couldn't bring herself to park and go
through it all again. And anyway—she told herself—
her patchwork sales had just begun to flow. Her situation was far better now. In fact, she'd probably do all
right.

Thus, she thought now, she had just let Rob get away
with it, the whole thing. Oh, she had secretly thought
that he'd pay one day in some Biblical, retributory way.

The memory—considering what had happened—
brought Rachel up short. *He has paid*, she thought.
Drew has seen to that.

SO ARE WE GOING IN, OR ARE WE JUST going to sit here or what?" They'd been out in front of Drew's mother's apartment for what seemed forever. The girl leaned forward and turned to look at Drew. Until then she'd been staring straight ahead. "Oh, hey," she said, when she saw that he was near crying. "You aren't going to change your mind or anything, are you?"

"No," he said, wiping his nose with a knuckle. 'I was just thinking about some shit is all." He wished he'd ditched the girl when he'd first thought to. He didn't like her seeing him this way, as if control were just a veneer, something that glossed his—what?— babyhood, almost.

She seemed to sense his discomfort, tried to brush off his show of emotion. "Yeah, well," she said, with a tougher edge to her voice, "we all have plenty of it, right?"

He had to stop and think back to figure what it was she was referring to, and then he remembered: shit, right.

Plenty of shit. He was up to his butt in shit, wading in it, like it was some kind of healing bath. He looked at the girl and wondered what the fuck she really knew about anything.

It triggered an anger that had been building in him right along. He brought himself up short and let an ironic snort serve as a laugh. "Sure," he said, "we all have shit. Like you have that smothering shit." He was repeating something she'd told him. About how her own folks evidently tried to win her over, keep her from doing the things she really wanted to do. And, right, they'd done it by loading her down with stuff like T-birds and trips here and there and everywhere, and custom-made boots. God, if he'd been half as lucky. If Rachel had given him anything, even, like Adidas instead of those asshole tennies that they sold in the supermarket. God how he hated those, especially with the way the other kids he knew were walking around with really good stuff. Rachel's excuse was always that he was still growing, and Rachel's word for everything he ever wanted was no. No. A reflex, Rachel on automatic pilot. And with a whole slew of reasons other than the one about him growing—the no-money reason or the it's-not-safe reason. He stopped asking for reasons after a while. After a while he figured out that what he wanted he had to get himself. That was one way to screw Rachel and her constant *No No No* . . .

He dropped his head forward, hid his face. Jesus, he was losing it and he couldn't, he couldn't, not having come so far. What was it, though, about No No No . . .

"Hey, are you crying?" The girl leaned toward him, her hair brushing up against him. He thought of angel wings and sat upright, pulled a little away. The girl took the hint, but not completely, just enough to keep her goddam hair and hands away. "Tell me," she said. "Come on."

It had to do with Rachel, of course, and with that one word, "no." It was what he was crying about all along, way down under, inside his mind and his heart, the word "no," *no no, no.* . . . It was as if he had to keep it down, that word and how it had culminated with regard to Rachel, keep the awareness and the pain from taking over the way rust took over, rust that you couldn't stop because whatever made it form was in the air.

"Drew." The girl made him pick his head up, look her right in the eye. "Listen. My mama said once when she was yelling at me that she wished she hadn't had me, I was that much trouble. That time I told you about? When I was riding the well? I swear, Drew, she was watching and hoping I'd fall off and die right there on the ground. I almost wanted to."

He told the girl, then, about the form that Benedict House gave to parents, a form that asked if the parent expected to take the child back into the home after treatment. Just a form.

It was one of those press-down-with-a-ballpoint forms so that you could make copies. Rachel had pressed down all right. She had pressed down hard, so hard the word had torn right down through the paper, so hard the word "no" still cut into him the way Rachel's pen had cut into every single fucking one of the sheets.

He remembered the way his psychodrama teacher had waved it at him, like the red cape that gets waved at a bull, "Look, Drew, see? Here's what your precious mommy has done now."

"You okay?"

He nodded yes that he was, but of course it was a lie. Then the girl made some asshole feel-better remark about how all of this might be happening because he wasn't eating right, wasn't getting enough sleep. "Sure," he said, swinging out of the T-bird and heading for Rachel's front door.

AS SHE DROVE BACK INTO THE APARTMENT complex, Rachel was reassured that the number of cars in carports and elsewhere had gone up tenfold, maybe more. The workaday world was at home now, turning on the evening news and preheating ovens and kicking off shoes. She now very definitely wanted to be part of that world. The opening of Patchwork would guarantee it.

True, she'd be arriving a little later than this, but just as she had tonight, she'd stop by the 7-Eleven for the local paper. But no. She'd bought a Houston paper. The local one was a morning paper, and she hated getting newsprint all over her hands first thing in the morning. She'd watch the news, and maybe subscribe to *Time* or *Newsweek* or one of those.

Odd, she realized. She was thinking of a future as though hers might be, after all, a safe and sane one. A few hours earlier, she'd thought of bolting as she had before, just picking up and running the hell away. Now she was entertaining the prospect of a deliciously mundane life. *Well, don't I deserve it?* she asked. *Don't I?*

The apartment, with its bright, autumnal colors and its cheery patterns, seemed to answer with a resounding yes.

There was Zachary's chair, a rich brown manly leather. She had watched him oil it once, kneading amber liquid into every crease. It seemed to her then an awful lot of trouble, but she knew it was the kind of trouble Zachary loved to take. He devoted the same sort of attention to the wooden furniture he owned: the enormous oak rolltop desk that took almost the full south wall, the mission table in the hall.

Now she was sorry she'd taken Peyton's keys. Was there a way not to go there? She couldn't think of any. If she stayed at home—and she felt all right about doing that now—Peyton wouldn't be able to get in later tonight.

Oh, well. She went through a mental list of what she'd have to take. Toothbrush, toothpaste. No, Peyton would have toothpaste. Makeup. A clean bra and panties. A pair of jeans. What else? A bathing suit.

She was about to go upstairs when she remembered that the laundry she'd done yesterday was still in the little utility room off the kitchen. Her jeans, in fact, were probably still lying heaped in the bottom of the dryer. Everything else had been dry.

Sure enough, there they were. She felt around the waistband and the zipper but wasn't sure if they were damp or just cold. It wouldn't hurt to run them through on high for five minutes or so. And besides, they had those awful wrinkles.

She wound the timer and pressed the start button. Then she began to sort through the other things, folding them as she went.

So little of it was Zachary's! He still sent his shirts out to be done, though she'd told him over and over again that she really didn't mind and even might enjoy doing them. Now she lined his socks up and paired them off. They were all alike, a navy-blue cotton lisle. Similarly, he wore one style and one color underwear: white challis boxer shorts. She found knowing this somehow touching and, at the same time, comforting as well.

She smoothed the folds she'd made, the soft vibration of the dryer lulling her into momentary calm.

But then she felt as much as heard some movement in the room beyond. She tensed, and strained to hear it once again. The dryer, however, made too much sound of its own.

My imagination, she thought. Her fingers, however, began to work even faster, though less efficiently. *Calm down, calm down,* she tried to counsel herself. She dropped the piece she was folding and leaned back against the wall. Eyes closed, she tried to let the soft vibration of the dryer soothe her as it seemed to earlier.

But no. Some slight but unmistakable sound from the hall beyond the kitchen's swinging panel door.

Her heart began to pound and a feeling of pressure overtook her, as though her head were being squeezed in a vise. She was trapped. She was there, in the utility room, with no window, no door, not even a place to hide.

All right, Drew, all right. She would face him, spit in his eye.

The dryer completed its brief cycle so abruptly that the silence almost made her swoon. But that's what it was: silence. Was she jumpier than she'd imagined, so much so that she'd invented sounds where there'd been none? Did that mean she'd imagined everything, even Rob's murder?

Just then she heard the door swing inward. It moved so slowly that its hinges creaked. Hearing, but unable to see it, Rachel felt that she just might swell and explode, her fear a growing balloon of a thing inside her.

The sound stopped. That meant the door was open and whoever it was—oh, why didn't she admit it, Drew, Drew, Drew—would step through it, on tiptoe perhaps. It was a game, the sort that Drew would have devised.

He would be inside the kitchen now, his hand along the edge of the door itself. That meant he knew where she was, knew he had her trapped in there. He had probably looked around all over the apartment so that he could seal her off this way.

Sure enough, the door swung shut.

All right, Drew, all right, I'm ready for you. She grabbed a wire hanger and bent its shoulder sides down, as if to use the hook as a weapon.

"Well, come on," she said, stepping forward firmly, even defiantly. She caught her breath, though, when she saw him, and she felt as though every ounce of daring and energy that she had possessed was quickly draining through her body and out her toes.

It was not Drew, not Drew at all.

"Zachary!" She felt that she would collapse into his arms with relief.

He seemed to sense that and stepped away. "Come into the living room and sit down, Rachel," he said.

"I'm so glad you're here," she said. "But I didn't see your car. I didn't know that you'd be back so soon. I thought you were"—she laughed nervously—"a prowler." As she spoke she moved past him, into the living room, where she sat on his fine leather chair. She actually had sat there only once before and she couldn't imagine why she was drawn to it now.

She now realized that he hadn't embraced her, held her; that he had coldly moved away. "Why are you here?" she asked. "And where did you park?" The apartment had two allotted spaces, and both had been empty when she drove up.

"Rachel," he said in an eerie monotone, "that isn't very important right now."

The last time anyone had used that tone of voice it was to tell her that her father had died. Odd that there should be a universal bad-news tone of voice. The thought made a bubbly sort of laugh rise in Rachel's throat. At least she thought it was a laugh. She certainly wasn't crying, though she was close to crying.

Did he know about Rob? Was he trying to console her? No, then he would have held her. But hadn't he been going to the Texas coast last night? To Galveston?

She looked inquiringly at him.

Zachary stood and watched her. He made no move of any kind in her direction. His face was blank, unreadable.

He doesn't love me anymore, Rachel thought, and this was coupled in her mind with death, with finality, with her father and with Rob and she didn't know what else. She began to cry, but softly, tears spilling down her cheeks and dripping onto her lap.

What was going on? She didn't understand any of this, not the way Zachary was acting, nor her own teary reaction to it.

Zachary dug inside his breast pocket and produced a crisp white handkerchief. Rachel yanked it open and blew her nose and wiped at her eyes and kept right on crying. Finally she was able to get hold of herself enough to demand that he speak. "Say something," she said.

"I don't know what to say," he admitted. "I'm . . . perplexed. To find out that I've loved you . . ." He let the sentence die, but not before Rachel had noted the tense.

"And don't you love me now?" Rachel cried. She stood up, hesitated, then pushed her way back into the kitchen. Once she had, she was sorry. Suppose he didn't follow her there? Suppose he just packed up and left without further explanation? After a minute, however, he came into the room.

She saw him look over at the rack of knives they'd recently bought. Did he expect her to be brandishing one of them? Slashing her own wrists, perhaps?

Rachel's sudden flash of anger enabled her to control her crying.

"I'm glad you've stopped," Zachary said.

Whatever else was going on, Rachel was most struck by the fact that he hadn't even held her when she wept. He'd never seen her weep before. How could he say he loved her, wanted to marry her, and then just stand and watch her that way? "What happened?" she asked, afraid. "What's wrong?"

"I would guess from your reaction that you know."

"My reaction! My reaction to what? To your not hugging me? To what? To not having the nerve to come in here earlier? My reaction to what?" She was practically screaming at him and she didn't care. She went back to the moment when she'd first heard the sound that had frightened her. *My God,* she thought, *it might have been better if it had been Drew.* Drew she understood; this was inexplicable. She continued shouting, "My reaction to what, Zachary? Are you planning to tell me?"

But she wanted to be in his arms. She wanted to say, *I've been through so much today. I've been through so much for years.* Instead, she waited to find out what it was that she'd done wrong. And it did anger her. The unfairness of it did. And the feeling foolish about having thought, so short a time before, that tomorrow Zachary would be back from his trip and would make things more right if not altogether right.

He seemed as angry as she, though he, unlike Rachel, spoke quietly, almost in a whisper. But Rachel hadn't known what his reaction to strain would be until just now. This was their first troubled moment. Zachary told her, "I forced myself to wait for you, Rachel. My first thought was to go away, just disappear from your life entirely."

This made Rachel toss her head and stare at him in utter amazement. But Zachary had no way of knowing that she'd actually done that once in her life and today had contemplated doing it again. She began to shake her head in a gesture of disbelief.

"Now," he went on, "I wish I had."

What was he talking about? Rachel knew she had to tell him, had to say, *Look, Zachary, I've got some catching up to do with you. I had a husband, Rob, and he was murdered last night sometime, and I have a son, Drew, and I think he did it. I also think Drew wants to kill me, and, Zachary, hold me, hold me, hold me because I'm scared.*

She stepped toward him, reaching out. She was struggling to keep from stuttering, and she didn't quite know what to say. "Zachary, I have a lot to tell you. I . . ."

He turned away. It seemed to Rachel the cruelest thing he might have done. "I'm sorry," he said, "but I can't . . . I don't . . ." And now he seemed to have decided on something. He turned back again, to face her. He looked her right in the eye, though, simple as that seemed, he did it with great effort. I don't believe you. I don't believe anything you say. I don't believe you, Rachel. I'm not even certain, at this point, that Rachel is your name."

But of course it was her name. She was about to tell him that, but Zachary averted his eyes. "Rachel, he was here," he said. "Drew. Your son. He was here."

Drew? Zachary had talked to Drew? Where? How? But Drew wouldn't give him the true picture, would color it to suit himself. Drew would make her sound terrible, sound awful.

And while these thoughts came coursing through her mind, she heard mere fragments of the rest of what Zachary had to say. That she'd made up being in the convent was blasphemous, worse than any other story she might have told. That she'd lied lied lied the way his first wife had, or maybe even worse. That she didn't trust him, didn't trust anyone, didn't deserve to be loved or trusted in return. But above all, above everything, was the awful awful fact that she'd denied the existence of her own son, her own flesh and blood.

But the overriding thing for Rachel was that Drew had been there, Drew had been this near. *Run run run*, her instinct told her, *run, Drew's here. Drew's coming, run, run, run, he's here* . . .

Rachel bolted past Zachary, almost knocking him to the floor. The kitchen door was still swinging back and forth back and forth as she made her way out the front door and toward her car. Then she was in it, on the highway, on her way to Peyton's and to safety long before, she was sure, Zachary had even realized what had happened.

ON SIXTH STREET, STARING INTO THE windows of the shop called Patchwork, Drew smiled at one of the pillows in the corner. His mother's love affair with the rhomboid was still intact. It was one of the first words he'd ever learned to spell, though he had to admit that the need for it didn't arise too often. He'd never even gotten to use it in a crossword puzzle.

The girl noticed his face. "That's the first time you've looked happy since we left your mom's place." She squeezed his arm.

He was sarcastic. "Yeah, well, I've had kind of a rough day."

"Not so rough. Besides, I did most of the driving." She pulled at him. "Come on, let's get a Coke or something. This place is closed. You can see she isn't here."

He let himself be persuaded, although what he really could have used right then was one of those little aerosol mouth sprays. Like Binaca or something. He felt as if his breath must smell like raw shrimp, though the girl didn't act as though it did.

He followed the girl down the street and into a little café with blue checkered curtains and real daisies in vases on the tables. "Nice," he said.

"That's what I like about Austin," she told him.

He wondered if she'd been here, to this very place, before. Then he wondered who with. Then he got the bright idea of offering a lot of that kind of information about himself, so that maybe, just maybe, she would respond similarly, the way she had earlier, back in the car *Oh, Benedict House,* he thought, *I owe you plenty. Plenty.* "You never asked me if I had a girl-friend," he started.

"I'm sure you have lots," she said. She gestured over at the waitresses who were standing off to the side kind of waiting for them to read the chalkboard menu. They were giggling at each other, over him, he knew. It happened all the time, and the girl, being no great dummy, had noticed.

She leaned forward, maybe to let the waitresses know he was hers. "Tell me junk that no one, no one else in the whole wide world, could know."

He gave a little whistle. "Hell, I wouldn't know where to start." He did know how to start, though. That was what psychodrama had been all about: secrets, deep down and dirty.

"I thought so," she said, and he didn't know what she might have meant except maybe to forget it. She pulled one of the daisies out of the vase and seemed about to begin plucking petals.

"Hey, don't." He took the flower away from her, put it back. "Look, the business about Rob Cassidy and about my mother and all, well, all that is true. The thing is, there's a whole shitload more."

"Like what?"

"Like, I've been in this, uh . . ."

"Prison?"

"No, not like that. It's more a rehab place. For druggies. It's kind of where you go to . . ."

"Like a halfway house."

"Okay. Kind of like that. Yeah, probably just like that. I mean, you live there and you get therapy and . . . yeah, a halfway house. Like that."

"My parents talked about sending me away one time, but I think it was only to scare me."

"Why would they?" He wanted to know. Especially since, except for that one little thing, that crazy story about her mother, what the girl had described was the Great American Family.

"I don't know," she said. "Because they thought I wanted to, I don't know, like, die."

"You mean kill yourself?"

"Uh huh."

"With drugs, right?" And he laughed. He had to laugh at them, parents, how they were all alike. "And that was it, just drugs?"

"No." And then she told him about how she'd taken her mama's car, a big old Buick convertible with cruise control. She'd set the cruise control on eighty and then she'd tried to drive the car without hitting the brakes, which would unstick where she'd set it. She'd ended up by wrecking the car, too. "The people sued my daddy over it," she said. "The people whose place I wrecked into, I mean."

"Why'd you do it?" he asked her. "Do you know?"

She nodded that she did.

"Well?"

Her answer was a little slow in coming. "I had seen my mama in that car one night when my Daddy was in Dallas? She was with this friend of his and they were sitting way too close. I mean way too close."

"And that's all?"

"I didn't hang around to see the rest. I just took the car the next day when she left it sitting there, keys in it and all. It seemed like she wanted me to. Like she knew I had seen her and she wanted to get rid of me, so I wouldn't tell."

"Oh, yeah." But it seemed to him unlikely that such deep psychological plotting had gone on. The girl's mom was probably just so glad to get her rocks off for once, she'd forgotten all about the keys. In any case, the whole thing seemed to him a dopey reason for taking the car and driving around like a maniac. He didn't have to say any of that, though, because the girl cut right in with a question.

"Hey, tell me something," she asked. "Okay? Meeting this guy. Your mom's boyfriend. I mean, didn't it seem big-time weird? So I mean, how did that make you feel? Was that weird or what?"

She was really hung up on this issue, he decided. "I don't know. I don't think it bothered me. I mean, it bothered me that he was a total surprise, like I hadn't heard a thing about him or about anybody else, ever, and suddenly, like, there he was. But I don't think it bothered me, no."

"You sure?"

"Sure. I mean, why should it?"

"I don't know. Because it's your mother, you know." She laughed uncomfortably.

It took him back to the intake interview at Benedict House. First his mother had gone in and then, when she'd come out, he'd gone in. She'd been sort of pink when she came out, he remembered that. And when he came out, he was pinkish, too. "Do you know what they asked me?" he'd said to Rachel, and she'd said, "Yes, they asked me, too." As if this weren't verification enough, he repeated their question, still incredulous. "They asked me if I ever had sex with you." Rachel said, "I know. They asked me, too." And he couldn't get over it. "Why would they ask that?" he wanted to know.

Now, after Benedict House, after everything he'd read and heard from the other people there, he couldn't believe this girl was making such a big deal over—what was his name?—Zachary. Or over her own mother sitting close to some dude in a car. "Look," he told the girl, "there's nothing Oedipal about this."

"What?"

"This guy and my mother," he said, louder still, "it means zero to me. Really."

And wouldn't you know. Right then, him screaming his head off, there was one of the waitresses right beside his shoulder. He, the girl, and the waitress laughed. The whole time she was standing there, the waitress at his table kept looking back at the one against the wall, like she had won something in being able to wait on him. He ordered iced tea for both of them.

Sometimes shit like this happened. He was objectively good-looking, but sometimes a really batty girl would go right off the deep end. Ordinarily that would have made him edgy, but this time, being with the moonfaced girl, it seemed okay. "It'll work out," he said out loud.

"What will?"

"What do you think?" He was more irritated with himself than with her, but it didn't come out that way. But maybe that way she'd be quiet and he could get some thinking done.

But she seemed to want to talk. "Were they divorced?" she asked.

"Who?"

"Your parents."

"Yeah. Eventually. My dad just took off."

She was predictable. "How old were you?"

"I don't know. About a year, I guess." Eight months and four days, exactly. They had made him find out, made him ask Rachel. *You may think it isn't important*, they'd said, *you may think, but it is, it is, it is*. And then they'd hammered away at him about it, they'd broken him down. *Were they right?* he wondered now. Or had they, maybe with some theory in mind, made it important?

You have to hate him, Drew. No matter what you say, it has to be there. This was his psychodrama teacher, her thin arms stretching toward him. *We have to get to it, Drew. We have to get it out. Get to it, get to the jagged glass edge of it, Drew.*

First Rob, then Rachel.

Pretty soon the jagged glass edge was very near the surface. For a time it was all there was. It was hard to do Rob, hard to be angry when he didn't know the man at all. Was it then that he had contacted Rob, sent him all of those cards? He couldn't remember, could only recall that the anger had come hard with Rob, but easy, oh so easy, with Rachel. Of course she—his psychodrama teacher—she was ever so good at evoking it. She'd had that form that Rachel had gouged "no" into and she'd had more, a kind of hate chant that she did: First Rob, then Rachel.

"So what was it like?" the girl asked. "Growing up, I mean."

"I don't know. Weird, I guess." Rachel with her

books. Dr. Spock. *Your Child from Six to Nine*. Rachel always looking for solutions.

"Was she mean to you?"

"Yeah, sometimes." Sometimes when he managed to get her really pissed off. Once she threw a book at him and the spine of it hit on the bridge of his nose. He bled hard, and she panicked, trying to hold his head back and run for water at the same time. Her own fear fueled his, and they were both almost hysterical. He thought he was going to die, probably because she was screaming, "Oh God, Drew, don't die, oh God!" He'd bloodied his nose before, but never like that, never blood coming out of his nose and his mouth together, blood in thick, fast spurts. He'd almost choked on it with his head back, and he thought he'd bleed to death with his head dropped forward. He couldn't remember how they got the bleeding stopped.

He had acted the incident out in psychodrama and they loved it. *That's good, Drew, that's what we want. And how did you feel about her when she did it to you, Drew? What did you want to do back? Did you want to hurt her back, Drew, think? You did, didn't you. Sure you did. Of course you did.*

He'd overheard Rachel telling someone about it, about that day. And she'd turned it all around. Oh, she wasn't lying, he knew that from her voice, but she'd turned it all around, remembered it all wrong. She'd meant to throw the book across the room, she said, and just then he'd stood up. The fact was, she'd aimed right at him, right at his face. She'd hit right on target, that was what. The day he'd overheard her, he'd felt like telling it his way, contradicting her, telling the truth. She'd deny it, of course. But then— oh, the justice of it, the irony and the justice of it— she'd get so mad that she'd probably do it again.

"How old were you when this happened?" the girl asked.

"I don't know. Maybe ten."

"Did your dad come to visit you or anything?"

"Never. Never anything."

She was wearing the strangest expression. A smile, kind of, on her lips, and a sad look, kind of, in her eyes. And she was shaking her head back and forth the way people do when they can't get over something.

"What are you thinking?" he asked her.

"That he sounded so nice on the radio. Rob Cassidy. Really. I thought he'd really be nice."

"Well." He drained his glass and looked squint-eyed at her. "You can't ever tell now, can you? About anyone."

SHE KNEW SHE HAD TO SPEAK TO ZACHARY, explain some of what was going on. Maybe he'd understand. She pulled up next to a pay phone and dialed her own number. He answered, thank God. She had tears in her eyes and in her throat. She'd realized, while driving, the ironic way the situation she'd constructed mirrored what Zachary had gone through with his ex-wife. She, Rachel, had lied, too. And just as his first wife had deprived him of a son, so had she. She was so moved by the import of all this that she couldn't even say hello. She only knew that she had to call, had to try, at least, to make things right.

"Rachel," he asked, "is this you?"

"Yes." Her voice was thin, tight. She held on to the silence, though, and—thank God!—Zachary did too.

Finally she was able to start. "It isn't that I was trying to hide things from you," she said, "it's just that it was all so complicated that I didn't know where to begin. And then, once time had gone by, I just couldn't. Because by then it seemed as though I had been hiding things."

"It's all right," he said.

"But there's so much," she told him. "You don't know."

"Rachel," he said, "come home."

"I can't!" She screamed it, then tried to regain control. But how could she tell him that her son wanted to kill her? How? "Zachary, I can't come home, not now. I can't."

"Wait there," he said. "Just tell me where you are and I'll come there and we can . . . puzzle this through together."

"No," she said. "I'll just go on to Peyton's for the night." But the fact that he offered meant so much, too much for her to continue speaking. She began to cry, with relief above all else. She tried to tell him that she'd be back soon. She tried to tell him that she loved him. She tried, but no words came. She hung up and sobbed back into the car.

A woman walking a cocker spaniel stood nearby. She smiled at Rachel tentatively, and that made Rachel cry harder.

While lack of caring would have made most people cry, quite the opposite got to Rachel. *Maybe*, she thought, *because I've had so little of it.*

HE STOOD UP AND STRETCHED. THE check lay on the table between him and the moon-faced girl. He watched her pick it up, wondering if she felt any resentment, paying. No. She was obviously used to it, never even gave it a second thought.

"Now where to?" she asked.

He had Peyton's address. Even a little map. Zachary had given him that and the shop address too. It was sad in a way. Zachary had said there were only two places he could think of where his mother might be. Two places. Shit. Drew hoped no one would ever be able to say that about him. "I guess we should swing by Patchwork again, and if she's not there, we'll try the other place."

"What if she went home?" Then she suggested, "We could call that guy back."

"I don't know," he said. Actually, Drew could tell, though Zachary it seemed to him had done a fine job of hiding it, that this was all news to Zachary. His very existence, news.

That made him very very pissed at Rachel, almost as pissed as he was when she ran away and left him there to rot at Benedict House. Right then, facing Zachary, he'd wanted Rachel to pay, and so he'd done exactly what he had to do, fixed her good with this guy.

Rachel had accused him of that all along, of putting on a sweet face to make her look bad, and he had come right back at her, saying she'd been bad all along, bad, bad, bad, bad.

At Benedict House, they'd called it Rachel's Betrayal. They'd acted it out in psychodrama, with one of the girls playing Rachel, running, running, running away from Drew. He'd caught up with her, and they'd had to peel him off her, had to stop him from bashing in the girl's face.

What a trip Benedict House was! He could still remember his teacher and a friend in the class holding him down while he strained to get at the surrogate Rachel. And she—his teacher—was saying, "Very good, Drew. We're getting someplace now. Keep it up, Drew, keep the fire alive."

When Rachel stopped coming he'd at first thought Rachel had died. Then, when he learned she hadn't, he wanted her to die. She'd run out the way his dad had, only it was worse because she was running from him and not, as his father had, from a situation, from responsibility and ties. They'd screamed it at him until he could hear it without screaming back: *Your mother dropped you here and then she left and then she sent a form saying no, no, no, saying that she never wanted you, never wanted you back.*

He told the Zachary guy about Benedict House, about the form. The guy looked like he was going to drop dead on the spot. What the guy asked, though, was about Drew's dad.

"He split before I had my first birthday," Drew said. Had the guy eating right out of his hand. Had to be careful to keep the hatred out of his face, though, keep the *Fix you fucking Rachel mother bitch* from shining through.

SHE WAS SURPRISED BY THE NUMBER OF PEO-
ple shopping at Barton Creek Mall. For a moment, she
thought she might be safer spending the evening there.
But no. Sooner or later the shops would close and the
security guards would shoo the last-minute stragglers
out and she would be alone, or nearly alone, in the enormous parking lot. *And besides,* she reminded herself, *I
have Peyton's keys. Without me, she can't get in.*

Rachel went to the drugstore on the lower level, buying the things she ought to have taken from home:
makeup, toothbrush. Then, though she'd planned to go
to one of the larger stores to make this purchase, she
saw some racks of clothing and decided she could save
some time. She bought a cheap pair of jeans, and tennis
shoes, and a T-shirt. She almost laughed aloud when the
clerk rang up the purchase. The whole thing came to
less than she would ordinarily spend on a scarf. But
what of it? At least now she could change into something casual. She couldn't very well arrive at Peyton's
with only the same things she had worn all day.

When she laid the bag on the back seat of the car she
noticed the flowers she'd bought earlier. She had thrown
the groceries away, but had forgotten all about the geraniums. Oh, well. They'd make a nice gift for Peyton,
she reasoned, and bringing such a gift would make her
visit seem more casual, less desperate.

Then she saw the flat tire. It was almost more than
she could bear. She could change it easily, of course, but
the timing of it! Then, almost in the same breath, she
realized it was far better to have to change it here than

out on Bee Caves Road or, worse, on the winding little sideroad where Peyton lived.

Count your blessings, Rachel told herself, thinking of the pitch of the hill and the fact that out in that part of the suburbs, out beyond Austin and beyond Westlake Hills, amenities like streetlamps were unheard-of. She had even once, sitting in the dusk on one of Peyton's decks, heard a coyote call, and then another respond.

Rachel snatched up her newbought things and went back inside the mall to get out of the now completely crushed chemise she'd worn all day and into something fit to change a tire in.

THIS PLACE," THE GIRL SAID, BOUNDING on Peyton's water mattress, waving her arms to indicate the room, the house, the property as a whole, "is intense."

"Yeah," he answered, standing at the wall of windows that looked out over the pool, the bougainvillea bushes, and the hills and cliffs and vast green spaces.

"I don't want to leave," she said.

"We don't have a choice," he said, "for now."

He could see why she liked it, though. It was, from every one of the levels, kind of like hanging off the edge of the world. But it was also very sparsely furnished, which made it seem less like someone's home and more like one of those Department of Highway places set up for tourists to get maps and stuff. Modern the way those places were, too, and very easy to "card" open. Like a lot of ritzy places, this one had a security system. And, like a lot of such systems, this one hadn't been switched on.

"She must be weird, though," the girl said of Peyton. "That picture, I mean, really."

Drew was standing in front of it, a poster-size blowup of a naked girl. It was taken from behind, and in it, the girl was looking at some run-down cabin in the woods. The door to the cabin was open and there was something on the ground near the door. Red, like a bloodstain. The girl had spots of it on what he could see of her feet, too. The thing was, this was a black-and-white photograph but for these spots.

"Would you believe," the girl said, but she couldn't keep a wounded note out of her voice. Jealousy, he guessed.

He could see why. The girl in the picture was more womanly than the skinny little moonfaced girl. If she had any extra weight at all, it was in her thighs, like one of those old statues tribes used, fertility goddesses.

He thought about how if he had a knife, he would ram the blade right into the mother part, the cunt. As it was, he only stabbed at the ass part of the picture with his thumbnail.

"Hey!" The girl came running and caught his arm. "I want to see the rest of the place," she said, "but not if it's going to make you go off."

"Okay." He knew she was right, and put his hand down.

"What I mean is, she"—the girl pointed at the wall—"didn't do anything to you, you know? You're misdirecting everything. She isn't the person you're mad at."

"Thank you, Joyce Motherfucking Brothers," he answered. "I'll take care not to behave bozoically in the future."

"Oh, you," she said, shoving him a little.

Off to the side of the house were a series of decks.

"Moon shoes," the girl announced, pointing to a contraption on the underside of an upstairs projection.

"What do you mean?" he asked.

"You hang," she said. "Upside down."

"Do it," he suggested.

After she had, he tried. He liked the sensation, even that of the blood falling down to his head.

"Your face is red," she said.

But he couldn't answer that hers had been too, he was laughing so hard. He was giddy with being upside down and giddy, too, with knowing that the chase was coming to a close. If he could have talked right then, he'd have told her that this was how it had all been—his life, he would have meant—for far too long: upside down. That, and how he was going to right it. But he was laughing, laughing, laughing so hard.

"You shouldn't do this too long," she advised him, a little knot of worry on her brow as she spoke. "Plus we'd better go."

"No, come here," he said. "Come closer."

She walked warily toward him. He reached out and unsnapped her jeans, but he couldn't get the zipper down. She did it for him, even slid the jeans down over her hips. He had to arch up, straining every muscle in his body, though, just to plant a kiss on her belly. Never mind doing anything more. "Bad idea," he admitted, kicking his feet free and flipping over and down. "What'd I say about not behaving bozoically?"

"What's 'bozoically'?" she asked.

"Like a bozo." Calling himself one made it much less true.

He left the girl out on the deck and went back up to the level where the bedroom was. There had to be a bathroom there, in the master suite.

For sure.

Strangest bathroom he'd ever laid eyes on, too.

All along it seemed to him that the whole house lacked something vital. Now, looking at the mono-chromatic bath, he knew what that was. The whole place was browns and grays, and the effect was like a color TV when something goes wrong with the thing, an electrical storm or trouble at the station, and it all becomes kind of faded brown and white. Or like those old old pictures, sepia. Anyway, this whole place was like that, lacking color, but the bathroom especially.

The first thing you saw was the floor, which was glass laid over plain gray concrete. It had an eerie luminescence, like scales. He wondered how long and what kind of experimentation it had taken to come up with such a god-awful creepy effect.

Next you saw the tub, which was punched down into the floor, nearly five feet across. It was tin and it didn't have any kind of shine. On purpose, he fig-ured. The welcome thing, though, was that there was an array of faucets and jets, which probably meant that the thing was equipped with a whirlpool.

Just what he needed.

There were no mirrors, which he found odd for a bathroom. And there was a small freestanding fire-place, a little pile of kindling stacked alongside.

He wondered how the place would be in dead of night, and he found a bunch, maybe ten or so, of recessed lights so tiny that they'd probably be just pinpoints. Like those tiny flashlights people keep on keychains, next to useless.

But the walls were the worst, concrete slabs that had been vaguely raked before they'd dried. Along one, as though someone had done it with fingers, let-ters had been gouged, rough letters more than a foot high. Up close you couldn't read them, but when you got far away, you could. Except that they didn't make any sense.

"What does it say?" The girl came up behind him, caught him on the sides of his waist with her hands. His cock hummed at that, but he didn't let on.

"I don't know. I think it's Spanish or something." The letters were N A J A and they were in there twice. "I think it means 'nothing.'" He remembered that from some book he'd read, one of the ones by the guy who wrote all about bullfighting and shit.

"No," the girl said. "That's *nada*. I don't know what this means. I don't even think it's Spanish."

Everyone in Texas knew Spanish some, the way everyone in Texas spent half their lifetime traveling around in cars. "Well, fuck it," he advised.

On a shelf beside the tub were tall jars with different kinds of powder inside. The girl took the top off a green one and offered it to him to smell.

"It smells like gin," he said. He didn't know why he had said it. He knew damn well what it was, it was juniper. "Get another one," he ordered.

The girl said, "I think this is lavender," and, without waiting to check with him, dumped a quantity of it into the tub. Then she fiddled with the faucets.

The tub began to fill with magenta water. There was some steam. The girl undressed him and then helped him ease himself down into the purpleness.

There was a bucket by the side of the tub, and he reached for it, found that it was full of natural sponges, the kind that look like brains.

"You're crazy," the girl said when he told her that, but she had a funny soft kind of gleam in her eye when she said it. She dipped a sponge in and squeezed the fullness of it out over his left shoulder, then his right.

Then she found a bar of soap, a fat white chunk that looked as though it had been made in a cave someplace. She lathered up the sponge and then lathered him up as well, taking off her jeans and panties and climbing in with him to do his back and then his chest.

That hum between his legs. That hum was like nothing he had ever felt before, the hum that broke window glass in New Orleans, sheared leaves off the trees in Taiwan, that hum, that. . . .

"Stand up," she said, "so I can do you."

He stood up, and he poked her belly with his hard, humming cock. She washed him, front, and back, and under his balls.

Then she knelt down in the water and she sucked his clean cock until he was afraid he'd come before he wanted to. He fiddled with the faucets until he heard the water pulsing through the pipes and then he made the girl get on her back and he parted her cunt with his fingers and then with his cock, too. They made vast purple waves, and soft magenta ones, again and again until he and she were heaving wet in a tin tub that all of a sudden seemed way too hot.

While the water was draining out, she took a long winding cord with a spray attachment on the end and held it up over them, showering them with fine clear water that was cold.

On the way back toward the car, she said, "I remember what they're called. Not moon shoes. They're antigravity boots."

"I like moon shoes better," he said, directing her to drive high into the hills, to a point where they could keep watch over the house. They'd do that for maybe a half hour at most and then, he said, if Rachel hadn't come, they'd try elsewhere.

RACHEL LET HER ENGINE IDLE AS SHE walked back to close Peyton's high wooden gate. As she'd promised, she didn't lock it, but it almost didn't matter. The gate conveyed a sense of safety even if, after analyzing the feeling, she had to admit it was purely psychological. *Do prisoners feel it?* she wondered. *Do animals in a zoo?* Was her view of safety a ruse, maybe even a trap?

Then, unbidden, an episode from her childhood came pressing down on her, one she'd never thought of before. The memory was even stronger when she closed herself behind the solid weight of Peyton's windowless front door.

Indeed, her memory was so complete that she could smell the cleaner that the janitor used on the floor tiles, a sort of green powder that he sprinkled everywhere and then swept up along with whatever else had been on the floor. It had acted, the powder, as a sort of eraser, she thought now. It was spongy, and lifted the soil from the floor, as an eraser might. It was an awful smell, unlike the smell of gasoline, which she sometimes sought. In fact, she'd been near the Esso station at the corner trying to catch a whiff of gasoline when—what was the little boy's name?—Dennis—when Dennis found her.

He started pulling at her hair, teasing her about its color. It was almost white back then, bleached by the desert sun. She had started running, running even then, and he followed her, calling her stupid things like whitehead and then pimplehead.

It seemed so dumb now, but her need to escape him had been potent, real. She'd run until her side hurt, until she knew she couldn't run anymore. Then, having come to the schoolhouse, she'd tried the door.

She'd expected it to be locked, because it was more than an hour since they'd been dismissed, but it wasn't locked, and Rachel had slipped inside. She remembered the doors closing behind her, huge wooden doors not unlike the gate to Peyton's property. And she'd felt safe. Totally and completely safe.

Then, to feel even safer, she'd closed herself into the cloakroom underneath the stairs.

The green powder had been in there, erasing the dirt from the floor. The green powder that had made her sneeze.

That was how the janitor had discovered her.

"I know you," he said, and she stared at him, at his nicotine-stained teeth, at something that was glistening on his mustache. "Yeah, I know you," he repeated, setting the broom aside and then standing there above her with his greasy thumbs hitched in his belt. The door to the cloakroom was ajar behind him.

But then the main entrance doors flew open and Dennis stomped in, still hard at the chase. The janitor reached to close the cloakroom door, but she was quick.

"I'm here," she called, pushing forward at the same time, actually brushing up against the janitor as she flew toward the vestibule, toward the boy who just minutes before had been her tormentor.

She never told Dennis, never told anyone, not even when her mother made such an enormous big deal about how important it was that she continue going to Catholic school no matter what it cost. Her father didn't think so, and they fought about it, Rachel's mother and dad, but her mother won out.

Wonderful Catholic school.

Now, Rachel shivered the memory away. She wasn't a child anymore and this wasn't a grade-school cloakroom but a house that Drew couldn't possibly know about, and, even if he did know, he would probably be unable to find it.

So relax, she told herself, rubbing her bare arms briskly. Why did Peyton keep the place so cool? It seemed such a waste to run the air conditioning at this pitch when she wasn't even home. At the same time, she didn't feel she had the right to monkey with Peyton's thermostat.

But she'd better not try to keep Patchwork that cold! Rachel thought.

Oh, Patchwork, Patchwork, just the sound of it made Rachel feel happy, feel strong. Just the notion that she'd come such a long long way since coming to Austin, fear-ridden, hesitating even to run a magazine ad lest Drew find her. Little things—like deciding to list her phone number—became big things. She remembered, too, what Peyton had said about opening Patchwork: that it would give her visibility. By the time Peyton said it, Rachel had gotten over her fear of discovery. She thought Drew and even fear itself long gone.

Knowing Peyton had helped, had helped enormously. Rachel didn't doubt that she would have come to stability on her own, but knowing Peyton had speeded things along. She would not have had the courage to open a shop or even think about opening a shop without Peyton. There was the money, too, but beyond the money was, pure and simple, the nerve. It wasn't the only time Peyton had enabled Rachel to face something she'd have been afraid to face, either. Peyton had been with Rachel when, after all these years, she'd run into Rob.

I should have told Peyton then, Rachel realized. It had been the perfect chance.

At Peyton's urging, Rachel had gone to a panel discussion at the University of Texas, something being offered by the radio, TV, and film department. Peyton frequently took advantage of the UT offerings but had never before asked Rachel to come along. Now, Rachel couldn't remember the reason for Peyton's enthusiasm, but in any case, Rachel had yielded to it and had gone.

She could feel it still, the rush of heat that overcame her when she saw Rob there. And worse! There had been no way to escape because she and Peyton were already seated when the panelists, Rob among them, filed in.

Rachel had felt near passing out. She squirmed in her seat and wiped perspiration from her forehead. She knew, just knew, her face was beet-red. She'd prepared to say she was having a hot flash when Peyton asked what was the matter but in fact, Peyton looked over at her and only smiled.

So, not only had Peyton not noticed, but neither had Rob spotted her. If she could just sit quietly, perhaps nothing would draw his gaze toward her.

She sat through the entire hour and felt that she would, indeed, weather it. She could not remember anything of what the panel had been discussing, either. She knew that Rob's portion drew the heartiest laughter, the loudest applause, but that was all. She'd made it.

Then came the questions from the audience. Rachel lowered her head as though searching through her purse for something whenever someone nearby raised a hand. But then Peyton asked a question, and asked specifically for Rob's answer.

He saw her then. He'd done a classic double take, shaken as much as she had been. Peyton had had to repeat whatever it was she wanted to know.

Rob made a beeline to Rachel's side before the room had cleared, and Rachel looked around for Peyton, for some of her cool, but to no avail. Peyton must have gone to the ladies' room or something; she was nowhere to be found.

In the end it was good to have seen Rob this way, good because in the intervening years and especially because of all the later trouble with Drew, Rachel had convinced herself that she was the bad one, the one who had created all of Drew's problems and thus her own.

Face to face with Rob, that feeling faded. Surely he was to blame, too. *I'm the one who stayed*, she reminded herself.

She never understood how Rob could've walked away. Was it because Drew hadn't grown inside him? Did that make it easy, make Drew separate and forgettable?

Because Drew wasn't at all separate from her, and she could prove it, prove the invisible but physical connection existed. She had told Rob about it, too, told him how, for instance, her breasts had begun to spurt milk when Drew as an infant, a hall and a room away, began to cry. It was a tie Rachel never would have dreamed possible, never had heard any woman talk about. And it had happened more than once.

But Rob only scoffed. Coincidence, he said. Rachel told him she was sorry for him, sorry that he couldn't be connected to his son as deeply.

As it turned out, he wasn't connected at all.

For a while, Rachel ascribed lack of feeling to all men, not just Rob. Men, she decided, felt nothing; women felt all. If she heard a man describing his love for or even interest in his child, Rachel would stiffen, thinking the man was lying, trying to make himself look better, look good.

Whenever Rachel heard about a man walking out on his wife, on his family, she was filled with rage. Whenever she heard of a man who wasn't paying child support, she actually imagined a barbaric revenge. *Cut his testicles off*, she'd think.

It wasn't that Rachel was mercenary, though money

mattered very, very much because she'd had so little. It was the total uncaring unfeeling un un un that not sending money implied.

And then, to Rachel's astonishment, there in the UT classroom, Rob was telling her that he was back in touch with Drew. He expected, she realized, to waltz back into Drew's life as though nothing had happened.

"Heard from the kid," he'd told her, as if they were the dutiful parents of a grown-up child. And then, reading the incredulity on her face, he'd added, "No, really. He sent me a bunch of Father's Day cards, can you beat that? Like the kid has really missed me. Really missed me all these years."

Rachel hated them both in that moment, hated Drew every bit as much as she hated Rob. Hated all men, in fact.

But then, in what now seemed an enormous moment of insight, she knew the cards had been a threat. Not an attempt at reconciliation, but a threat.

She'd felt goosebumps rising, but Rob went on about how he was going to make things up to the kid, how he'd have Drew over, give a party, maybe introduce him to some girls.

Sure, Rob, you do that, Rachel had thought, rubbing the goosebumps away. Drew would have called him an asshole or a dildo, his favorite words of opprobrium. And he would have been right.

"So how old is the kid now?" Rob was asking. "Nineteen, huh? Like a year for every card?"

Rachel couldn't take any more. She excused herself to go off in search of Peyton, and Rob called after her, "Hey, no hard feelings, huh, Rachel? You can come on down too. It's a real nice place, right on the water. Here, I'll draw you a map."

Rachel stood while he sketched the map on the back of one of his business cards. She nodded when he

handed it to her, stunned speechless. She wished she
had the nerve to confront him, actually scream at him in
front of all these people, *You think you can abandon us,
never send us a dime, and then make up for it by having
us over? Having us come to a party at your goddam
beach house? You can rot in your beach house, Rob
Cassidy.*

If anyone had deserved to die it was Rob.

But Rachel must have concealed how she felt quite
successfully. At least, Peyton hadn't seemed to notice.
Peyton had rattled on and on about the panel, finally
saying that she'd thought, from his voice on the air, that
Rob would be younger than he was.

"He was kind of cute, though," she added.

Rachel had been silent.

"You don't agree?" Peyton probed.

"No," Rachel said, summoning up a pejorative phrase
from her own era, her own days of weighing who was
cute and who wasn't. "I thought he was too plastic."

Peyton had laughed, it seemed to Rachel, longer than
the comment warranted. *Maybe the word "plastic" had
changed its meaning,* Rachel thought, *the way "gay"
has. It would serve Rob right.*

Now, walking into the downstairs powder room at
Peyton's, Rachel wished she'd taken that opportunity to
confide in her friend. *I've been selling her short,* Rachel
thought. *Peyton would understand.*

But actually, Rachel wondered if anyone who hadn't
borne children could. On the other hand, because her
love was so mixed with hatred and because mothers
were expected to be sweet and wonderful and under-
standing no matter what, and because she still felt some
residue from the period when society held that there
were no bad children, only bad parents, Rachel couldn't
decide if Peyton or Zachary or anyone in the world

would understand, and as a result she just kept everything to herself.

With cause. She'd once seen some parents on the *Phil Donahue Show,* each with different theories of raising a child. The woman Rachel had especially liked told an anecdote about how her son had called her by her given name instead of calling her "Mother" and in response to this she'd told the boy, "You're just a crummy six-year-old and you're going to call me 'Mother.'" The thing was, there was love and humor in her voice and Rachel had laughed when she heard the woman say it, but another woman on the panel and then several people in the audience had stood up to say that calling a child "crummy" at the age of six could do permanent damage to his self-esteem and they'd gone on and on until Rachel had wanted to scream. And then, even worse, a man in the audience stood up to say he'd stopped dating a woman, a single parent, who had "cursed" her child, and, when he'd explained what had happened, the woman had three times asked the child to answer the door because she herself was in the bathroom and finally she'd had to do it herself anyway. In response, she'd said, "Damn you," to the child and the man, who'd been at the door and who'd heard, simply told the woman then and there that he couldn't continue to see someone who'd curse her own child. This man had been applauded by several others in the audience. It made Rachel wonder how on earth she could ever tell anyone of the awfulness, the screaming and the threats and the language worse than any she'd ever imagined herself using ever, that had passed—and often—between her and Drew.

And how could she ever expect anyone to believe that Drew wanted to kill her? She'd had a letter, a letter saying that perhaps it would be better, perhaps it would be safer for her to avoid seeing Drew right then. Avoid upsetting his tender homicidal psyche.

Rachel wished she'd kept the letter, because she couldn't remember now exactly how it had been phrased, but there was no way to forget the upshot of it, which was that Drew hated her guts, wanted to kill her even then, and acted out, over and over in psychodrama, hurting, killing Rachel.

Even that might not have been the end for Rachel, might not have made her turn tail and run. But the same day that the letter had arrived, something else had happened, something that fortified what the letter contained.

She'd been sewing all morning, taking a break only after the mail had come. The mail, in fact, was her way of signaling the break, and the mail, after all, was the source of her work.

The letter from Benedict House, however, was at the top of the pile. She read it twice, maybe three times, and then crumpled it up and then smoothed it out again. It made her angry and it made her sad, but it hadn't, not yet, made her afraid.

Until she walked into the bathroom and found herself gawking at the sink.

The basin was filled with blood, at least two inches of blood. It was almost too red, against the blinding white of the basin, to be real. Rachel stood there staring at it, like staring at an accident or a dead thing on the road.

Enough!

Rachel reached and put her hand down into it, feeling for the rubber stopper. When she yanked the metal pull, the blood bubbled up as far as her wrist. She ran the water over her hand and sloshed it sloppily on the sides of the basin. Then she got the can of cleanser out and she scrubbed and she scrubbed and she scrubbed as the fear grew.

Someone had been there, someone had come while she was sewing, someone, someone . . . Drew. Who would dare but Drew. And he could do it. It would be easy enough, with Benedict House just an hour away. Too close. Too close. She could only think, *Too too close, run run run.*

That was what had propelled her away from everything she owned; away, no forethought, no word to anyone, not even any real packing to speak of.

She had taken the packet of orders in her old Coach bag and she'd grabbed her bag of fabric scraps and she'd done something with the letter from the school, she'd stuck it back in the envelope and stamped it and put it out in her box thinking, *Here, here, RETURN TO SENDER, here, this is the end of it, I'll have no more to do with it, with him.*

She'd driven until the gas gauge had read empty for a long long while and then she'd seen a farmyard with a lot of derelict cars rusting there and she'd simply pulled her car in among them and that was that. To her knowledge, no one had ever found it, nor had she heard a word about herself being missing, being sought. Even the woman who picked her up on the highway never asked her what was wrong or why or even if she was running away.

That's what comes from being unpopular and a hermit, she thought now. Then there had been no Zachary, no Peyton, no anybody except maybe the people on the street who heard and pretended not to hear Drew screaming at her or her at him or both of them at once.

Kingsville was such a small town. Rachel doubted that she could have gotten a job there if she tried. She felt like a marked woman in Kingsville, the woman with the uncontrollable, drug-taking, drug-pushing son. The woman who screamed all the time. It was a blessing that she'd thought of patchwork, thought of selling it through the mail. To those who answered her ad, she must have seemed dimpled and sweet and countrified, a quiltmaker instead of what she was: a wife who had failed, and then a mother who had failed.

Once she'd run, once she'd constructed a new life, the old one seemed never to have existed. Until this morning, when she'd heard about Rob.

HE AND THE GIRL HAD POSITIONED themselves on a cliff above Peyton's property. From the spot he'd picked, they could see the gate and the upper garden and the roof of the house and various decks and terraces, and the whole of the little swimming pool that jutted out on yet another cliff, a larger one than theirs.

"Was that her?" The girl had to ask because, except for a kind of gasping sound that Drew had made when Rachel had emerged from the car to shut the gate, he'd said nothing, but nothing at all. "Dre-ew," she whined.

"That's her." He said it just to shut her up.

"Well, what now?" She seemed impatient. Probably wanted him to screw her again, and furthest thing from his mind right now.

She repeated the question, and he said, as coolly as he could under the circumstances, "We wait."

"Oh, great," she said. She looked around at the brush, the dust. "And exactly what are we going to do if a rattlesnake shows up?"

If he had been in a joking mood, he'd have laughed. Now, he half wished one would show up. "How about fire ants?" he asked her. "Ever been bit by one of those? They can get all over you before you know it. And people are allergic to them, too."

Her eyes were getting bigger, rounder, as her imagination took hold. He liked the effect he was having, and he kept right on. "No shit, man, people, they swell up. Imagine what it would be like, being puffy all over. Your face, your eyes puffed closed, your cheeks swollen out like—"

"Knock it off," she said, turning away from him and clapping her hands over her ears. "I've been bit by them and I know I'm not going to swell all up."

She was getting too loud, too shrieky, he decided, so he'd better quit. He got in one last shot, though, whispering so she'd get the hint about making less noise. "What about scorpions or, hey, a tarantula, what about one of those? We've got 'em all right here. Or, fuck, you could sit on a cactus."

It was all true. He found himself wondering why anybody lived in Texas, himself included.

"Hey, I mean it." The girl's temper seemed to flare up right in front of his eyes. Her hair actually lifted with some kind of current just a little, too.

It made him aware of her hair anew. Traveling with her, bickering and talking this way, had made him numb to the beauty of it. But maybe there was more to it than that. Maybe there was what had happened in the bathroom, while they'd been getting it on together. In any case, he figured he'd stop tormenting her for a while.

"Look," he explained, "I've been waiting a long time for this. This is my mother, you know? You've been telling me all this crap about your folks and you haven't heard one goddam word I've said about mine or you wouldn't be carrying on like this about bugs and snakes and dumb shit like that right now. Plus, if we aren't careful, she'll hear us. She can probably hear every word we say up here." He suddenly lapsed into silence, wondering if that could be true.

"Look, I'm sorry," she said, "but it's just that all of a sudden, this is really, I don't know."

"Then get lost. You can leave me here. Just fucking get lost."

She seemed to be weighing this, but Drew didn't have time for any of that. Out of the corner of his eye he saw movement, and when he looked down, sure enough, there was Rachel crossing one of the terraces, a flower pot in each hand. He raised an imaginary rifle and watched her through imaginary sights.

RACHEL HAD REMEMBERED THE GERANIUMS and had gone back to her car to bring them inside. She had tried them in various locations around several of the rooms, then finally thought, *No, it's too dark in here, they'll have to go outside.*

She suddenly knew exactly where to put them, too. She walked out across the deck and set the pots on a ledge where she knew they would catch lots of sun.

She stood back to admire where she'd placed them, but suddenly felt very vulnerable, very exposed. She looked around, but saw nothing, only the gathering evening gloom.

She went back inside and then came out on another, lower terrace. Inexplicably, she felt better here. Safer and—though this seemed to her a contradiction, one she could not understand, much less rectify—more alone.

She opened a canvas sling chair and sank down into it.

Better still.

And now she directed herself to concentrate on the scenery. *Is this meditation?* she wondered. *Sort of guided thought?*

The humidity was high, causing mist to catch between one hill and the next. It was lovely, all in clearly delineated shades of a deep, greened gray. As the darkness came, however, hill and mist and sky merged into one dark, solid mass.

Perhaps a quilt like that. In panels. First the hills all bright in sunlight, then toasted red as the sunset, then gray-green and all mist-shrouded, and, in the last panel, dark, dark and deep. Wait. She should have six panels. She needed two panels more.

Rachel waited for the stars to come out, but none appeared. It was as if she and the house had been covered by an enormous blanket, something thick enough to block all light. Fine. A star-and-moon panel, and then what? One that would be solid black.

Can't have that, she censored. *Funereal, gloomy, can't, can't.*

Yet neither the thought of black nor the pronouncement of "funereal" had the power to frighten Rachel now. Something reassuring here. She felt the way she used to feel when she'd put up candles for a hurricane and, though they hadn't been used, the storm was past and she'd done right, she'd been ready. Maybe even strong.

Right now, for instance, she could very easily have gone back into the house to put on a welcoming light. She didn't choose to, in part because she knew that Peyton would not be back for quite a while, in part because the totality of the darkness was comforting rather than fear-provoking. She sank into the darkness, or wanted to, accepting it the way she would have an anesthetic.

Rachel found she was quite exhausted, and why not? It was as if she'd been buffeted back and forth throughout the day: first doubt, then certainty, then anger, then fear. Rachel had, throughout her life, found decisions as difficult as they were inevitable. Today, it seemed, she had made—and then retracted—a great many.

Now a new one pressed its way into her thoughts. Perhaps it would be wise, she now felt, to call the police, tell them of her relationship with Rob and her suspicions regarding Drew and be done with it. Let them investigate. Let them protect her if, indeed, the situation called for that. Wash her hands, in other words. Once and for all, relax.

At the same time, she could not imagine herself implicating Drew. She could not imagine herself—and not solely because she might be wrong—siccing, as it were, the authorities on her son. The idea, the very idea, brought out something fierce in her, a kind of atavistic need to protect her young.

Then why was she running from him?

Another atavistic need: to protect herself.

Did scientists wonder which need was the more powerful? *I could tell them*, Rachel thought. *Let them talk to me.*

Yet Drew accused her of turning him in, accused her of having him held against his will at Benedict House. And he was right; Rachel had pulled out every stop to have him sent there. She'd heard about the place on the radio and on the television news, she'd read about it in the local paper. It seemed to her at the time that there was no other answer for Drew, no better way to get him to change, to help him.

Just as Rachel wavered now, she'd wavered then, measuring, weighing all of Drew's actions against some book-learned standard of normalcy. She hadn't had any brothers or sisters, she hadn't even baby-sat, so she had no idea what was right and what wasn't. Drew learned to play on that when he was older, either to scare her or to get her to let him do things she'd be inclined to say no to.

When she'd figured out that he'd been doing that—lying to her, for instance, in order to go to the beach with the other kids—she'd been outraged, thinking it a terrible deception. Later—when he didn't seek her permission to do anything at all—it seemed insignificant.

Once he even stole her keys and took the car, bringing it back with sand all over the inside, and with a huge gash in the upholstery in back. There must have been twenty dented beer cans, too, on the floor. After that she hid the keys or carried them on her person.

Yet she'd observe Drew with his friends—boys and girls both—and she'd see another side of him, a side that was friendly and fun, a side that people not only liked but were drawn to, and she'd think: *It must be me*.

Drew could, if he wanted to, have people orbiting around him. She had seen it often enough. When he wanted to make people laugh, they split their sides, and when he wanted to tug at their heartstrings, he could do that too. Even she, who knew him so well, knew his lies and his sense of humor, would sometimes, even guarding against it, end up in his thrall.

One time he told her that he had been working with gasoline and that a lot of it had spilled on Drew's clothes. He said he went to a friend's car and changed and then right after that, the friend had lit a cigarette and that his clothes, his jeans and his shirt and his underwear had gone up, whoosh!, indicating yard-high flames with his hand.

Rachel had uttered a gasp, the way maidens in melodrama do, and it had been too much for Drew, he'd laughed and laughed, saying, finally, that he'd made the whole thing up. But if that was so, where were his clothes? She never saw the things he had been wearing that morning after he'd told her this tale.

Also, if she, knowing what he was like, could fall for his stories over and over, imagine what it would be like for someone new to resist, to even be neutral to them. Well, they couldn't, that was clear.

He's such fun, he's always fun, he isn't like anyone I've ever met. She'd heard that from everyone, from everyone he wanted to charm, at least.

But they were never his friends for very long. It was as if Drew ran through people. Nonetheless, there were others always to take the place of the ones who weren't around anymore.

And they gave him things, Drew's friends. He never lacked for anything he ever wanted, money to go into Corpus or even as far away as Dallas for a rock concert. Clothes. Tapes and records. One time a trip to Cozumel, one hundred percent paid for by some friend.

She would overhear him talking to his friends and she would marvel at the way he joked and laughed and talked. Whenever she tried to talk to him, he answered in monosyllables, the tone of his voice harsh and cutting. She had cried once over it, and he had told her it was because she never really did talk, all she ever did was lecture and nag, lecture and nag.

But everyone was having trouble. It seemed as though every magazine she picked up had an article about teenagers, about runaways, about druggies. One day she wondered, *Why doesn't Drew run away?* She imagined how calm her life would be without him, and yet when in the next hour they had an argument and he'd stormed outside, she had followed him, afraid he would go for good, begging him to come inside and stay until he was over his anger, over whatever it was that had set him off. She was always apologizing to Drew, too.

At the same time, he didn't seem half as bad as some of the kids she'd read about, like the girl who'd been killed in New York City by the punk star Sid Vicious. Compared to that girl, Drew was normal, Drew was fine.

Rachel bought books, too, about truly evil people, and, yes, compared the way they were to the way Drew was.

It seemed ironic that Rachel, who had started out with all the "right" books about child-rearing, books like Dr. Spock's, would end up reading about psychopaths instead.

Her reading scared her. She learned, for instance, that almost all psychopathic killers had things in common. One text, in fact, had reduced them to a rhyme: bed-wetting, fire-setting, animal-getting. The question was, did Drew have them too? The bed-wetting, yes, he had for sure, but what about the others? She could remember him getting in trouble for playing with matches at school and once again for tossing firecrackers into the supermarket. But was that fire-setting? He had done it with some others kids; were they psychopathic too? And what about animal-getting? Did bringing that dog home, if those people were right and he had stolen it, count? Or was it being cruel to animals that they meant? And what about its foot? Had he hurt the dog's foot?

And did it mean all animals or just cats and dogs? Because she could remember one time at the beach Drew had picked up a live crab and had poked at it with his finger, sort of daring it to pinch, and when it did, he had cursed at it and hurled it away. Was that animal-getting?

What about the fire that had been set in the principal's office at Drew's old grade school in Kingsville? Over three thousand dollars' damage, the radio had said. Was Drew responsible for that? She'd heard that on her way out of town, the day he'd evidently slipped away from

Benedict House just long enough to put the blood in the sink. Maybe it was animal blood.

Or had there never been blood in the sink? Had Drew, that day, been to Kingsville at all? She ought to have called Benedict House to see if it was possible to check, but she hated Benedict House, hated their letter, hated their philosophy, hated the dirt on their floors and the holes they'd let kids punch into their walls.

But she'd kept reading, Rachel kept reading, and by the time she'd finished, she was scared to death, and worse than that, Drew had picked up some of the books and had figured out why she was reading them. One time he had marked a passage about mass murderer Ted Bundy as a child, "I'm like that" in the margin. Rachel had felt her stomach turn when she read it, and Drew, who had been hiding where he could observe her reaction when she came upon the passage, leaped out and whooped with laughter. She had laughed too, awash with relief, but then when they had stopped laughing, he became very serious and said, "I really am like that, Mom."

She threw that book at him. It was either an astonishing coincidence or something she'd been meant to throw, but it turned out all wrong, all wrong, the book had hit him and she'd half scared him and herself both to death.

Anyway, whatever had seemed wrong at one point would eventually seem insignificant in the face of what came next, and next, and next. Until she'd wrenched herself away from Drew entirely, she'd been caught up in what felt like a whirlpool carrying her down to a deepening, never-ending sadness.

Numbness, too, like the numbness that keeps the dying from really feeling their pain.

Rachel could remember when all she had left was acute disappointment, that someone as smart—indeed, even gifted—as Drew should have made nothing of it. It was unthinkable that he should be failing in school when children who were log-stupid passed. She could name the names of at least a dozen of them, dumb as dumb could be, all doing well. Why couldn't Drew pass?

"Make sure he does his homework," one of his teachers advised. But if he lies and says he doesn't have any, what then? For a while she took to calling his math teacher for the assignment each day, but even though she stood over him, he dawdled at it, in the end doing it in a form of gibberish which guaranteed that the teacher wouldn't accept it, wouldn't even be able to read it. Why? What grade had that been? She couldn't recall exactly, there had been so much turmoil for so long, but she did know he'd been young then, and she'd believed he'd change.

It wasn't as though his problems were ignored. She could still hear the break in his English teacher's voice —a young Mexican-American man who had been for a while her only hope, someone who recognized Drew's potential and seemed to want to work with it, Eddie, Eddie something, Eddie Garza. "I was like that myself," he'd told her early in the semester. "Macho, tough, liked to strut my stuff." To Rachel, it was like a movie: handsome caring professional, troublesome but talented boy. But she knew how the movie ended and she waited and watched the young teacher's hopes quashed along with her own. "I tried everything," he said. "I designed a whole unit around something he seemed interested in. Look." He turned over paper after paper, blank, blank, blank. "He did nothing. Not one word. He sat there and looked as though he was working, but he turned in these blanks. . . ."

Rachel wanted to hug Eddie Garza, hold him, cry with him, thank him for trying. Most teachers didn't,

wouldn't, but this one had. And look what happened.
Look what happened. Rachel hated Drew at that moment, hated him for being her son. She wished Eddie
were her son, or anyone, just not Drew Cassidy, not
Drew.

Was Drew on drugs then? She doubted it. He was just
what she'd at first called dragging his feet. Dragging his
feet. It sounded so simple, so normal, so fixable.

She could endure disappointment, however acute.

And disappointment was normal. All parents had
dreams for their kids. All parents wanted something that
the kids resisted, even refused.

In her own case, after Rob left, her parents—though
fortunately they were far enough away—were sorry for
her. She'd failed at marriage, and marriage, in their
eyes, was what she had been raised to succeed at, at
least in the surface staying-together way that they themselves had. She hid from them the worst about Drew,
lest they discover that she'd failed at motherhood, too.

Now her dad was dead. He'd never find out. She still
lied to her mother, though she didn't know why. There
had never been anything resembling real emotion in her
parents' house. Perhaps that explained why Rachel had
not fled the turmoil sooner.

Rachel did attempt to lighten her load by trying to rid
herself of expectations about Drew, or at least by scaling
them down: *If he doesn't end up in jail, be satisfied. . . .
If he doesn't kill himself, be happy. . . .*

Easy to try, impossible to do. The expectations, or
maybe hopes, were always there, always.

They were playing a game of Scrabble one night.
How old was Drew? Twelve, maybe. Outside it was
pouring, the tail end of a Brownsville hurricane whipping through Kingsville, turning the sky slate-gray,
making huge murky pools at every intersection. The
electricity had gone out, and Rachel had lit two kero-

sene lamps and a little gas heater. It was almost cozy, mother and son on the rug on the living-room floor, Drew keeping score, and Rachel holding the dictionary.

Drew had spelled N-E-A-P and Rachel claimed there was no such word.

"You're crazy," Drew said. "It's a tide."

"I don't believe you."

But this wasn't an argument, this wasn't nasty, this was just the sort of talk that came with a game of Scrabble, and in fact Rachel felt good about it, felt whole, and knew that Drew did too.

"I challenge," Rachel said, opening the dictionary, sure that Drew was bluffing.

"Go ahead. You'll see. It's a tide." Waiting, cocksure.

Rachel found it, started reading, "A tide of minimum range," her voice catching, tears beginning to fall, "occurring at the first and the third quarters," on her feet now, dropping the dictionary; but remembering the rest, "of the moon."

She ran to the bathroom, bent over double, sobbing. Drew pounded on the door, "Mom? Mom, are you okay?"

But she wasn't okay, she wasn't okay. How could she be okay? She didn't even understand it fully, but she knew there was something heartbreaking about it, about having a son who would know a word as obscure, as esoteric, as "neap" and yet that same son, same son, would be failing every single subject in school. Would do no work, complete no project. Would lie and cheat and play hooky from school . . .

"Hey, Mom. Come out of there. You're scaring me, okay?"

Rachel sniffled, blew her nose in a towel, looked at her sad red eyes, and opened the bathroom door.

"You gonna finish the game or what?"

She nodded yes.

"It's cold in here," he said, almost as though he was trying to distract her. As though she were the one in need of help. "Where's the matches?" he asked, finding them and lighting the heater in the bathroom, too. "Come on. Let it warm up in here. He took her arm and led her back into the living room as if she were feeble.

She had seen that side of him, the nurturing side, though not often enough. Often he would lose patience with her, calling her psychotic and suggesting that she see a shrink and get some tranquilizers. She felt like yelling back, "Why don't I just buy them from you?" but she never did.

And sometimes she felt like telling him that he was the reason she cried, but again, she didn't.

No wonder then that he thought she was crazy, crazy Rachel, crazy Mom, crying suddenly, unpredictably, at the oddest things, at things like his knowing "neap."

How stupid to be thinking of this now, Rachel told herself, walking back toward the shadows of Peyton's bedroom. Especially since things got so much worse.

Rachel reached for the light switch and then thought better of it. Again, the feeling of concealment comforted her. What was it Peyton had said? "Just float." It was a super idea, a version of hydrotherapy. Rachel changed into the inexpensive leotard she'd bought and went downstairs to the lowest level and the pool.

HE HADN'T EXPECTED THE GIRL TO TAKE him seriously when he'd told her to get lost, but she must have, because she stood up, dusted herself off, and started scuffing back toward the place where they'd left the car.

He had a sudden fear that Rachel would emerge from the house again, would see the girl and then spot him as well. He couldn't have that happen before he was ready, and he wasn't quite sure what "ready" meant.

That was what the girl was bitching about, about waiting, and yet if he didn't wait, he could screw the whole thing up, get Rachel scared, get her running again, lose her.

So he let the girl have the lead, and he even, in the end, had to concede that she was right to get off that bluff before the darkness fell entirely, He could just imagine himself trying to keep from yelling when he'd tried to get a boost by catching hold of a prickly pear cactus or something worse.

He'd been unprepared for what seeing Rachel after all this time, even fleetingly, even from so far away, would do. He'd felt a physical reaction, a sort of ringing in his ears, the kind of thing he'd expect from a blow.

For one thing, she looked so fucking small. Somehow, in the time that had elapsed, he'd made her bigger in his mind's eye, and now there she was real, and fucking tiny. In fact, it seemed to him now that he'd been taller than Rachel for years and years, since he was thirteen at least. He'd forgotten that.

"What are you thinking about?" the girl asked him. He'd gotten into the passenger side of the car and had just sat there. She'd gotten into the driver's seat, but he hadn't handed her the keys. She'd waited, not wanting to ask for them because of the depth of his reverie. Finally, though, her curiosity got the best of her.

He found that when she looked at him, he had to

quickly rearrange his face, knowing that his expression had to be way too intense. Christ, he could remember catching someone at Benedict House looking that way, looking that way at him. It was his psychodrama teacher, too, and it had been the first time he'd reckoned with the way she felt toward him.

Surprisingly, he tossed his head back and laughed, answering the girl right off. "You want to know? I'm thinking about weird women. You, my mom, all the weird women I've ever known." And then he laughed again and lapsed back into himself.

"I don't know that I'm so weird," she said, pleasure tingeing her words. He knew why; it was because he'd said women instead of girls. First time anyone had ever referred to him as a man he'd felt it too. She went on to ask, "How was your mom weird? Aside from splitting, I mean."

"I don't know how to explain it. It was like she believed in magic. Yeah, that's it. A kind of television magic."

"I think *you're* weird," the girl teased.

It felt good to be with her this way, even now, with Rachel down there and Rob already dead. It felt wonderful. Drew sank back toward his door and raised his arm to pass over her head and across the back of her seat. It was tight, but he'd made a sort of pocket, and she scooted as best she could toward him, resting her head against him. "You smell like chocolate," he said.

"Better than the way you smell," she answered.

"And just how do I smell?" He waited expectantly for her reply. There was nothing he liked better than trading affectionate insults. To him, this cemented their relationship the way nothing else, not sex, not dope, not anything else could have.

"You smell..." She debated, then chose. "Like some old boots my daddy used to own. Rough-out boots. Pigskin."

He wished he could drop his other arm around her. Wished the car wasn't so cramped.

"Listen," she said, "let's get out of here. Let's drive away, to Mexico, maybe. Let's—"

"I can't," he interrupted her. "I don't even want to." But of course he did. She didn't know it, though.

She squirmed away from him, sat upright. "I don't think you're telling me everything. About your father, fine, I believe that because I heard it on the radio, so fine, but about your mother I just don't know. I mean, you say you have to find her, you have to get to her, and then, I don't know, you just *sit* here once you do. I just don't know what to think, and there's something about this whole thing..." She leaned back again, resignedly. "I don't know. I just don't know."

NO MATTER HOW WARM THE NIGHT AIR, NO matter how warm the water, there was something shivery, always, about slipping into a pool. Rachel slid as slowly as she could, barely stirring the surface, hoping that this time she wouldn't be cold, wouldn't feel the goosebumps racing over her body, but of course she did. She huddled against the pool's edge until the feeling passed, and then edged her way to the side at the deepest end.

She pushed off and crossed the pool with her face beneath the water. Then she treaded her way to the center of the water and rolled over floating, as Peyton had suggested.

The movement of the water was slight, and rhythmic. She thought of amniotic fluid and then wished she hadn't. *Drew, Drew,* she cursed softly at the starless sky.

It was a good thing that she made her living as she did, at home, at the sewing machine, or tucked in a chair, handstitching. A good thing because she would never have been able to get dressed each day and go into an office like a normal person. She would never have been able to concentrate on anything that engaged her mind as well as her hands.

The needlework was instinctive to Rachel; her hands just went and did it while her mind was free to brood.

And brood was all she did, all she was doing now.

Drew accused her of partaking in a belief that family life should be as pat, as problem-free, as life on the set of a sitcom. "Television magic," he called it. She remembered him opening the fridge, opening the fruit bin, tossing oranges one after another around the room. "This shit!" he was yelling. "You believe this shit is going to make some kind of difference."

And in a way he was right.

The first time she'd gone to Rob's apartment, way before they were married, she remembered being utterly appalled. There was nothing in the fridge, nothing in the kitchen cabinets, nothing on the walls. As though Rob had been waiting just for her, and she believed that yes, her arrival could make a difference, rescue him, put fresh-squeezed orange juice on the breakfast table and cheery curtains on the kitchen windows, prints framed on the wall, wildflowers in a Mason jar on the windowsill.

She'd never lost her belief in that, even when Drew

did all he could to stomp on it, all he could to take it away from her, make it seem superficial.

She'd run around the kitchen picking up the oranges, putting them back. "You don't want anything nice," she'd screamed. "Nice things are wasted on you."

Once she'd run away, she'd made her theory work. She'd surrounded herself with the little things that mattered to her, things she'd once hoped would matter to Rob and to Drew. She was sure it was those things— picking flowers, squeezing oranges in the morning, and straightening things up at night—those things that had drawn Zachary to her, for instance, and Peyton, too. More examples rushed in upon her, small, yes, but not trivial. She almost recited them aloud: cloth napkins, salad forks alongside regular ones. *We're the same kind of people,* she thought of herself and Peyton and Zachary. Rob and Drew, on the other hand, could live like animals.

Oh, she could just imagine what that beach house of Rob's must have been like, even if he'd had someone come in to clean. She could well remember the way he'd leave a bathroom, grub-ringed tub, towel clumped to mildew on the floor, globs of toothpaste congealing on the sides of the sink. She could see his place, all right, dust bunnies and pretzel crumbs all over the living room, clothes dropped where they'd been removed.

Rob, to tell the truth, just disgusted her, disgusted her in every conceivable way. But when had it started? Could it happen that way with Zachary, too?

She couldn't imagine it. There were already a few things about Zachary which irked Rachel, but they weren't the kind of things that would make her wish that he would disappear. She had, however, wanted Rob out.

Maybe, she thought, *he picked up on that. Maybe that was why he'd left.* But no. She'd hidden it so well.

She'd smiled and cleaned up his mess and tolerated his lovemaking.

Rob.

Everything he did got to her. He would clip his toenails in the living room and let the little nail ends fly wherever they flew. She was forever finding nail ends stuck to the fibers of the rug.

What else? *Oh, why think of any of this, why do that to yourself? Just float, float. Don't think about any of this.*

But the fact was, the thoughts were rolling, sour and souring. *Oh, God, even his death hasn't helped, even that hasn't wiped any of this away.*

She had thought about Rob dying long before he did die. She had imagined she would feel just the way she'd felt when, during their life together, she'd returned to the house from, say, the grocery and found Rob unexpectedly gone. She would walk around the empty house and revel in the fact of his absence, light candles, play records loud and late into the night. She would change the sheets on the bed and she would lie on them, glad not to smell his smell. *Rob is gone*, she would think. *Rejoice, rejoice.*

What was the last thing Rob had thought? Had he made an Act of Contrition? Had he thought, This is it, this is what I deserve?

Oh, God, am I saying it was right for Drew to take Rob's life, if he did do that, if Drew was the one? Is that what I'm saying? But who else could it have been? Who else?

She heard something then, over and above the lap of the water. It was a sound from above, a sound she knew, a scrape. The clay pot. The scrape of the clay pot on cement, the same scrape she'd heard just minutes earlier, when she'd placed the pots on the upper terrace ledge.

She jerked involuntarily at the recognition. Water washed up over her face and down into her throat. She slapped at the water and felt her legs pull at her, weigh her down. She coughed and paddled awkwardly to the side, where she clung, trying to regain her breath.

LISTEN, I DON'T WANT TO TELL YOU. I'M afraid to tell you, afraid that you'll take the side my mom is on. Think I'm lying, the way she always thinks I'm lying."

"No, I won't," the girl said.

He could tell she meant it. But instead of feeling relief, he felt anger. He could almost hear Rachel's voice, yammering at him. "Sure they believe you, they believe you for a while. Everyone believes you, but they all find out. The way I found out."

Rachel was talking about his getting away, away from her and the house and all the fighting and the nagging that she did. A couple of times he'd managed to find someone to take him in, an old coot out in the country who needed chores done and then later the parents of a friend of his.

In the first instance, things had just gone awry. The deal he'd made with the guy was that he was supposed to do ten hours of work a week for his room and board. But it always came to more than that and the guy kept complaining that it was less. So he started keeping a sort of time card, and it didn't make any difference because then the guy started ragging him about all the food he ate, as though he was eating it on purpose, not because he was hungry but just to break the guy.

He told the guy, fine, he would find something else at the end of the week, but the whole time he kept thinking, like a little kid, about what Rachel would say if she knew. Well, he figured, he would lie to Rachel and get away with it, but like the next day, next fucking day, who should arrive there but Rachel, and at the worst possible time, too. It was like she had the radar that would get her into any situation where she could say to him, "See? See?"

That day, man, that day stood out as one of the all-time horrible ones in his mind. The guy had an old horse, a mare, and it was his job, part of his hours, to feed it morning and night.

He liked doing that. Liked the fact that every morning and every night, here was this mare standing there waiting, and it was so easy, you just knew what she wanted and you gave it to her and she was happy.

He used to listen to her munching away and he'd think, *Why can't it be that way with people? Why can't you know what they want?* Thinking of his mom, mostly, the way nothing ever came out right between him and her.

But here he was, in this new situation, and here it was happening again. He and the guy ended up pretty much the way he and his mother had, just kind of at each other all the time, and he couldn't help but wonder if that didn't prove that what Rachel had said was right. That everyone "found out," as she put it, about him eventually.

Still, there was the mare. She liked him. She was pregnant, too.

One morning he'd gone out to feed her and instead of being there, waiting, she was way up in the field.

He put the grain in the bucket, thinking she'd come down, but she didn't.

So he walked up there, and as he walked, he started feeling clammy, like, what if he got there and she had a broken leg or something, but when he got there, it wasn't like that at all.

She had given birth during the night, and there it was, the foal, still in the membrane, dead. The mare had been licking at the foal and she'd managed to get the thing, which looked like a huge bloody Baggie, off his nose. It hadn't mattered; it was still just dead.

Drew hadn't known what to do. He knew that he had to do something, that he couldn't just let the mare stand up there forever, that he couldn't just let the dead foal stay there either.

He took his belt off and he put it around the mare's neck and he led her away, out of the pasture, into an old run-down stock pen. She turned right around after he'd put the rails back up and stared up at the spot where she'd been.

Then he went to get the pickup truck to take the foal away. He hadn't wanted to tell the old man. He felt telling the old man would be worse than any of it, than finding the foal or having to touch it.

But he couldn't get the foal up on the bed of the truck. It was the membrane as well as the animal's weight, and the fact that the dew was still fresh on the membrane around the animal's body, slicking it up.

Meanwhile, the mare just stood in the stock pen staring up at him. He wasn't sure if she could see that far, see, actually, what he was doing, but it was enough to unnerve him and that didn't help matters any when it came to lifting either.

Then, all of a sudden, there was the old man yelling at him, yelling about what he'd done to the foal and how good for nothing he'd turned out to be, not even able to lift what had to be only a hundred pounds or so and how he'd have been better off trying to do the work by himself.

He figured the old guy was just shaken up by this dead foal that he'd counted on being able to sell, and he'd just started hollering at him, "Shut up, shut up, shut the fuck up," his shirtsleeves and his jeans all slimy and bloody now and the mare still standing there watching.

In the middle of this, Rachel's car came banging up the road. He said to the guy, "Open your fucking mouth and I'll slit your throat." The guy got the message, even grabbed hold of the foal, and together they slung the body up onto the tailgate.

Rachel was out of the car now, coming close. Behind Rachel, over her shoulder he could see the mare keeping vigil.

"What are you doing here?" He advanced on his mother. "What the fuck are you doing here?" he asked, his voice wringing itself out on the words, like it used to back when it was changing.

Rachel looking from him to the old man and then spying the foal. Rachel's head bobbing around in confusion. Rachel saying something, he couldn't remember what.

He just wanted her out of there, wanted her away. Didn't want her hanging around, commiserating or puking or whatever the hell she would do. "Get the fuck out of here," he said, knowing that she wouldn't be able to handle that, what with the old guy there and all. He would holler her off, and he was doing it, she was turning around to head out of there.

But she turned and then she saw the mare, staring, staring, and she froze in her tracks and started bawling how she was just like the mare, bewildered, just the way the mare was and how she was dumb dumb dumb in the face of it, only knowing that something was bad wrong, the way the mare knew.

The all-time worst day of his life.

Rachel was an asshole, didn't know anything, always thought the worst where he was concerned. She probably thought he'd killed the foal, strangled it or something. He ought to write Rachel off, not spend his time finding her, but just write her off, forget she existed the way she was able to forget that he existed.

Of course, first she had to stash him at Benedict House.

Maybe that was why he had to track her down, sit her down in a goddam chair and look at her face to face, no turning away now. He wanted to see her expression, to see her eyes get round and her mouth flop open when he told her about the place, about how his father was dead right now because of Rachel's putting him there.

"But why did she?" the girl asked, and her question startled him. He hadn't realized he'd said this thing about Rachel out loud but thought he had been thinking about it in a kind of stream.

"Because," he said hesitantly, "there was an accident. Except that my mom didn't think it was. My mom thought it was something I did, something I was even glad about."

"Was somebody killed?"

"Yes. A girl. My girlfriend. A girl who..." He reached up abruptly and balanced her chin against his fingertips. "Oh, shit, I don't know."

He'd taken the dead foal to the vet in Bishop, and the girl was there with a puppy to get its shots. She knew all about horses, and before the vet even came outside she was there with him, her eyes wet, looking up at him and telling him how this sometimes happened, happened a lot in fact, and how there wasn't anything anybody could have done about it.

SHE HAD DRIPPED THROUGH PEYTON'S ENTIRE house only to find that a marauding housecat had been on the terrace investigating and rubbing against the newly placed pots. She was feeling cold and very foolish now as she eased back into the pool.

Just float, she counseled herself, drifting again. The water smoothed out, and the clouds in the sky parted just a bit to reveal a pinprick star or two. But try as she might, Rachel couldn't clear her mind of the thoughts that jammed it now. Like storm clouds gathering, she realized.

She kept herself afloat by flapping her palms occasionally. *Odd that I have to,* she thought. Usually the water would pillow her for long periods. The tension, she decided. The tension and the ever-returning, all too easily triggered fear.

Even when she was trapped in Kingsville there with Drew, the fear had not been constant. Once or twice he'd gone to live somewhere else, not storming out in anger but actually making arrangements of some sort, and then she'd been relieved. The tension, the fear—it had lifted.

Once he'd moved into the country to that old man's tumbledown spread, and even though she'd known it couldn't last, for the man was known to be a miser and a crab and an impossible person to work for, she was glad to have Drew in someone else's hair. But if that was true, why had she driven out there that grim, awful day?

God, she still felt hollow when she thought about that mare. The animal was grieving, she'd known it, and what pulled at her even to this day was the way she'd felt that same grief too. Drew was alive, yes, but he was just as lost to her as the foal had been to that mare.

Right after that, Drew had left the old man's place, but he'd moved away again almost immediately.

The second time he'd moved in with a grubby redneck family, moved into a peeling frame house too small for the people without Drew there. She'd driven by it, repelled by the barren yard, rusting car parts heaved randomly about it. There was even an overturned trash can with a skinny mongrel routing through the contents. *Fine. If he prefers that to me, let him have it*, she had thought.

But that ended too.

Then his girlfriend's family had taken him in. She wasn't even certain where he'd met the girl, but there had been girls all down the line, since he was, oh, twelve, thirteen. They'd call him up and giggle and if he wasn't at home, they wouldn't leave a name.

This girl was his first real girlfriend, someone he went out with, and didn't pretend indifference to.

When he'd moved in there, Rachel found it impossible to raise her usual objections. She couldn't possibly look down on them, because they were educated, maybe even rich. They ran a boarding stable for horses. Rachel had often driven by it, a little green oasis bordered by a hand-hewn mesquite fence.

Once again, Rachel had thought rescue. They'd save Drew, redeem him, do what she could not.

Drew spent more and more time there, and indeed,

did seem to change. He was hardly ever surly or smart-alecky, he laughed a lot, made jokes. Rachel's feelings were mixed. She was glad, yes, but ashamed, too, to have had such a change wrought by strangers. The fact that they could have success with Drew where she had none convinced her it was something awful she had done to make him the way he had become.

But now he wasn't that anymore.

They invited Rachel over, the parents, and she drove there, up what for South Texas seemed an anomaly, a driveway, fence-lined and straight.

The house was caliche, with saltillo tile floors and a tall beamed ceiling. They—the mother, father, daughter, and Drew—stood on the verandah to watch Rachel up the walk. They are what I'd always hoped to be, Rachel realized, trying to hold her head high. Trying not to feel how superior they, and Drew included, were.

The girl's father clapped an arm around Drew's shoulder. "We've taken this boy under our wing," he said. "I think you'll notice a big improvement."

Wasn't it what Rachel had been hoping for? Wasn't it? She'd smiled at the girl's father when deep inside she'd wanted to spit in his face. How smug he was, how smug and righteous he and his whole family were. But then she looked at Drew and saw something in his eyes and she knew that it wasn't any simple conversion, she knew there was a plan there, something Drew was after and would get. Their money? Maybe that was it. Drew would marry the girl, it was that simple. Even if it was a plan, so what? It was a good solution to everything, to everyone's problems.

She saw the way the girl looked at Drew, saw the adoration in her eyes.

IT WAS AN ACCIDENT, TOO. FUCKING wheel came off the car. If it hadn't been, they'd have charged me with manslaughter, and they tried, too."

What he remembered most was the noise. The radio blaring, the sound of the empty beer cans clattering against each other.

"Funny," he said now. "I didn't even make the connection, but she had a little two-seater, too. And hey, it was an oldie, just like yours." He got excited about it, as if it were a good thing rather than a reminder of something awful that had happened. But they told him at Benedict House that that was what he had been doing, glossing over things instead of facing them, confronting. "It was a bug-eye, you know, a Sprite? A '61, I think. It'd been her mom's, and they'd kept it up, and then, on her sixteenth birthday, they'd just handed it over to her; just like that. Did you, by any chance, get this car on your sixteenth birthday?"

The moonfaced girl just smiled.

"Anyway, it didn't have a trunk, it had this kind of empty space where a trunk should have been. A boot, she called it. Anytime we had a beer we tossed the empty back there and pretty soon they just rattled around. It wasn't full, because her dad had the yardman empty it out from time to time when she was asleep or something, but we always had a semi-stash back there, so there was this noise. This constant noise."

He went on. The moonfaced girl might not have

been there any longer. He was remembering for himself rather than for her, and everything that he remembered was good.

She'd taught him to ride, and it was a funny thing, having a girl teach you something and not resent it. But she wasn't saying "Here, you've got to learn this," but instead "This is the neatest thing in the world and I want you in on it."

They would take the horses out when the moon was full and they'd let them walk side by side and every now and then his leg would squoosh up against hers and he'd apologize until she figured out he had to be doing it on purpose.

She had shown him one small grassy place where the horses never minded being tied.

They went out in her car, too.

"The roads are straight down there," he said, "straight as arrows, and we used to look for curves. A sports car's gotta have curves, right? Well, we found a good one on the Chapman Ranch Road, and we used to go there just to rev around it. Only the wheel came off the car and it went over. . . ." He flipped his hand from palm down to palm up, the way it had happened.

He had run toward the only light he could see, a tenant house out on the ranch, and he'd banged and banged at the door and the Mexicans inside only looked at him with suspicion. "Open the door!" he'd screamed, and he'd even broken the glass with his fist, but they wouldn't open it, and he kept thinking about the girl who was back there, dying probably, and how he had to get some help.

Finally, when he'd given up and turned away, one of the Mexicans had come out and then some others behind him. He'd begged for a phone, but there wasn't any, and in the end he and the others had piled into a panel truck and driven back to where it had happened. No noise now, not any.

Together they'd lifted up the car and there she was, still in it, dead.

A couple of the Mexicans had crossed themselves and started praying.

The next thing he knew he was back at the dingy little police station in Bishop, waiting for he didn't know what. For Rachel, probably.

SHE WAS USED TO BEING WAKEFUL AT NIGHT in those days, and it didn't really bother her because her schedule was her own and she could just as easily sew at night as in the daytime. There was something mean about this particular bout of wakefulness, however, because she didn't seem able to concentrate on anything, not even on the essentially mindless activity of sewing. She paced around, tried to find something on television, then gave up.

The phone startled her, and she answered right away because she was so close to it, not even taking time to steel herself. And she should have, she should have, because it was a woman's voice, a voice she didn't know, and it said, "Your son. Your son, your awful son, has killed my daughter." The last three words were hard, hate-filled.

Rachel pushed at the disconnect button, but didn't have to. The line had gone dead immediately after the announcement had been made. It never occurred to Rachel that perhaps it was a crank call, or a mistake. Instead, the words *I knew it, I knew it,* corkscrewed through her brain.

She sat down, she stood up, she paced, she sat again, she picked up the phone and then put it down and then picked it up. Her hands were heavier than she'd ever known hands could be, and her feet, too, and then the head on her shoulders, heavy, heavy, weighing her down.

She had to do something. She didn't know what to do. She paged through the thin Kingsville phone book and found the number of the people in the caliche house.

What had Drew done? Had he shot her? Stabbed her? Strangled her?

The girl's father answered. His voice was calm, even soothing. Yes, it was true, she was dead. There had been an accident, an auto wreck.

"But where . . . are they at the hospital or what?"

The answer was preceded by a sigh. "They didn't take our girl to the hospital," he said. "They took her to the funeral home."

Was that possible? Did that ever happen, that they wouldn't even try to save someone? Could that be?

He read her silence. "That's where she is now and that's where we're going."

"What about Drew?" she asked.

"The police have him." He took a long breath. "I've got to go now. My wife needs me. I'm sorry for the way she . . ." And then, midsentence, he hung up.

Now Rachel was panicked anew. Which police? She called the station in Kingsville, and after she'd explained was told to call Bishop.

On the way there she feared what she'd find, Drew battered and bruised, Drew held without receiving the medical attention he needed. She drove faster than she'd ever driven in her life, grateful for the long straight roads and for the fact that no one, not a single car, was out to get in her way.

She felt the same need to defend Drew arise as had

arisen when the couple who owned the dog Drew had found had said that Drew had stolen their dog. What did the girl's mother mean, that Drew had killed the girl? How dare she imply that it was Drew's fault, that he had somehow engineered it? And why had she called Rachel, compounding the horror of the accident, making it somehow Rachel's fault?

A man who wasn't in uniform had gone to get Drew. She hadn't even had to explain who she was or why she was there. When Drew appeared in the doorway, she had rushed to him, had hugged him and, that quickly, had been repelled.

He reeked of alcohol. Reeked. She wanted to bang her fists on him, beat him, punish him, make him pay.

Instead she hugged him harder, hiding what she was feeling.

When she met his eyes she saw that they were networked with red veins.

She signed some things—or did she?—it seemed she had. On the phone they'd told her to bring the deed to her house and she'd done that and it somehow figured in Drew's release.

And then they were in her car on the way back home. The confinement made the smell of booze seem stronger, if that was possible. She rolled her window down, but it didn't help much. Then she asked Drew to roll his down and he ignored her. She didn't ask again, just suffered with the smell.

On the way back he began to talk, began to tell her about the way the car had flipped, about the way he'd been thrown free and the way he'd known that the girl was trapped beneath it.

"Her hand was sticking out, I could see it, and she called my name and I went as close to the car as I could and she grabbed my pant leg." His voice seemed to tick like a metronome, with that kind of monotony, as though the speech was boring him even as he recited it. "I lifted the car up and I held it there, kind of bracing my back against it, and I waited, thinking someone would come. Then I couldn't hold it anymore and I had to set it down and I told her I was doing that, told her I would go for help, get help somewhere. For all I know, I set it down on top of her. For all I know, she would have lived if it hadn't been for me."

"No, no, baby, that's not true." Tears ran down Rachel's face as she drove on, her words soothing him. She hated herself for the anger she'd felt when she hugged him, hated herself for all the sympathy she'd ever withheld.

He went on, talking about the Mexicans and about being taken into Bishop by the police. Then he said that he had been upstairs with one of the uniformed men, alone. "After I told him what happened," Drew had said, "he took off his holster and he rolled the whole thing up, the belt and the gun and the holster, and he pulled out a drawer and stuck it in there. Then he kind of looked at me, I mean, made sure that I was looking back at him. And he left the room, Mom, left me in there with that gun. Like he was suggesting that, I don't know, that I ought to kill myself or something."

She knew then that he was lying. She didn't take the road that led toward Kingsville proper, toward their home. Instead she headed toward the hospital. "I think you should be checked," she said. "You might have something wrong with you, something internal."

Instead she hoped to persuade them to keep him, persuade them to get him the kind of help he needed. "Don't you see?" She ended up begging an intern who seemed to her incredibly, but incredibly dense. "Don't you see how sick he must be, to be *lying* at a time like this?"

Finally they got someone on the phone, a psychiatrist

from Corpus Christi. She screamed years and years of anguished suspicion and fear and resentment into the mouthpiece, never once stopping to wonder what anyone overhearing her might think. Never once wondering if Drew himself, in some examining room, could hear as well.

But that was how she'd gotten him into Benedict House, on the strength of that call and a visit the following day when Drew's entire history was taken, all of it, the whole thing.

How old was Drew? Seventeen. Still a minor. Still eligible for the program that Benedict House offered. She begged him into it, would have done anything, paid anything, to get him in.

And having him there evened out the days, made her realize how jumpy she'd been, even when he'd been away from her before, how every time the phone had rung or someone had knocked on the door she'd thought: *What's Drew done now?* Benedict House, because it was so official, somehow, took that burden away. They were responsible for Drew. She wasn't anymore.

Rescue, again, but a more realistic form of it than ever before.

Still, Rachel made the one-hour drive to Corpus every Sunday to visit him. As much as she thought she wanted to, Rachel couldn't quite let go.

AT FIRST I HATED HER FOR STICKING ME in that place. The kids were so fucked-up, more fucked-up than I had ever been. After a while, though, I got to like it, got to sort of be in charge."

It was just as easy, maybe even easier, in there. Everybody liked him, but more than that. Everybody there was more or less anti-parent. You could say anything you wanted, and nobody would shoot you down.

Hell, in psychodrama they encouraged, even demanded it.

"You remember I was talking about weird women," he asked. When she nodded, he went on, "Well, the one who taught the psychodrama thing was one of them. Weird as shit."

He'd already talked about some of the things that went on in the sessions, but now he told her about the teacher, Paula, who'd inspired them.

"She seemed really young, like she was one of us, except that she wasn't because she had her college degree and all. But she really liked me, me especially, said she knew all there was to know about me. I made some remark about how my files didn't say anything, and she said, 'Fuck the files, man, I'm talking about the Essential You.' She talked like that a lot, part cursing and part this mystical kind of stuff.

"When I first got sent there I got all weird about my mom. I mean, they'd say one bad thing about her and I was ready to punch them out. I couldn't remember any of the nutso things my mom had done, only the good stuff, like her baking cornbread with jalapeños in it and shit.

"My psychodrama teacher, she would say, 'She's evil, Drew, and you have to be purged of her.' See what I mean about the way she talked? Except that she was really convinced that I wouldn't be okay until I could hate Rachel or act like I hated Rachel. Until I could act out killing her and killing my dad, too. Symbolically, of course.

"For one thing, she made me call them by their

names, not my mom and my dad but Rachel and Rob, because she said that would be easier. I don't know, I couldn't really get into it, and partly, I know, it was to give this psychodrama teacher a hard time.

"Then she tipped me over to her side. She got Rachel on one of her visits to flip out so that I could remember what she, Rachel, was really like. I was in my psychodrama teacher's car with this girl from the class? I remember that the place was practically deserted because there was some kind of trip that was scheduled, only a bunch of us didn't go on it. Anyway, I had my teacher's car and she set the whole thing up and I was driving. As far as I was concerned the wreck was something I just never wanted to remember again, but anyway, she, my teacher, said it was important, the key to breaking me out of this goody-goody bullshit I was feeding myself about my mom. You remember? It was exactly, *exactly*, what you were doing about your folks. It's normal, probably. Except it isn't if you want to face reality. Break free.

"So I'm there, on the ground, and I'm driving like my teacher told me to, going up on curves and shit and carrying on. No big deal, but the kind of thing that would freak my mother out. Rachel came around the corner and she saw this, and what do you know? It's just like my psychodrama teacher says.

"Rachel yanks open the car door and she doesn't pay any fucking attention to the girl who's sitting there at all. And she yells something like 'You've killed one girl. Isn't that enough?'

"And there it was, out in the open, what Rachel thought of me. And I remember thinking, *Fuck you, bitch*, and how my psychodrama teacher had been right about her all along, and I yelled at her, "Fuck you, Rachel!" using her name that way. And then I got out of the car and started pushing her around until she got back into her own car and drove off. I said, like, if she thought I was a killer, fine, fine, I'd be one, I'd kill her.

"She used to visit me every single Sunday, but after that she didn't come anymore. Then my teacher showed me that form that she'd gouged out, 'no,' like I was never going to set foot inside her fucking house again, as if I'd ever want to."

The girl rested a hand on Drew's thigh.

"This," he said, "it's the first time I've seen her since that day."

The girl squeezed. Drew picked up her hand and rubbed her fingers over his lips. "So," he said, "do you begin to get the picture?"

FROM THE OUTSIDE, BENEDICT HOUSE HAD looked like a mansion, two stories, pink stucco, with a tile roof, a view of the bay, a long paved drive lined with tall, swaying palm trees. Inside it was a wreck. There were holes in the plaster, broken banisters on the railing of the stairs. The air, too, seemed musty and foul, as if no one had opened a window in years.

Still, Drew, after an initial bout of hostility, seemed to like it there. Drew's room, in fact, seemed cheerful when compared to the rest of the place.

He'd collected several cactus plants from who knew where. And various bones, including the skull of a cow. He'd made one of those cactus-and-bone gardens so common in Texas, but with a special twist. Because it was indoors, he'd used various plumbing pieces—the cracked basin of a sink, a commode—to contain the plants. Rachel had been truly impressed.

"You could be a landscape artist," she'd told him.

This was her third visit, the first time she'd been allowed to venture from the first floor to the third, where he'd been given a room.

"Good behavior," he'd explained.

After that the conversation got risky. He asked about the girl's parents: Were they trying to get a manslaughter charge pinned on him?

No, she told him. The fact that the wheel had come off had made that charge untenable.

What about the fact that he'd been drinking?

She didn't know, but she'd been told that no charges would be brought. He didn't ask about a civil suit, although Rachel feared for a while that one would be lodged. She expected the girl's parents to file it against her, since Drew was a minor. She was so naive about the law and so afraid to find out anything for sure that for months she went on imagining that somehow, because of the wreck, all of her earnings and everything she owned would be taken away from her.

I did feel that way, Rachel realized now. *As if I would have to pay.*

It riled her that Drew felt nothing, paid nothing, cared about nothing, or so it seemed, except whether his own neck was safe. He never mentioned the dead girl. It was as though she had never existed.

Still, she could have lived with that, could have gone on making weekly visits and noting Drew's progress, had he not begun to change from polite and guarded to more on the order of the way he had been before—argumentative, defensive, occasionally just plain nasty. What Rachel thought was, *So it wasn't just the drugs, it was us, him and me.* The thought saddened her.

Then she'd driven there to find him careening around

in a car with yet another girl, and she'd lost all control. The minute the words were out of her mouth she regretted them. She let him push her around and then she drove away and then she got the letter from the school about the way he felt about her. And she'd gone there and filled out that form, and her rage had weighted the pen and she'd torn the word "no" into the page where they'd asked if it seemed likely that Drew would return to his home. Except that they'd called it "the" home, and that was it for Rachel.

This isn't "his" home and it isn't "my" home, she'd told herself, walking from room to room in the Kingsville house and hating it, hating everything about it. *This is "the" home, and I can leave it, I can run, I don't need to stay here and I don't need to drive up there to Corpus to see a son who not only doesn't want to see me, but wants to see me dead, wants to kill me*. Then the blood.

And so she'd left, never looked back. It had been so incredibly easy she wondered why she hadn't done it years before, done it before Rob had.

Having come to the end of the train of memory that had pursued her, Rachel felt as if something inside had collapsed, given way. So deep into her thoughts had she been that the water—the fact that she was still in Peyton's swimming pool immersed in water—surprised her, lightened her, made her smile as she reached up over her head and drew her legs up in an elementary form of backstroke that she'd practiced as a child. She glided beetlelike through the water noting that now several stars had appeared. They stood out in relief against the darkness of the sky, the water, the house.

"I'm free," she said out loud, and at that precise moment, as if to belie her statement, the underwater lights came on, outlining her there in the pool as if she were quarry.

Rachel boosted herself over the lip of the deep end, but too late, she knew. Whoever was there—and she heard rustling, footsteps, someone coming near—had seen her, marked the spot where she'd emerged and stood dripping.

She felt a hand on her wet, naked arm, and heard, "Rachel!"

It was Zachary, only Zachary, and Rachel collapsed against him. He stepped back and held her at arm's length, laughing softly. "You're all wet, my dear." Then he guided her to one of the chairs that stood poolside. "I hoped you'd change your mind and be back by now," he said. "I was worried."

Rachel rubbed her arms. "I'm freezing," she said, standing up. "I've got to get a towel." She stepped past him, padded along the concrete, slipped inside the house, and walked toward the closet where she knew the towels were kept. Again, she felt Zachary beside her, and again she jumped.

"Rachel, we've got to talk. . . ."

My God, she realized, *I'm afraid of him, too, afraid of Zachary, and why?* There was no reason, none that she could fathom or find. Still, she told him, "No. I've got to be alone. I've got to sort this out for myself before I can talk to you about it." Especially since his first response had been so cold, so unlike any that she would have imagined that it stunned her. "I don't know anything about you," she said now, her voice accusatory. "I don't. Not really."

It seemed a stupid thing to say, especially since it was she who, acknowledgedly, had lied to him.

Then all of a sudden she remembered him telling her about his name and how it was so very Texan. How Zachary Taylor, the general and maybe even the President, had had something to do with Texas, as had Zachary Scott, the movie star. "Oh, Zachary, Zachary, I'm sorry," and, wet or not, she threw herself toward him. "Really, I am."

He took the towel away from her and began to knead her hair and then her shoulders. And then, he began talking about her own name, about how, in the Bible, Rachel had wept for her children and would not be comforted.

THE GIRL TRIED TO LIGHTEN THINGS UP, teasing him. "Weird girls, huh? You're gonna blame everything on us women."

But Drew didn't tease back. "There was only one weird guy. A fag."

"Really?" she asked. "Did you sleep with him?"

"Be serious."

"Then how did you know he was a fag? For sure, I mean."

Drew laughed at what he remembered. "It wasn't anything about the way he acted. It was . . . well, we used to do a lot of hugging at Benedict House, you know? A lot of body contact. They even showed movies about it, about how important it was."

"Movies?" Her eyes grew wide.

"Yeah, movies. Like this one they had about people who were screaming crazy and then they'd calm down whenever someone came and put their arms around them. Kind of like a human straitjacket, except that it worked. You saw it up there on the screen."

"Well, fine," she said, eager to get to the part that had interested her, the part about the homosexual, "but what about the guy?"

"You know the way when you hug somebody you're not interested in sexually you kind of dip your backside out away from the person?"

"No."

"Sure you do. Hell, I used to do it with my mom all the time. And she'd do it with me, too. I remember one Christmas when she hugged me just before I went to bed and I could see her in the mirror, her rear end poking out so she wouldn't be touching her groin up against mine. I even pointed it out to her, because she wanted to know what I was laughing about. I just kind of turned us sideways and then showed her in the mirror."

"And?"

"And then she laughed too."

"But the guy," the girl insisted.

"Yeah, well, he was crazy, He would always have us hug and then he'd tell us how important it was to give a whole hug, none of this mooching back that people do, and then he'd do it, tuck his rear end up, and everyone would see him and laugh because we all would recognize ourselves, recognize that we did that. And then we'd walk around the room and he'd reach for me and he'd say, 'Here. I'll show you how I want you kids to hug,' and then, right in front of everybody, he'd grind himself right into me, as if by doing it there in front of the whole room, it was okay. Or, I don't know, maybe I was supposed to like it and show up later on at his room. But anyway, that's the one weird guy I've come up against, I mean, weird enough to match the girls I've known."

The girl was coiling her long, long tail of hair around and around on top of her head. It was fine hair, and it made a mound much smaller than he would have thought. "What happened to him?" the girl asked.

"He got fired. A couple of teachers got fired. Him, the teacher from psychodrama . . ." His face tightened and he changed the subject without explanation or apology of any sort. As though whatever mental process he had gone through had been visible to the girl. "You almost ready?" he asked her, leaning across to tap the ignition keys. He thought about suggesting that maybe they ought to coast to the bottom of the hill, but then he figured that steep as it was, she might not be able to control the car. It would be like her cruise-control game, she would take her foot off the brake and they'd roll to their deaths without gears to hold them back.

Better take a chance on being heard.

The girl placed a hairpin with her fingers, holding yet another in her mouth. When she'd removed it and added it alongside the first, she said, "Mmmmhmm." But she didn't sound ready, she sounded sleepy, like she'd like to curl back up against his shoulder, in his arms, and just forget about everything but herself and him.

But she started the car and managed to turn it around, though it took several swings back and forth to do so. When they passed the gate to Peyton's, she slowed and looked over at him with her eyebrows up to ask if he wanted to stop.

"Wait here," he told her. "Don't shut the engine off, okay?" When was the last time they'd bought gas? Wouldn't that be a crock, to be stuck there, tank empty? Wouldn't that be something?

He got out of the car, and he left his door wide open. It was then that he saw the glint of another car farther on down the road and off to the side.

He hesitated, and the girl leaned out the window and urged him to go on. So this was it. This was it, the payoff, the thing he'd come all this way to do.

He cracked the gate and slipped inside. He couldn't hear a thing, not the T-bird's idling engine, nor his heart, nor his footfalls. It was like being in a soundproof room, a studio, maybe, or a coffin or a womb.

THE LIGHT IN THE POOL CAST TERRIBLY DEFI-nite shadows into the darkened room where she and Zachary stood. It frightened Rachel. Never mind that she told herself it shouldn't, it just did.

"That's absurd," Zachary told her when she shared that thought, and he tugged at the strap of her leotard as if to help her remove it.

"No," Rachel said, pulling the strap back into place. She felt affronted and said so, that he'd even hint at sex, at *sex*, not comfort, at a time when she needed comfort most. She was right to be afraid, to be more than afraid, to be angry.

But sex, Zachary said, could be comfort, too. "Ra-chel," he continued, his voice taking on what she thought was a measure of threat, "you're acting very silly, very silly indeed," pulling at the strap again, as if she were a little girl.

That cloying green vestibule smell rose up again, rose up around her, and she shivered. Did memories ever die? Still, her nipple hardened just before his fingers moved over it and then his mouth. "Rachel." He kept saying her name, and she let him slide the leotard wet and cold down the length of her body, though she stood there without stepping out of it lest she assist.

"Rachel." He made her spread er legs with his hand

and then he kept his fingers there and he plied her with them.

But the panic that she felt was growing, and it kept her from the response he sought, the response he must have thought was usual for her, since she'd had it every time until this time: that soft sticky yearning flow.

Now she was tight, dry, and her skin felt gummy and the wet leotard felt heavy on her feet. Why, she wondered, couldn't he tell? Why wouldn't he stop? What did it mean? That he, like Rob, like that janitor at school, he was brutish too? She'd been right to be afraid, she would have been right to actually go into a convent, lock herself away from men and peril.

Rachel jerked away from him and bent down and picked up her soggy suit. She was going to try to put it on again, but she didn't trust him to let her. She raised her hand, begging him to stop.

He took a step toward her, and she let that hand fly, let the flatness of her palm catch him full in the face, not even his cheek but hard against his nose and his chin, and she even thought she'd felt the edge of his teeth.

He reeled back, and she, clutching the suit in one hand and wondering about the dim resounding pain in the other, ran back out toward the pool. She pushed through the bougainvillea and tried to get into the leotard, but she couldn't keep her balance, couldn't keep the dampness of the fabric from resisting her pulling it on, either. So she crouched there in the rustling leaves and blossoms, enormously aware of her bare back and the night air immediately behind her, where the hillside began. It sloped swiftly, was far, far too steep for her to gain a foothold there.

"Rachel?"

She could see him walking now around the pool. He seemed to think she'd come out if she heard him, and she could not help but wonder why he would think of her as that stupid.

"Rachel, come out. Rachel, I know a lot has happened today and I know you have a lot to tell me, too. Come out, Rachel, let me see you. Let me talk to you."

He sounded as if he'd rehearsed. Or—what was it the doctor had said about Drew, about the vague way Drew had behaved right after the accident? That he was in a fugue state. That was how Zachary sounded: like someone in a fugue state. A disturbed and yet detached state of mind.

"Rachel? Rachel?"

The more he called the more she determined never to come out. The more she was sure that somehow none of this had been Drew at all but that all of it, all of it had been Zachary. *Oh, I am going crazy,* Rachel thought, *I am going crazy after all.*

Drew had accused her of it often enough. He had. And maybe he was right, maybe he was the sane one and she was the one who . . .

"Rachel, if I leave, I won't come back. Do you understand that, Rachel? If I walk away from you now, I'm going to go on home, gather up my things, and never see you again, Rachel. Do you hear me? This is your last chance."

He waited and she waited and she wondered if maybe she wasn't throwing away her only chance for happiness and sanity. Despite the way she felt right now, the way things seemed, maybe she was wrong. Maybe it was something she'd made up or even dreamed. Maybe the business with the janitor at school had never happened, and maybe there had been no blood in the sink. Maybe she *had* been in a convent all those years.

"All right, Rachel."

She heard him walk away, heard him go into the back of the house and then out through the front. She thought she heard the gate as it opened and then waited to hear, but didn't, the door and then the engine of his car.

Not gone, he was *not gone*. She forced herself into the leotard, snapping the fabric against her skin and yanking at it. The straps remained twisted and she couldn't get the crotch exactly right, but she didn't care, she didn't care about anything except being ready to run.

Her fear with Zachary out of sight was really rampant now, as if he could appear out of nowhere beside her, behind her, his breath on her shoulders and then on her breast and his fingers probing.

Not gone, but out there, waiting, deciding. He had to be. She knew he hadn't driven away, because he couldn't have done so without her having heard him. Any moment now, any moment . . .

HE'D MOVED QUICKLY THE HELL OUT OF there once he'd seen what was going on, his mother and that Zachary guy, all set to get it on. The guy was rubbing his mother's shoulders with a towel and his mom was wearing a bathing suit and pretty soon the guy had put the towel away and was yanking at the strap.

It just wasn't anything he wanted to see, his mother getting it on.

He remembered that that was what had tipped the moonfaced girl when she'd gone off driving like some crazy, her mother and some guy. He'd sort of made fun of the girl, in his head at any rate, for getting so bent out of shape over something so basically dumb as her mother sitting up close to someone, but now he understood it, the intent was there, right there in the air.

He didn't want to tell the girl about it and didn't, but got back into the car saying only that someone, not even who, had been there.

The girl didn't hassle him about it, just drove on down the road. When they got to the main road she turned off to the right and then right again on the first side road she had come to.

It turned out to be houses under construction, four or five of them as far as he could see. It wasn't a development the way you usually think of suburbs, but five really ritzy each-distinctly-different kinds of things. The girl pulled up in front of one of them, a domelike cedar house that he wouldn't have wanted to live in if you paid him.

The girl said, "You have to get some sleep before you go back there and finish this."

And he said, "Hey look. I have to do something, I know." And they got out of the T-bird and walked inside the partially finished house. Like it had been waiting there for them, Drew thought.

SHE CROUCHED IN THE SHRUBBERY THAT edged the pool, growing more aware of the physical pain she was feeling. Her lower back ached from being bent so long, and the soles of her feet felt as if they'd been raked. She began to consider coming forward, out to the edge of the pool at least. She would have earlier but for the underwater light that would give away, at once, her position. Nevertheless, an age had elapsed, or what felt like an age, and she hadn't heard a single sound.

Then, from within the house, "Yoo-hoo, anybody home? Rachel? You here?"

It was Peyton. Not Zachary, not Drew, but Peyton, Peyton. Peyton, her friend. Rachel half crawled, half leaped out of the bougainvillea, her back revolting at the sudden movement so that she found herself moving awkwardly, like a woman who'd been aged in a flash, as in time-lapse photography. "Peyton! Peyton!" She shouted the name with each breath she took.

Peyton pushed through the doorway with her arms wide. One look at Rachel made her face gather into a look of fierce concern. "Rachel, honey, what is it?"

Rachel rushed to her friend and wept uncontrollably, her shoulders heaving. Peyton steered her as gently as she could into one of the lawn chairs and then squatted down beside the chair, patting Rachel occasionally, clucking now and again—soothing Rachel from the depths into a more shallow, manageable form of sorrow.

"Feel a little better?" she asked. When Rachel nodded, she stood, dusting off the gauzy flowing gown she wore. "Good," she said. "That means I can go inside and get us something to drink." She kicked her sandals off and headed back toward the house, taking one last glance at Rachel to reassure herself that her friend was indeed all right. "Be right back," she shouted, perhaps a bit too cheerily.

Rachel slumped in the chair, feeling that she'd spent her lifetime allotment of tears. She rubbed at her eyes, sniffled, and, in general, assumed a pose of utter misery.

That was what she felt, too. Misery. And disgust at herself. At her own behavior.

Not the show of tears. That she didn't mind very much, but at her fears. Her unwarranted fears.

First Drew, Drew, her own son. She'd run around Austin all day long in mortal fear of losing her own life at his hands. She'd been convinced that, having murdered Rob the night before, his mission now was to also murder her.

Then, without any evidence, without any warning, she'd shifted her terror and affixed it to Zachary. *Poor Zachary!* Not only had he known nothing about Drew, nothing about Rachel's former husband, Rob, but now, without any reason whatsoever, he was being treated as if he were a threat, as if he, in fact, were out to kill Rachel, too.

Maybe no one's out to kill me, Rachel thought. *Maybe it's all in my head. Something I imagined, something that isn't any different from the back-and-forth, back-and-forth that I've been going through all along, for years now, about this, about everything.* About Drew, about whether he'd hurt the dog or not, about the sink, about the blood in the basin of the sink, even that if she were totally totally honest.

And immediately, all of the insults Drew had shouted at her seemed not insults at all but revelations: "You're psychotic. You're crazy. You're nuts. Why don't you see a shrink?" Maybe Drew had been right all along. Maybe she was the one.

Wait. Rob had been murdered, she had heard it on the radio, it was not made-up, it was real. And his body had been wrapped in a patchwork quilt, a quilt that she, Rachel, had likely made. A random killer would not have done that. Drew would have done that.

Or Zachary.

No, *not* Zachary. Zachary knew about her patchwork, knew about that, yes, but hadn't known about Rob. *Drew,* not Zachary. But Zachary hadn't driven off, she had listened for his car and and she hadn't heard it. Zachary was still out there, he was still—

"Here you go." Peyton attempted to press a frosty glass into Rachel's hand, and Rachel started so that the glass shattered at Rachel's feet and the contents, so cold that they burned, splashed up to her knees.

"Don't move, honey, you'll cut yourself," Peyton said, and Rachel stared down and realized that Peyton was barefoot too. Rachel opened her mouth to apologize, but trying to talk only made her start to cry again.

"Be right back," Peyton said, evidently unconcerned about walking where the glass was or that she might step on some of it. "The broom is on the way."

I hope she bears with me, Rachel thought. *Here I am, hysterical, making a mess and breaking things.* She already despaired of ever seeing Zachary again, considering not only what her behavior had been but the very final way he had responded to it. *If I leave, Rachel . . .* It was almost as if the echo of his voice hung in the air around the pool.

Rachel stood up and immediately heard the glass shards shifting. She remembered her promise and sat anew. Then an enormous spotlight went on and Peyton came out again. She was wearing shoes of some kind and she had a broom in one hand, a drink in the other. She handed the drink to Rachel and began sweeping the chunks of heavy glass back into the bougainvillea.

"I should get a dustpan," Rachel said.

"No, it's fine this way. If I push hard enough, the glass'll roll back off the edge behind. Shhh. Listen and you'll hear what I mean." She swept, and Rachel thought she heard the chunks of glass slipping down the slope into some brush below.

"I didn't hear you drive up," Rachel said.

"These hills are funny," Peyton explained. "Some things, like the glass, you can hear real well. Other things, like a car in the driveway, you can't hear at all. One time a service man claimed he sat out there blowing his horn and I swear I didn't hear him. On the other hand, he may have gone to the wrong house. I can't imagine not hearing a horn." She finished sweeping and stood, leaning on the broom and looking at Rachel, who was still processing the information about what the hills did to the sound. Zachary *was* gone after all. Not out there waiting, but gone.

"You look better, hon," Peyton said, "you really do. Well." She straightened. "Guess I'll fix myself a something too."

"What is this?" Rachel asked. She was glad she hadn't ranted on about Zachary still being there.

"A little herbal concoction. Don't worry. It isn't alcoholic."

"It feels alcoholic." Rachel laughed. "I swear, I'm dizzy."

"Good." Peyton reached for her glass. "Then I'll get you another."

"Wait," Rachel said, and Peyton, on her way back toward the house, turned to see what Rachel wanted. "I don't want another one, really." Peyton shrugged and once again headed away. "Peyton, I mean it," Rachel shouted after her. "I don't want . . ." And then, realizing how upset she was becoming, she let the words die.

But not the thought that she was becoming intoxicated. That she couldn't shake. For her own survival, she couldn't let that happen. She couldn't risk another drink of whatever it was that Peyton had given her, whatever strange herbal drink.

Some eerie music lifted from somewhere within the house. A single bagpipe? No, a sitar. She could remember that much from her younger days, from the Beatles and their flirtation with Indian music. Hadn't Peyton been a child then, back when the Beatles were popular? Rachel always meant to ask Peyton about her

fascination with East Indian music and food and artifacts, but somehow or other, always forgot.

When Peyton came outside again, Rachel saw that
she had ignored Rachel's refusal of another drink. She
bore the same glass, and held it out, though Rachel held
up a hand to fend the drink away, shaking her head no.

"It's water, silly," Peyton said. "But there's this to go
with it." She held up a capsule, and Rachel squinted to
see what it was. Peyton anticipated her question. "It's a
tranquilizer. And don't tell me that you don't need one.
You do. Just the way you're carrying on right now while
I'm offering it to you is enough to convince me of that."

"No!" Rachel said, with force.

"Rachel. I hate acting this way, but believe me, you
have got to take this. It's for your own good." She held
out the water glass, and Rachel closed both of her hands
around it. "Good." She watched as Rachel sniffed, then
tentatively sipped the water. "What is it? Do you think
I'm trying to poison you?"

How had Rob been killed? Rachel wondered suddenly. Did she know that? How? She stood up and
looked about herself, as if to find a route of escape.

"No." Peyton laid a firm hand on her shoulder. "You
just sit right down. We've got a lot of talking to do, but
before we can even begin, *you,* Rachel, are going to
take this pill." She said the last five words with heavy
emphasis, and Rachel yielded to it, held her hand out for
the proffered tranquilizer. Peyton watched her swallow
it, then pulled a chair of her own near the one that Rachel occupied. "Now," she said, "maybe you can tell me
what this hysteria is all about."

The pill itself hadn't taken effect, but the idea of the
pill had. Rachel felt a wave of calm sweep over her.
Indeed, there was a soft night breeze just then to suggest
that. "I don't know where to start," she said truthfully.
She looked at her friend but found that the harsh light

behind her had blackened her face, illumined only her silhouette. "That light," she said.

"I'll get it." Peyton rose, went toward the light.

Rachel realized, then and there, that she couldn't possibly begin to tell about Rob or about Drew or about anything so long ago, so complex. She would talk, she decided, about Zachary. Peyton knew Zachary, or at least they had been together on several occasions, though neither had seemed anything but minimally friendly toward the other. Zachary, yes. If she told Peyton that they'd had a fight, that would explain it all—the tears, the irrational behavior.

The light beneath the water went out, and then the spot. It was dark again, the way it had been before Zachary had arrived. Before Zachary . . .

And there were the tears again, only this time for the fact that she and Zachary wouldn't marry, wouldn't even see each other anymore. She sobbed bits of the confrontation out to Peyton—her irrational fear, and Zachary's reaction.

"I don't get it," Peyton said. "You were hiding from him?"

It did sound stupid, but what could Rachel do, short of spilling everything—Rob, Drew? "Yes," she said. "I was hiding. I can't explain it. My mother used to take me to school very early, long before it really opened, and I used to hide there too." She'd thought it an explanation, but she had to admit that it made her sound crazier than she had before. She laughed softly, hoping that Peyton would as well.

Instead Peyton sighed. "Okay, so you were hiding. What then?"

"Zachary kept calling me, asking me to come on out. And he said that if I didn't, he would leave for good." The tears again, the tears.

"And?"

"And I didn't come out, and he left. For good." She bent forward as far as she could. She buried her face in her hands. She waited, wondering what Peyton would say.

"You're better off without him." It was a flat statement, and, Rachel thought, a cruel one. But Peyton continued, "I know it doesn't seem that way right now, but believe me, hon, you are. You don't know what you've been like since you met him. You've changed, believe me." She raised her voice in mimicry. "'No, I can't go to the movies, Zachary's waiting.' 'No, I have to get home and make dinner.' Really, it's been Zachary this and Zachary that. I say you're well rid of him. No kidding, sweetie, you are."

"I know you don't much like him, Peyton, but . . ."

"I like him fine. I just happen to like you much better. He's wooden, a stick. I don't know what you ever saw in him."

Peyton had never spoken of Zachary this way, and Rachel realized that had it not been for the pill, she, Rachel, would be very very angry. What business did Peyton have talking that way? And why would she? Zachary was a wonderful man, not a stick at all, but warm and . . . Her fear of him seemed so absurd now, so long ago, so far away.

"Look," Peyton went on, "you just said it yourself. He came here and you were as upset as can be and what did he do? He walked out on you. He up and *walked out on you.*"

It was true, but Peyton didn't know all of the circumstances; didn't know that Zachary had only just found out about Drew. Oh, she wished now that she'd never started talking to Peyton, wished she'd gone through with her original plan to just disappear again, go to Mexico or somewhere. "Peyton," she said, hoping to halt all further conversation. Before she could get another word out, Peyton stood up.

"I think we ought to hit the sack," Peyton said. "I've said too much and I'm sorry. No kidding. I am."

"It's okay," Rachel answered.

"The guest room is made up. Grab yourself some towels. You know where they are."

Rachel smiled gratefully, and the women parted for the night, Peyton to her bedroom upstairs, her aerie, as she called it, and Rachel to the lovely glass-walled guest room.

Rachel looked out at the darkness and was glad for the tranquilizer now. An hour earlier and she'd surely have imagined eyes, Drew's eyes, looking in at her. She lay back on the futon bed and tried deep, deep breaths, the very sort that Peyton herself would have advised.

And they must have worked, because Rachel soon was asleep. It was a shallow sleep, however, a troubled sleep with much restless movement.

She woke up because she had to go to the bathroom, woke up with a start because she had to adjust to unfamiliar surroundings, had to realize that she'd awakened not in her own bed, not with Zachary, but somewhere else, in someone else's house, yes, Peyton's, yes, yes.

In this state of growing recognition, Rachel padded toward the powder room. Voices sounded somewhere on the edge of her hearing, voices she knew. Peyton's voice, yes, but . . .

Then Rachel suddenly was wide awake, awake and ready once again to flee. Could she be wrong? She listened intently, even went closer to the staircase than she should have, and she hadn't been wrong, it was Drew she heard, it was Drew. Drew had taken Rob and he had, for all practical purposes, taken Zachary, and now he was talking to Peyton; now Peyton, too, would cease to be her friend.

She was angry, angry at Drew for getting away with this, angry at him for disrupting her life earlier, certainly, but again, now, even now. She started up the staircase, wanting nothing so much as to tell Drew off, tell him to go away, tell him . . .

But she was near enough now to make out the words, make out what it was Drew was saying, and what Drew was saying, over and over again, was: "I want to kill my mother I want to kill my mother. I want . . ."

Rachel turned, but slowly, and headed back to the bedroom. She dressed hurriedly, and slipped outside. Which way? Not the gate, which would mean she would have to pass alongside the full length of the house, but where then? It would have to be the slope.

Meanwhile, the pressure of her bladder was immense. She would have to relieve herself, especially before climbing, or maybe even sliding, down the hillside over which the house was cantilevered.

She took her jeans down and crouched, aware of something prickly against her buttocks. Then she couldn't start. Finally, but all too loudly, her urine began to flow.

She was sure she was peeing on her shoe. She grabbed at some leaves and wiped herself and started to stand to raise her jeans when the huge glass windows on the highest level were swooped open.

Rachel looked up, but couldn't see. And she couldn't move for fear that Peyton and Drew would hear her. *God, I'm like an animal now*, she thought. *Always crouching, hiding, like prey*.

She felt a sharp bite on her buttocks, and she stood up without thinking.

No sound from above, no sign that they'd heard her.

Encouraged by that, she pulled her jeans up, fastened them, but didn't dare yet move on.

I want to kill my mother . . . her mind replayed his words. There was no comfort in knowing she'd been right about Drew all along. The knowledge, or maybe the residual effect of what Peyton had given her, made her suddenly weary.

She tried to sharpen her senses again, but she'd been kept alert by the fact that she had to go to the bathroom and then the sound of Drew's voice in the other room. The alertness had come like a bolt and now it was gone and the fact that it was the middle of the night and she'd been given some sort of sedative came to the fore. She was almost sleepy and she knew that if she didn't get up and move she just might fall asleep, the way those who are freezing to death are said to, sleep and then die.

But the window was still open wide above her, and there was still the threat that Peyton and Drew might hear.

Think of something, she told herself. *Keep your mind occupied.* She forced the names of quilt patterns, but could only think of those that sounded terrible or terrifying: Fly Foot, Devil's Puzzle, World Without End. Even the quilt called Hand of Friendship, which sounded so lovely, had alternative names like Crow's Foot, and Bear's Paw.

Just then, from above, she heard Peyton cough softly and then, with the same swooping sound, pull the windows closed.

Rachel was ready, on her feet and alert again, as if her body had been saving itself and its awareness for now.

She tried moving sideways down the slope, but it proved too steep for that. She began to tumble, and reached to balance herself, feeling, as she did so, the sharp spines of a prickly pear cactus on her palm and in her fingers. She almost shouted at the sudden pain, but realized, for her safety, that she couldn't. In fact, she slowed her progress, scuffing with her feet until she could wait and listen.

The hills were eerie, dark and quiet, with occasional

rattles and chirps and coyote calls. It was hard to believe that this section was just minutes from downtown Austin, yet that was the case. The much-touted, much-sought seclusion of the area now seemed to Rachel an enormous obstacle, a threat.

If she were to scream, who would hear? Drew. Not a rescuer, but Drew. She had to keep going then, had to keep sliding down, down, until she came to civilization—another house, a phone, a lifeline.

She began edging down the slope once more, feeling the soft shale fall before her, hoping not to hit another cactus or some equally spiny mesquite. There were other forms of plant life to be avoided: thistle, briars, and so on. Zachary had told her once that Texas offered a veritable minefield of vegetation.

She stopped herself again, this time by letting her knees drag after she'd managed to grab hold of some strong sort of vine. She clung there and listened, thinking for a moment that she'd heard some movement on the hillside above. Yes, a soft fall of earth came after, proving that was so.

Would it be Drew? Would Peyton have come with him? Would she be captured like some hunter's prey, maybe frozen there in the beam of a searchlight and then—what?—shot?

The movement stopped, but Rachel, meanwhile, was able to determine that it had been far too slight to be the movement of another person. It was an animal, perhaps, or maybe even a lizard or a snake settling in for the night. The latter thought—which earlier might have terrified poor Rachel—now provided succor.

Rachel continued the long way down, realizing that the slope was easing somewhat and that the vegetation felt bushier, more tame.

Indeed, she found herself in a bed of thick, leafy

growth—ground cover of some sort. She was in someone's garden! She'd find help here, she was sure.

There was a low stone wall where the vegetation ended, and Rachel stepped over it onto what seemed a flagstone walk. Straight ahead, she saw a little light. There seemed nothing more. It was a reflection, in either a large glass window or a pool. She made her way toward it.

It was a house, one of those magnificent glass-walled houses that magazines often feature, tucked there in a notch in the hills. Rachel concentrated on waking the inhabitants by tapping on the glass, first at one pane, then at the next, and the next, and so on. Finally she strained to look within and saw that what little furniture there was had been shrouded as though the inhabitants had gone on a long journey. She stopped tapping and instead began trying to find her way inside.

But everything was locked, of course. Then she had a brainstorm. What if she attempted to break in? Wouldn't a house like this one have an alarm hooked up to it? Wouldn't it ring at the police station and wouldn't they then send police officers here?

With that in mind she grabbed an enormous brass doorhandle and began shaking on it with all her might. It barely budged. Next she searched for a rock or something with which she might shatter one of the panes of glass. In the darkness, she found none. Finally, she searched out the driveway leading to the house and began to pad along it, hoping that would lead the way to safety.

But she was tired. She wondered if she dared to stop and in the same moment knew that she had to. She stayed on the narrow paved drive that she had found, however.

When she listened now, she heard the familiar night sounds muted by the thickness of her own exhausted breath. It seemed she'd stopped just in time. Another moment and she might have fallen, might have lost consciousness, might not have been able to catch her breath. She tried to concentrate on calmness. On stealth. She tried to banish the fear that fueled her.

Off in the distance, a car's headlights cut through the darkness. Too far, much too far. She couldn't even imagine what roadway that might be. Route 360? Wouldn't there be more traffic if that was the case? On the other hand, it had to be four, five, in the morning. If that was so, even Route 360 would be almost deserted.

That made her wonder if she'd ever find help.

She started moving again, walking now, though at a good pace. She felt sure that the driveway would lead to the same road that she'd taken to get to Peyton's. That meant if she turned to the left when she reached it, she'd soon be on Bee Caves Road and able to get to an all-night store or at least a telephone.

Then she froze, aware of a presence just ahead of her. She wasn't even certain how she knew, but she did, and she yielded to what must have been pure instinct. "I need help," she said, in a voice that would have persuaded even a stone-hearted soul. "Please . . . ?"

A slight stirring in response.

Rachel stared hard, trying to see who it might be. It wasn't Drew, she was sure of it, she'd have known had it been Drew. But it wasn't a presence that inspired her to feel she was safe, out of harm's way, either.

Movement again, and then Rachel knew. It was an animal, a large one.

Then she did, very definitely, hear a car, and did, therefore, know that the road she sought was just scant feet away. Around a bend, perhaps, but there, within a minute's reach.

If whatever it was didn't tear her to pieces.

Very slowly, she took a half-step forward. There was a low, unsettling growl in response. A dog!

She was so taut, so reliant on her senses, that she would have sworn she could discern the pads on the dog's feet plop-plop-plopping softly toward her.

No growl now, but a definite odor, foul, like the smell of a dog who's been rained on, but ten times heightened, a dog that's rolled in dead things, in garbage.

The dog stopped. She hadn't then really seen it, only the suggestion of its form in the night. The smell was more real than the sight.

Rachel tried to breathe through her mouth. Was it a watchdog from the glass-walled house? But no, who would have left it behind? It had to be a wild dog, a dog that spent the night marauding and the daylight hours recovering from the effort that it took. "Poor dog," she called. "Poor dog."

The depth and threat of the animal's growl only increased.

She saw it then, as if it had only now materialized, a spirit dog until now. It stood about five feet away, regarding her, deciding. She thought to drop to the ground, to cover her head with her hands, or roll herself into a ball, but which? And so she just stood there wondering if she smelled as bad as the dog did from her fear. Her arms hung down at her sides and she wondered if moving them into some more defensive pose would be a mistake, as bad as running would be.

But wasn't running better than this?

The dog came closer, and Rachel could see now that it was bearlike, huge and round and black. The sort of dog that ought, she thought, to be rhythmically flapping its tail. The sort of dog that ought to be friendly, tongue lolling, paw extended, a dog that should be good with children, know tricks.

Hand of Friendship, Bear's Paw.

Right up next to her now. She could feel its hot breath on the back of her hand. It sniffed her hand, sniffed it audibly, then the right leg of her jeans and her shoe.

Odd that the smell of it had gone away. Either she'd gotten used to it or it was far less noticeable up close.

She remembered hearing that if you turned your palm to a dog, it would know your intentions were friendly. Was that true? The dog had walked behind her now, was sniffing the backs of her legs. She had a sense of bulk, not the wiry thinness of a wild dog, but the thickness of an animal that was well and regularly fed.

When it came around in front of her again, Rachel leaned forward, turning both palms out. The dog jumped backward, raised its hackles, dropped its shoulders as if to leap. Rachel had moved when the dog did, she had wrapped her arms around herself as if something so stupidly simple could help.

Perhaps it was a submissive gesture, a flag of surrender, she didn't know. The dog began to whine and rock from side to side as if to play.

Rachel took a step away, and the dog came forward too, though not aggressively at all, its body loose, almost flopping, without the warning stiffness it had shown minutes before.

Rachel felt she'd broken some mysterious animal code. She didn't know what she'd done, but only knew she had done it, had exercised her will to survive and won yet again.

She wanted, smell or no, to run her hands deep into the animal's fur, chanting, "Poor dog, poor dog," with great gratitude, but she didn't dare. The dog accompanied her on the last part of the drive, padding along a few strides to Rachel's right. It went its way as Rachel started down what had to be the same road she'd used to get to Peyton's. It just disappeared.

Maybe she was wrong to ever be afraid, ever be afraid at all. Wouldn't it be wonderful, never to be afraid?

HE COULD TELL THE GIRL WAS VERY AGI-tated, because she was pacing, the heels of her boots sounding hollow knocks on the hardwood floor.

Amplifying the sound was the emptiness of the house, no furniture, no nothing, not even glass in all the windows. They'd gone around lighting a book of matches and used them all, checking the whole place out.

He pretended to be asleep, and maybe he did sleep at that, because when he opened his eyes, the sound of her heels had stopped and he couldn't see her moving from one room to the next.

Just before he decided to curl up there on the floor they'd had an enormous argument, and he'd ended up telling her that she was the one who had fucked up everything, that if she hadn't been there, everything would have turned out right.

Now the sound of her T-bird warming up came through. Damn! But he couldn't blame her, really. Still . . .

He was up and outside just like that, but too late to stop her. He wondered if he ought to run and shout. But her taillights were pinpricks by now, so what was the use? No way he'd ever catch her.

So what now?

He could go back to sleep, he needed sleep, he knew that now, if only so he could think straight. He'd felt so blurry earlier, almost as if his words were coming in a slur.

Maybe the girl hadn't just split. Maybe, he told himself, she'd gone to get coffee, gone looking for someplace that was open. One of those goddam stores she was always looking for, a 7-Eleven or a U-Totem, it was like she spent half her life in those stores. That was probably it. She'd seen that he needed jazzing up and she'd gone out looking for someplace where she could get him some coffee. She hadn't wanted to wake him was all.

More likely though was that, if she wasn't pissed off by what he'd said, she was just plain sick and tired of his turning back and forth, back and forth, like one of those big old fans arcing through the same old stale air no matter which fucking way they turned. That was it. She was fed up with his bullshit, and in fact he was fed up with it himself. Totally and completely ragged out by his bullshit. If he could feel that way, imagine how it had to be for the girl.

But meanwhile, what was he supposed to do about his mother? Stuck here in this house, the T-bird and the girl both gone, what was he supposed to do?

RACHEL TRIED TO MAKE HERSELF THINK about the road now, about the likelihood of anyone's being on it. Where did it go when it went past Peyton's? Rachel wasn't sure, but she knew that it wasn't posted with the No Outlet signs that marked dead ends. Someone might conceivably come along, and if not, she knew for sure that a more or less main road was at the bottom of this one.

Rachel wondered then just how disheveled she must look right now. Wondered if anyone with any sense would ever pick her up or stop to listen to her story. She had no money, she realized, nor any identification. It was all back at Peyton's, and Peyton probably didn't even realize she was gone.

A new sound. Thunder. Rachel looked to the sky. A solid ceiling of clouds had formed overhead. No wonder it had seemed so dark! Never mind that she'd watched the stars when she'd been floating in Peyton's pool. Texas weather was like that. She'd known the temperature to drop maybe even thirty degrees or more in an hour. She'd known rain to fall while the sun was beating down. There was even a joke about the changeability— something about how if you didn't like the weather, you should wait a few minutes. But now, with rain pelting her, it didn't seem very funny. Rachel was as wet as she'd been in the pool and five times as cold. She started running, and coughing, too.

She saw the headlights first, and moved to the side, but the driver slowed so drastically, Rachel knew she had been seen. She ran toward the driver's window and said, "Can you help? Oh, please, please, help."

Before the driver could answer, Rachel ran around to the passenger side and slid in. It seemed so cozy inside. So warm and safe and cozy.

"I know you must think . . ." Rachel began, but then the coughing overtook her again.

The driver was a young girl. She turned the little car with ease. She smiled at Rachel in the soft cockpit light and said, "You're welcome," when Rachel was able to choke out, "Thank you." A pretty girl, round-faced, with long, extremely long brown hair.

FROM FAR AWAY HE HEARD AN ENGINE over—or maybe under—the sound of the rain. It was the kind of throaty noise a sports car would make. It was the Thunderbird, his mind raced on, it had to be. The girl, coming back.

So she hadn't just given up on him, written him off, after all.

He ran outside in the downpour and listened more carefully, just to be sure. Hell, yes, it was the T-bird, all right.

He'd fix her, though. He'd hide, that was what. He'd hide and when she came inside to find him, she'd think he'd awakened and was gone.

IS THERE SOMETHING," RACHEL ASKED, "A phone or place where I can make a call?"

Even as she asked, she wondered whether or not she'd need a quarter. Would she? She had planned to call the emergency number, 911. Still, she'd better have a quarter just in case.

She'd have to ask for one, she realized, and even now, in a situation like this, it embarrassed her.

Again, she wondered how she looked. The girl kept sneaking glances at her, so she really must have looked a mess: dirty, wet, bedraggled.

Then Rachel mustered her courage and said, "I don't have any money, not a cent. I . . . it was a domestic argument, I had to leave..." Her words slowed as she tried feverishly to invent a story that would be believable.

The girl didn't seem to require one, however. Rachel couldn't even tell if she was listening, really. She seemed sort of smug, pleased with herself, she had that kind of look on her face.

The girl made a turn off the main road onto what seemed a newly paved street. Yes, there was even some heavy equipment there by the side of the road.

"I have to use the telephone," Rachel explained, and she couldn't remember for the life of her whether or not she'd said that before. She thought, *she must be taking me to her own home.*

She saw a scattering of houses, dark, every one. She thought perhaps the storm had knocked the electricity out. Then again, it was the middle of the night, but still, people did leave some lights on, a porch light or something.

The girl pulled up in front of a house that seemed to Rachel unused, but nonetheless she followed the girl up the walk. *She must just have moved here,* Rachel thought, *with her parents. But of course, of course, they'll have a phone.*

Then the rain stopped so suddenly that the hollow hush that followed seemed an ominous thing.

The girl walked through the open door and stood aside, and Rachel walked in past her, and knew instantly from the emptiness that this was wrong. Rachel turned to the girl, turned to ask the girl to explain, but the smile on the girl's face, so satisfied, so beatifically pleased, told her it would be a waste of time.

What was going on here? Was there something wrong with the girl? Was she stupid or retarded or what? She wasn't able to understand what Rachel had been saying, that was it. She was foreign. She didn't speak any English, that was it.

The girl left Rachel in the front room and went into the one adjoining it. Without even thinking it through, Rachel spun around and rushed out of the house, stepping off the walk and sinking and slipping in the mud that surrounded it. She went down to one knee and felt the thick ooze of it through the denim of her jeans. She used her hand to right herself. Now even the terrain was against her. She stumbled on, and then she felt herself about to slip again when two strong hands from out of the dark grasped her shoulders and steadied her.

She turned. He was taller than she was, broad, and he smelled familiar. He was . . .

"That's right, Mother. It's me."

Rachel stopped breathing. Time itself seemed to stop.

He put an arm around her as if this were a long-sought family reunion, and he led her back toward the house she'd run from. He'd caught her. Drew had caught her after all.

Rachel let herself be led. She felt suddenly devoid of energy, of will. She felt already dead.

"You amaze me," Drew told the girl, closing the door, closing Rachel and himself and the girl inside. Rachel wondered at the softness in his voice. That was new. Some new and more convincing act he'd learned, no doubt. The slight twinge of anger that the thought created began to revive Rachel.

"It was easy," the girl said. "I thought I'd have to go on up there, to the house, but just after I made the turn, there she was. No kidding, Drew. It was like it was meant to happen or something. I just turned and . . ."

"There she was," Drew finished for her, looking, in the predawn light, not at the girl, but at his mother.

HE HADN'T BEEN THIS CLOSE TO HER IN —what?—years, that's what. And now here she was, delivered like a package, by the moonfaced girl. Like it was meant to be, the girl said, and that was how it felt, meant to be.

He had to hand it to the girl, she'd just gone out and done what he'd been fucking around about. And she wasn't lording it over him, either, wasn't putting him down for not being able to get his shit together on this.

Anyway, none of that mattered now, because, like the girl said, there she was.

Rachel was looking at him like he was something out of a horror movie, *Night of the Living Dead* or something, all eeked out, not glad to see him, not grateful that he was alive and tall and healthy, not any of the things he'd hoped when he'd dreamed this scene, dreamed it looking out at Corpus Christi Bay watching the clouds move and the sailboats tilt in the sea breeze. It was so like a picture postcard that it had been easy to picture-postcard up the way things would be with his mom when and if he ever saw her again.

Looking down at her from that cliff, that hadn't seemed real, and coming close to her when she was with that Zachary character, well, that had messed him up too bad to tell how that felt. This, though, this was the real thing, this was where he could see the little lines around the corners of her eyes.

Her mouth was all screwed up, because of how

mad she was. And she was yelling her head off, too, not that anyone could hear her, what with no one living nearby.

The rain. It had beaten on his shoulders, and was still rolling off his hair. It was cold, so cold he thought that it and maybe the moonfaced girl who was inside the house kind of watching was keeping him from going crazy, what with the way his mom, the way that Rachel, was carrying on.

Nothing like that picture postcard he'd envisioned at all.

"Stupid bitch!" he screamed at Rachel. "Stupid, stupid bitch!" And he came in driving her backward across the floor, like some maniacal dance, him tramping forward shouting, and her screaming right back in a tight falsetto voice, but moving out of his way,

"Drew..." The moonfaced girl stepped between them, and he pushed her aside.

"No," he said. "Get out of my fucking way."

Rachel, meanwhile, had reached the wall. She clapped her hands against it and was outlined there like a specimen on a page, one of those little butterflies, or a velvet-winged moth. She must have recognized that, because the wall—the fact of the wall—did shut her up.

He could hear her breathing and his own. The girl might not have been there at all, she was invisible, she'd receded in importance if not in fact. This was his mother, by God, it was her belly that he'd lived in. Her fucking belly.

"I don't mean shit to you, do I?" he said.

Rachel whimpered. He didn't know what that meant, but it made him mad.

"Not shit!" He reached up as if he was going to

crack her one, but then he didn't. A sense of this having happened time and time again in the past washed over him. He knew from the way Rachel had barely juked that it must have, must have, that he'd really want to smash her good and then he'd chicken out, something would stop him.

"I'm trying to get through to you," he said. "Can't anything get through to you? Can't you remember anything? Can't you remember..." He broke off, not knowing what it was he was trying to say, but seeing it, seeing it clearly, something that had happened when he was just a little boy.

It was back when his granddad—Rachel's father— had died. The morning of the funeral, he, Drew, sat stiff and upright, oppressed by the dopey little suit Rachel had made him wear. His grandmother sat on one side of the kitchen table and his mother, Rachel, on the other.

They weren't talking, Rachel and Gram, not at all. Gram's hand rested palm down near a candy dish or an ashtray, he wasn't sure which. He saw Rachel reach across and lay her own hand on his gram's, and saw, too, that his gram flinched back, as if Rachel's hand had been hot as a coal.

"Growing up," Rachel had said to him later, "growing up, I always thought she hated me. That I was just a pain in the neck, someone she had to—but didn't want to—take care of. Right then, when I tried to comfort her, I knew I'd been right. And I'll tell you, Drew, it was something I never wanted to know."

That was exactly what Rachel was doing to him right now—just what her own mom had done to her —but there wasn't any way he could break through and make her see that. Wasn't any way at all.

"I've come all this way. . ." he tried.

"From Galveston," she said. The cutting edge in her voice!

"That's right." He put his face right next to hers. "Damn fucking right!"

RACHEL DIDN'T KNOW WHERE SHE FOUND the courage, but she stayed right there, right there where she could feel the spray from his spit in her face. And when he'd finished foul-mouthing her, she'd yelled right back at him, right back. "I'm the one who stayed. You forget that, don't you? I'm the one who stayed through all of your. . ." She couldn't think of what to call what she'd been through with him, there just wasn't a word, not a single word that could say. "Your shit! Your shit!"

Her fists went out and pounded at his shoulders until he grabbed her, both her wrists. Then she tried to kick, but the way he had her wrists, she couldn't reach. He shoved her back against the wall, and she hit hard.

"You listen, bitch," he said, and something snapped in her, something absolutely came undone.

"No, you listen." She advanced again, fists flying. "You listen to me."

It became very clear to her suddenly that he wasn't going to kill her, wasn't going to have a chance, because, by God, by God, she was going to kill him first. She was going to take him by the throat and . . . oh, it was a pleasurable thought, she would love to do it, love to squeeze the life right out of him and yell, "Die, Drew, die, die," stabbing and pounding and . . .

He grabbed her wrist again, and he pinched some spot that made everything but the pain he was causing blank out of her mind. "Stop," was all she could say, and even while she was saying it, she was dropping to the floor in front of him.

Now that she was on her knees he let her go. "Don't get up," he ordered.

She shook her head no. What kind of maniac was he? And what kind of girl did he have with him, what kind of girl would watch a son do this to his mother? She tried to see the girl, but without being obvious about it, without having Drew see that she was looking. Could the girl—any girl?—be impervious to something like this?

"You calmed down now?" Drew asked.

Rachel nodded yes.

DON'T THINK ABOUT RUNNING," DREW said. "Don't be afraid of me. Don't be afraid at all."

"Is that what you told your dad?" Rachel asked. "Is that what you said to him? So that he wouldn't fight back?"

"What the fuck? My dad! Man, you are sick, Rachel." He spoke her name with venom. "I can't believe you, Rachel. Sick, sick, sick." He knew he was losing it, knew she'd never calm down again if he did. Knew she'd never listen to what he had to say. At the same time, she got him so pissed off, he just couldn't believe it.

What he told his dad!

He felt just the way he did at Benedict House that time, just the way he did when she'd said to him that shit about how he'd killed one girl already, about how one was enough. He wanted to say, *I hate you*, *Rachel*, *hate you, you bitch*, and then just let her take what was goddam coming to her, but even while he was thinking that, he knew that he wanted to save her, too.

He took deep panting breaths to try to catch hold of himself. When he felt he had, he said, "Look. We've got a lot of shit between us, that's obvious, but at the same time . . ."

But Rachel looked away, and he sighed, torn again between wanting to bash her in the face and wanting to make her listen to what was going to happen.

"Mom. Please. Forget everything for now. I don't care what you think five minutes from now, you can hate me, you can never see me again, I don't care, only listen right now. Listen to what I have to say, just that, all right?"

Rachel turned back to face him, her face all screwed up with hating him and fearing him and God knew what else. "Is it the same thing you said to Zachary? The same thing you said to Peyton? Will you tell me whatever it was you told them? Whatever it was that turned them away from me and back toward you?"

She was hysterical, he thought, making no sense at all. Or else she had flashed back like some acidhead, back to the days when she used to accuse him of getting everybody on his side.

He would have to be super-careful, super-calm for this. "Mom," he said, real soft-like. And he just kept repeating "Mom, Mom, Mom," like a mantra, hoping that he'd lull her and get through to her.

RACHEL TRIED TO KEEP FROM LISTENING TO the sound of Drew chanting "Mom, Mom," like some magic incantation that would overpower her.

She thought she would go crazy. He had never done this before, one word over and over like that. Thank God he'd never tried that. She surely would have cracked.

"Shut up," she yelled. "Just stop it." She held her palms over her ears and began a chant of her own: "Shut up, shut up, shut up." When she stopped and took her hands away, he had stopped too.

And he was looking hard at her. "You ready to listen?"

Yes, she nodded, worn out.

The girl sat down on the floor beside her, her long bony arm around Rachel's shoulder. Rachel felt like yielding to her, turning to her for comfort. But that would be crazy, crazy, she was on Drew's side.

Rachel sat stiffly, resisting.

"Mom," he said. "I know I gave you a rough time. No kidding, I really know it. And I know, right then, that Benedict House was just about the only thing you could do. Look at me. I mean it."

Rachel looked, but it took every bit of strength that remained. She nodded agreement.

"The thing is, Mom, it was kind of a strange place. Some of the people there, they were kind of . . . far gone. Do you know what I'm saying?"

She didn't, didn't want to know. Unless he was saying that he'd learned from them, the far-gone ones. Was that what he was saying? "Your father . . ." she began. "Rob . . ."

"That's what I'm trying to tell you," Drew said. "First Rob, then Rachel. That's what I'm here for. That's why I . . ."

"Tracked me down," Rachel finished for him. "You tracked me down. First Zachary, then Peyton. You just tracked me down."

"Hey, wait a minute," Drew said, sensing her hysteria rising again. "Wait a minute, I had to. I had to find you to . . ."

"And did you get Peyton to help you? Did you win her over too? Was she planning just to hand me over to you in the morning, or what?"

"What are you talking about?"

"You!" she accused. "I heard you talking to her. I heard you telling her, for God's sake, telling her you wanted to kill me, kill me just that way you killed him, just the way you—"

"Jesus Christ, Mom, you're crazy, you're really crazy, you know? I don't know what the fuck you're talking about, but you'd better listen to me now, because if you don't . . ." His voice was breaking, as if he were going to cry or scream, she didn't know which.

She wanted to baby him, pat his back, offer him a sip of water. She also wanted to push him away from her, push him just as hard as she could, and run, run, run screaming away. "You're lying," she said, "You always lie."

"I'm trying to talk to you. Trying to talk. The way you tried, with your mother, remember? Remember how she jerked away?"

Rachel looked stunned. For a moment she wondered how he knew that.

Rachel turned to face him. "You tell me exactly what you told my friend Peyton tonight and then you tell me, exactly, what her reaction was." It was a test, she thought. A test.

"I told you, I don't know what the fuck you're talking about." His voice was tinged with the whine of exasperation.

HE'D COME UP AGAINST THIS—WHAT the fuck was it?—this gulf, this fucking impassable gulf between them every single time, every single time he tried to get through to her. And it didn't matter how he prepared for it, how he told himself it was going to be, it just happened, happened this way, every time.

Fucking impassable gulf, miles wide, miles deep.

But what seemed so sad was, he didn't want it there, and he doubted, he really doubted, that she did. What did that mean? The worst thing: that it was there, that it really existed, that it was something that neither one of them, not he, not his mom, could ever cross over.

How did shit like this happen? How could people stand for shit like this to keep going on? It would almost be better to be hatched out of an egg, never have a mother at all.

"Get up," he said. "Get up and get the fuck out of here. I never want to see you again at all." And he turned away.

"I don't think he means it," the girl told Rachel. "He said that once to me and he—"

"I mean it all right," Drew said. Then his voice fell almost to a whisper. With his back still turned, he said, "Let her go. Let her die."

"But . . ." the girl began, her arm still around Rachel's shoulder. Then the girl shouted as Rachel tore free, heaving the girl so that she lost her balance and fell to the floor.

"Bitch!" Drew whirled and reached for Rachel, but too late. He could hear the squish of Rachel's footsteps in the mud. He ran to the doorway and stood there, listening. Then he started to sob. He stood there and sobbed and hollered into the night. "Mom. Mom, you have to listen. Mom, you have to believe me this time, just this once. Mom." Then all at once, his voice seemed to break, to give way.

The girl had boosted herself to her feet and had stood behind him through all this. Now she reached for him.

Drew squirmed away. "She can go to fucking hell," he said.

"Oh, sure," the girl said, persisting, reaching up and kneading his shoulders.

He shrugged her away, though not harshly this time. He even smiled a bit. "Come on," he said, walking toward the doorway. "Let's get her. She can't be very far."

HEADLIGHTS. WERE THEY DREW OR WERE they someone else, someone safe? She couldn't take the chance, even though the lights were coming not from the direction she'd run from but from the one that she was running toward. Still, it could be a trick, another person he had in on this.

She would have to veer off the road, veer away, into the stubble and the brush, and hide there like an animal until daylight. Except that she wasn't fast enough, she'd been slowed by her own fatigue. The headlights were upon her. Rachel fell before them as if the beams themselves had brought her down.

"Rachel." Peyton's voice, Peyton trying to lift her. "What's going on? I went into your room to close the windows and you—"

"Drew," Rachel interrupted, barely able to speak and sounding delirious when she did. "Drew . . . here . . . he . . ." She staggered to her feet, looking at Peyton and wondering why Peyton would be smiling, almost a crazy grin, at a time like this. She let herself be helped into the passenger side of Peyton's Mercedes. "He's going to kill me. I know he told you, I heard him, heard him telling you. He's going to—"

"Don't talk." Peyton pushed Rachel's legs inside, then closed the door. "You're sopping wet," she said. "I have a blanket in the trunk—"

"No!" Rachel clutched at her. "No time!" Her eyes met Peyton's, and she could see that Peyton understood.

"Okay," Peyton said, going around and climbing in. She leaned across Rachel for a moment, though, and fished through the glove compartment. She produced a flask and handed it to Rachel. "Just a minute," she said, fumbling with her handbag and then unscrewing the lid of a small brown bottle.

Another one of Peyton's pills. She didn't have the energy to resist. She took one pill and washed it down with whatever was in the flask.

Peyton watched maternally. Then she drove off, though not in the direction of her own house.

"Good," Rachel said. "Police." She was so tired, so tired, she was glad that Peyton had figured everything out, that Peyton was taking her not back home but to the police.

"Just lean back, Rachel," Peyton told her. "Get some sleep."

They passed the side road where Drew and the girl had taken her. She thought she saw the headlights of the girl's car. Before she could say anything to Peyton, though, she was swept with a wave of great fatigue. She felt the way she used to on the bus from Kingsville to Corpus Christi, almost unable to keep her eyes open, lulled by the roll of the tires beneath her, the mild and soothing vibration of the open road. Rachel drifted as though at rest, no thought of Drew or danger intruding.

Something about the car, something about being with Peyton, but more the car, its solidity, the way it seemed sealed against the weather, against the rising dawn. Rachel closed her eyes, and felt the tension around her mouth begin to ease.

Occasionally she would open her eyes, but without shifting her position. Once she saw the lights of Austin proper still on in the distance and knew that Peyton had decided to drive downtown, to the big glass-and-brick terminal that was near the interstate. That was wise of Peyton, she thought, drifting again. Go right to the heart of the wheel, the main police station, the top.

She dreamed of other lights, the lights of the petrochemical plant in Bishop, on the road to Kingsville. It sounded awful, when she tried to tell anyone about it, like Peyton, for instance, who hadn't ever seen it, because everyone expected a petrochemical plant to be ugly, and it was ugly in the daytime, all the pipes and tubes and columns and chutes, but at night! At night it was a fairyland, a host of tiny twinkly lights that silhouetted every projection. Tinkerbelle's castle, or maybe Tivoli, which she'd never seen in person, only in a movie once, a long time ago, back when she was herself a little girl.

She awakened suddenly, aroused by Peyton's shuffling on the seat beside her. She was disconcerted, partly because she expected to see Austin again, perhaps even be in Austin, almost there by now, but they were out in the middle of nowhere.

She turned to ask Peyton about it, but Peyton had found whatever it was she was looking for—a tape— and was swerving slightly as she attempted to place it into the tape deck.

The headlights hit a road sign, and Rachel knew then where she was: on FM Road 2222, the road to Lake Travis, the road that curled away from the city and up into the hills. But why?

The hiss of the tape as the leader fed through the heads kept Rachel from asking. Then Peyton said, "Say it. Come now, you must. Just once. It'll be easy, you'll see. Only say it now. . . ."

Rachel furrowed her brow and looked at her friend, whose face seemed angry, staring straight ahead.

Then Drew's voice, very hesitant: "I want to kill him."

And Peyton's: "Who?"

Drew: "My father."

And Peyton: "His name?"

Drew: "Cassidy. Rob Cassidy."

Rachel's entire body was locked in terror.

Then Peyton said, "And now your mother, Drew. Say it."

And Drew, laughing. "That ought to be easier. I have some experience at that."

Peyton: "Seriously, now. . ."

"I want to kill my mother. I want to kill her, kill Rachel. Kill her. . ."

Rachel screamed and reached for the tape deck, jamming her hands against the controls. Peyton tried to stop her, but Rachel had hit against several of the buttons, and now the tape had ejected and Rachel was pulling at it, pulling at it.

The tape unraveled like spaghetti, and Peyton swerved, trying to get it from Rachel, then finally gave it up in order to keep the car on the road.

HE HAD FOLLOWED THE MERCEDES BEcause it was the only car around, and also because the girl insisted that the passenger in it looked like his mother. He wasn't sure, but he figured it was possible, and something possible was better than the enormous range of possibilities if that one didn't pan out. Otherwise, his mother could be anywhere.

Behind the Mercedes, he became more convinced that the girl was right. For one thing, there were two women in the car. For another, the one he thought might be his mom was fighting with the other one, the goddam Mercedes fishtailing all over the road.

He pulled over to the side. "Quick," he told the girl. "You drive."

"Why?" she asked, getting out when he did and very efficiently making the switch. The Mercedes was way the hell in front by now.

"Because I want you to pass that car. I want to see who's driving."

I DON'T NEED YOU FOR BAIT ANYMORE," PEY-
ton said, letting Rachel win the battle over the tape,
reassuming her dignity as if she'd never lost it while
struggling with Rachel. "I have Drew back now."

What did she mean? Rachel felt as though she must
be having a nightmare, but for the casing of the tape that
she held in her hand. Rachel tried to gather the long
unraveled ribbon up so that she would have some evidence, some proof. But of what?

And suddenly she realized the significance of part of
what had happened: that Drew, who wouldn't admit
he'd talked to Peyton earlier that night, actually *hadn't*
talked to her. What she'd heard was this tape. Peyton
playing this tape.

"And are you getting it, hon? Is the whole thing coming clear to you?" Peyton asked, turning sharply, almost
a jackknife turn onto yet another stretch of road. The car
bounced along, the suspension pillowing the effect.
"Well, the whole thing's almost over, Rachel. The
whole thing."

Something about her delivery kept Rachel very very
quiet.

THEY WERE GAINING ON THE CAR HIS
mother was in, but he couldn't let the girl get too
carried away. "Just keep it steady," he said, "and just
go right past like we're in a hurry or something and

then keep on going, don't slow down or drop back, okay? And the other thing is, get fairly close when you go by. Not so close that they'll look at us, but close enough for me to see, okay?" He wished the hell he could be driving, but there was no way he could do that and look too.

The girl was pulling out now to overtake the Mercedes. "Okay, easy . . . easy," he said, like he was coaxing a balky horse across a stream.

"Well?" The girl pulled the T-bird back into the right lane. As Drew had instructed, she kept up her speed. The Mercedes was dropping behind. But Drew hadn't answered, so she said more pointedly, "Well?"

"I can't believe it," Drew said. "I guess I knew it the whole time, but I can't fucking believe that I was right."

He leaned back into the seat and thought how much better it would have been to be wrong. But that picture back at her house; he'd remembered her shape. After that picture, he'd pretty much known for sure. Even back before then, when he'd found out about his dad and about the quilt, he'd known. It was what had pushed him on.

"Wait a minute," he said, looking back along the highway. "They've just turned in."

The girl pulled across the road, then went into reverse in order to turn around. She was whirling the wheel and was just about to pull forward again when they saw the headlights of another car.

Great. Here they were, blocking the guy's lane.

And, oh, shit. It was a cop car, too.

But wait a minute! Wasn't that a stroke of luck? A cop car! Who'd have thought that he'd ever be grateful for one?

Except that the asshole girl pulled forward and

then jerked around it and off to the side. He saw a flash of caliche, which must have been the drive where the car carrying Peyton and his mom had gone. But before he could even assimilate all of this information, the girl stalled out and leaped out of the car, leaving the door hanging wide. He said, "Hey," but she was gone, like some alley cat into the night, just flat out gone, and there he was, staring right into the belly of one of the cops.

"Hey, listen, you guys," he said, trying to open the door but finding that he'd have to bang the one cop in the knees to do that.

Then there was another one on the driver's side.

The one at his window squatted down and said, real meanlike, "No, you listen. You listen good."

Christ, they treated him like he was some kind of piece of shit, not even wanting to let him talk and then listening to him like he was a mental escapee when they finally did let him say his piece. He felt like if he had a gun he would blow their fucking heads off and never think back about it again, they would deserve it. After a while, he stopped trying to explain.

They made him stand beside the car and they'd patted him down. Like he was a criminal or something.

He was telling himself to hold on, hold on, but even while the words were floating through his mind, he felt his fists rise up and come down again on the roof of the little T-bird.

The police officer didn't take very kindly to that, and now Drew was standing with his hands cuffed behind his back. He was shouting, too, and not making very much sense.

Did he have the registration for the car?

No, the girl had it.

What girl?

And dammit, wasn't she gone? Wasn't she vanished and wasn't he being told that he'd stolen the car from some bigwig down in Galveston?

"That's bullshit," he told them. "It's the girl's car, it's hers, it's hers." But she was off into the woods someplace, nowhere to be found.

The little bitch. It was her fault they wouldn't listen to a thing he'd said about Rachel, about Peyton, about anything.

The cops pushed him into the backseat of the cruiser and locked the door. If only he'd known the girl's name. That was the thing that made his whole story look shaky. They'd asked him and he'd hemmed around and finally admitted that he didn't know and then they'd looked at each other, the cops, and then one of them said, "Let me get this straight. You were with this girl all day..." And just the way he said it told Drew that it was hopeless. That he might as well just shut up and let them take him wherever the hell they were going to.

Along the way, though, he made a final try.

"Look," he said, "you just don't seem to realize. This isn't a joke. This total whacko has got my mother. She was one of my teachers, okay? That's who that is. That's who's got my mother." It did sound crazy, now that he was listening to it himself. It did.

He went on anyway, he had to. "That's right. She's a real case, too. All this kill-your-parents shit she used to drop on us. I'll tell you, I thought it was like she said, that we had this stuff inside ourselves that we had to get rid of, but uh-uh, she took it way too far. Way too far."

They didn't even turn around to look at him. Like

what was their problem? Were they used to stories like this?

"Look," he tried again. "That Rob Cassidy thing. The murder, down in Galveston. Hey, look, that was my dad. This teacher killed my dad, too. She used to tell me that she would, she used to chant it at me, shove it down my throat all the time."

He remembered what the girl had said about the time she was at UT. That the psych majors were always the weirdest ones. That it was like they were going into it to find out what was wrong with themselves.

He sank back, staring at the mesh screen between him and the cops. They hadn't even glanced back there at him. It didn't fucking matter what he told them. In fact, he'd probably be a lot better off if he didn't talk at all.

And why should they believe him? His story sounded pretty weird. Especially weird if they hadn't actually seen this psychodrama teacher when she really got going. Even at Benedict House, they wouldn't listen when he told them what she was doing, how she was looneytunes. She'd probably still be teaching there if Rachel hadn't mailed the goddam letter she wrote right back to the school. He didn't know, in fact, if the school had fired her because of what was in the letter or because she'd used the director of the place's name. Probably the latter. They, just like the cops here, probably didn't give a flying fuck about anything that was really sick and wrong, but just about their asshole rules.

IT WAS ODD THAT THE THING SHE WAS MOST worried about, as Peyton steered the car up the rutted caliche drive, was whether or not they would wreck. The caliche, wet from the rain, was treacherously slick, and the car kept sliding. The ruts were deep and the undercarriage would scrape.

Then they came to a rushing stream of water, a flash flood from the earlier downpour, but did Peyton stop? People had been swept away in water like that. Rachel had seen it on television. You weren't supposed to drive through swift-moving water, and Peyton ought to know that. Rachel watched Peyton's eyes narrow and a look of determination cross her face as she drove the car through the torrent.

Miraculously they crossed the stream safely. They passed through a clearing, and the headlights and the rising daylight illuminated an old hunting cabin tucked into a notch between two hills.

Peyton got out and stretched, as if this had been a pleasant but tiring vacation drive. Rachel got out and tested the ground beneath her feet: wet brush, with squishy footing beneath.

She realized then what she'd instinctively been doing. She'd been testing the ground to run.

She listened. There was a hollow, rhythmic, metallic sound she couldn't place. As she walked toward the cabin she grew nearer the sound, and nearer, nearer still, until she knew what it was, a windmill croaking, croaking.

She had the feeling that she'd been here before, but of course she hadn't been. Unless in the depths of your mind, she thought, you see the hour and the place of your death.

But she couldn't believe that Peyton would kill her. Why would she? What had she, Rachel, ever done to Peyton?

But what had Peyton's relationship with Drew been? Were they in it together? Both of them planning to kill her? Maybe she was already dying, dying from the pill Peyton had given her—that, plus the stuff she'd washed it down with.

She thought about the windmill, about the water it produced. Was it good water or would it eventually go bad?

They'd driven back, back, back from the highway so very far that Rachel was sure she could be murdered here and never found. Was this what they'd planned? Peyton and Drew.

But still, Drew had been telling the truth about not having been at Peyton's, it was the tape of Drew, not him in the flesh. Oh, God, and that was what had made up her mind! She had been wavering in his presence, wavering, leaning toward believing him, until he'd come up with what she'd thought was a shameless lie.

At the cabin door, Peyton turned and made a gesture toward the road they'd been on. "This was all my parents' and my grandparents' place," she said. "They started out with nothing, right? But they bought up all this land with every penny they could lay their hands on. And everybody laughed at them, too, because it was so hilly here, so rocky. It was good-for-nothing land, the kind of land you'd expect a cedar-chopper to buy."

Cedar-chopper meant redneck, only maybe worse than that. A little worse than that.

Peyton turned back to the cabin and indicated it. "I grew up here."

Rachel didn't know what she was supposed to say.

She herself hadn't grown up in luxury or splendor. What was she supposed to say? She did know that the land was worth a fortune now. It was prime development land, especially since it fronted the route to the lake. She remembered that Peyton had said her money came from real estate.

"I guess you could say they gave me something, then," Peyton went on. "My own parents. Of course, they didn't give it to me willingly. I had to, uh . . ." She halted, tried to sound coy. "Nudge them a little bit."

"Nudge them," Rachel repeated, as though to draw someone out at a cocktail party. It was almost laughable —what she'd thought of coming up the drive, about the car wrecking, and now this, so unconnected, unreal. And the setting, the backwoods cabin, the creaking windmill, the sopping wetness of the grass and trees and ground. And now the lecture on real estate.

Then Peyton said, "But I freed myself, changed my life. It's what I wanted for Drew, too. What I wanted him to know." She pushed past Rachel at the cabin door. It swung forward.

Rachel thought, *The cabin, the picture on Peyton's wall,* and she thought of something Peyton had said a long time ago about picturing Rachel in a cabin, maybe even the first time they'd met, sitting in that deserted little Indian restaurant, a restaurant that had long since closed.

Peyton smiled at Rachel and changed her demeanor, her tone. She spoke brightly now, like the Peyton of old, telling Rachel, "Well, you'll see."

YOU CALMED DOWN ENOUGH TO MAKE your call, son?" The desk man looked like he might have doubled as a Santa during the Christmas season, gray-haired, with tiny wire-rimmed spectacles that he wore low on his nose.

Drew nodded at him, determined not to be swayed, determined not to be won over into anything resembling friendliness.

That was actually the secret behind Drew's toughness: he was won quite easily by kindness. He guarded against that and thought now, with an ironic sense of triumph, that no one had ever lucked onto that secret.

Oh, maybe the girl had, in her way, At least she'd kept on being nice to him no matter how rude or surly he became. She'd stuck by, until now. Now the fucking little bitch had run off leaving him to pay for her asinine thrill-seeking. God, he should have bolted the minute the thought that she had stolen that car occurred to him way back by that stream. He should have known there was no way she could have afforded a restored little T-bird. God, he was an asshole, pure and simple.

And the cops didn't believe him, didn't even believe the girl existed. No chance in hell they'd believe him about Peyton, about Rachel. It would be just like it had been in the cop car; he could talk until he was blue in the face.

Santa pushed the phone set at him.

Drew sat down and drummed his fingers. Then he asked for a directory and looked up Rachel's number.

THE SAME SWEET INCENSE SMELL THAT HAD filled the shop washed over Rachel when Peyton opened the door. They both stepped inside, where the light didn't seem to reach. Briefly, Rachel thought of overpowering Peyton, smashing a rock or a tree branch across her shoulders or her head. What could she use?

But her memory of Peyton's strength, Peyton lifting her limbs while she was doing yoga, slowly, powerfully, with no betraying quiver, no sign of strain, made her hesitate. And then she thought of Rob, Rob trying to fend Peyton off.

Because that was what this meant, didn't it? That Peyton had killed Rob? But why? And what had Peyton meant about getting Drew back? What did she know about Drew?

Peyton switched on an overhead light, and Rachel looked at her, hoping that the sight of her friend in full light would yield some answer, some explanation. Was this Peyton, the Peyton she knew?

"I think you know by now what I look like, Rachel," Peyton said. "So why not turn your attention elsewhere? Over there, for instance." She swept her arm in the direction of the far wall, where an enormous, but enormous, quilt had been hung.

Rachel gasped at the sight of it, but it was a gasp wrought not by beauty but by some inexplicable sense of—what? Revulsion, really, the sort that she might feel in the presence of a cockroach or a hairy spider. But more than revulsion, fear, but not just ordinary fear but an instinctive kind. The kind that makes you jerk your body back away from something before you've even seen clearly what it is. Different from the kind she'd felt hearing Drew's voice or upon finding out how she'd heard Drew's voice.

And yet the quilt was beautiful in a way, too. Could that be? That something a person would be afraid of could also be thought of as beautiful? And more, there was something familiar about the quilt, familiar and yet quite alien as far as even modern quilts were concerned.

The pattern had struck Rachel first, the odd, clown-face pattern, two deep sad oval eye shapes and a contradictory upturned line that seemed a grin. Something about it haunted her, teased her memory.

The quilt seemed appliquéd, and when Rachel drew closer, she saw that it was. The stitches were impeccable, as were the variously sized little oval shapes, oval shapes that ran together at one end but were apart at the other. And the colors were so odd, monochromatic, brown on brown on brown, deep mud brown and light cocoa brown and a rich heavy umber.

She looked at Peyton and thought Peyton's eyes unusually bright, unusually gleaming, as if Peyton's interest in all of this had been stored up for years and years and years and was fierce, animal-keen.

"What do you think, Rachel?" She seemed breathless, and yet at the same time, it was, Rachel thought, as if they were contemplating a purchase or consignment together, something innocent.

But there was nothing innocent about it, about being brought here through the predawn light, brought to this backwoods place and shown this quilt and now asked to evaluate it. It was crazy, so crazy that Rachel thought she ought to play along, do whatever it was that Peyton wanted her to do.

Rachel pinched at the fabric of the quilt and tried to act as she might have if they were on a buying visit.

Peyton pushed Rachel back out of the way and slapped her face. "You're so stupid, Rachel," she shrieked, her voice not like her real voice at all.

The slap stung, but it also cleared Rachel's mind enough to admit the part that wasn't crazy, but sad. "You were never my friend, were you," Rachel said. It was not a question. Nor was it anything that Rachel would, in a million years, have chosen to know. It was wearying, the thought, it wore everything down flat. How many times had she felt betrayed in the past twenty-four hours? Too many. By Drew, she'd thought, and then by Zachary, she'd thought, and then, in a minor way, by that round-faced girl who'd seemed a rescuer but who instead had taken her to Drew. And now this. Now this! "Never my friend," Rachel repeated, as if to burn the words and the idea home. She was alone again. She'd alienated Zachary and Drew and now she was alone with someone who was not her friend, never her friend.

"Stupid, stupid, stupid," Peyton chanted. Then she walked up to the quilt and she pulled it back along the rod that held it, pulled it to reveal the wall behind it.

Rachel saw that the wall was covered with photographs of Drew, of things that had been his, with letters that he'd written, and drawings that he'd made. Rachel remembered him asking her to bring them to Benedict House. He'd given them to Peyton, then, or else she'd taken them.

It had been an enormous cardboard-boxful, a box that a portable TV had been in. Drew's baby quilt. His battered little brown teddy. Even his baby shoes. A yo-yo, a Duncan yoyo, green with a black shimmer. All up there on the wall.

Rachel was dumbfounded.

"The tape, Rachel." Peyton reached forward.

Rachel looked down at her own hands and was startled to see that she still had the tape she'd attempted to destroy. The tape with Drew's voice. In automatic fashion, as if she were far too stunned to think of saying no, she handed it to Peyton, and Peyton examined the long brown jumble that protruded from its casing. She glared at Rachel, then placed the tape on a small wooden table in the center of the room.

Rachel turned and tried to appease her. "Peyton," she began, feeling an odd mixture of emotion: sadness and sympathy and fear and even a lurking anger.

Peyton turned to look in the direction of Rachel's voice, but when Rachel saw her eyes—how blank they were, how devoid of humanness, of everything but shine—she knew there was no point talking, there was nothing to say.

"He would have been mine," Peyton said quietly. Then, with sudden bitterness, "But you had to send them the letter, didn't you, Rachel? You had to make them fire me, send me away."

Rachel made the connection at once, the letter she'd received from the school, the letter that had come the day she'd seen the blood, the letter she'd balled up and then smoothed out and then stuck out in the mailbox to be returned to sender, returned to the school! "I didn't know," Rachel said, torn by the knowledge that she'd run from Drew, run away when she ought to have driven there, driven to Benedict House to rescue him. Oh, Lord, Drew in this woman's clutches!

Peyton, still mad-eyed, had begun to talk about Drew, about how he'd looked when first she'd seen him, angry, the way she herself had been angry; thwarted, the way she'd been too. And how handsome he'd looked, how fine, how proud she'd been to tutor him and be with him, shape him. "If it hadn't been for you, Rachel, you . . ."

Peyton's eyes flashed hatred, and Rachel was glad to see it. The glassy stare, the vacancy, had been frightening beyond all measure. If she could just keep Peyton from slipping back into that emotionless, more terrifying state. How could she do that? How could she keep Peyton's anger fueled?

Jealousy, she decided. That would be the way. She remembered how her own anger had flared when it seemed to her her role as mother had been usurped by the father of that girl Drew . . . in the accident. "You'd have had to hate me anyway, Peyton," she dared. "Because Drew loves me. Whatever happens, I'm Drew's mother and he loves me."

Peyton's face colored.

"That's right, Peyton," Rachel went on. "You didn't shape him; I did." She began to examine the pictures, the artifacts, convinced now, by the way Peyton came up close to her and glared, that the tack she'd taken was right.

"Look at these pictures, Peyton, look here." She walked over to one of Drew at about the age of three, standing proudly beside a wagon. "I bought him that wagon, and I took that picture. I was there! I was there! I can even tell you what I was wearing and what kind of day it was. Imagine that, Peyton, I can remember everything, remember it all completely if I care to, because I'm Drew's mother and I was there."

She waited, watching Peyton's face. Then she went on, "And this one . . ." She walked to another, and another and another, until finally Peyton reached up toward the one Rachel was pointing at and ripped it from the wall before Rachel could comment on it.

"None of this is so," Peyton said, clutching the picture, her voice taking on a childlike, taunting quality.

"You hated Drew, Rachel, because he told me. You were mean to him. You were mean."

"Oh, but I wasn't," Rachel said. "If anything, I was easy on him. Easy, why I—"

"You bloodied his nose. You threw something at him and you bloodied his nose."

"An accident!" Rachel screamed, but she knew that it was not an accident in Drew's telling of it. The memory of that awful day, blood arcing from Drew's nose and his throat, might have halted Rachel now, had she not been in sight of a photograph which brought back to her, not those moments which were ugly and which she wished she could erase, but those which had been whole and good.

Unlike the others, this photo had been torn in half. What was left was Drew, maybe five or six years old, on his belly, laughing down at something in the sand. Rachel remembered well that they'd been at the beach and they'd been lying side by side and Drew had been putting sand in a little metal pail. That was when he'd found his first sand dollar, and he'd shown it to Rachel and they'd both examined it. An old woman came up to them afterward and told them that she'd snapped their picture and she asked for Rachel's address so that she could send a copy of the shot. "It was a wonderful picture," the woman went on, and Rachel realized when the photo came that it was the most perfect picture that she and Drew had ever had taken together or most likely would. The woman had captured a look of bright wonder on both their faces, a profound resemblance not only of features but also of perception and mood.

Peyton had torn Rachel out of the photograph. Rachel could use even that. "Look here, Peyton." Rachel squinted at the ragged white edge. "Look, here's my hand. I was there, too, with Drew. Let me tell you about that day. It was bright and clear and sunny, and so I fudged on the work I had to do and as soon as we could, we went up to Corpus and then across the causeway to Padre. We'd never done that before, and so Drew was terribly excited, and I remember him pointing at the pelicans that were there in the shallows. You could see them from the bridge. Drew kept pointing at them and bouncing up and down, and I'll tell you, Peyton, I was probably yelling at him to stop, but it didn't change anything about that day, not the love I felt for him or the love he felt for me—"

"Stop it," Peyton said, pushing herself a step closer.

But Rachel kept right on as if she hadn't heard. "See here? In this little corner of the picture? That's suntan lotion, Peyton, because I remember buying it that day. I remember how Drew cried when I put it on him, saying that it burned, and how I told him it would burn a lot more if he didn't—"

Peyton came up to Rachel, eyes blazing, and pushed her backward, one, two, three quick steps. She grabbed Rachel's shoulders and shook her so roughly that Rachel's teeth clacked together painfully. Then Peyton yanked Rachel over to another part of the photo collage, and she directed Rachel's attention to the pictures that were tacked up there.

"Here, Rachel, tell me about these. Come on, Rachel, what do you know about these?"

Rachel had trouble focusing, but when she did, she saw that they were Polaroids of Rob. Very recent photographs. Rob when he'd evidently only noticed Peyton—puzzled, curious, yet annoyed. Rob when Peyton had evidently struck some sort of blow. Rob injured, his eyes questioning, then dying, perhaps, the questions grown faint and a bright stream of saliva from his lip to his jaw.

Rob dead, his eyes frozen and hard, a sort of foam now at the corners of his mouth, his skin tinged blue.

Then Rob's head poking out from beneath the quilt, the quilt, the magnificent sunburst she, Rachel, had labored hours and hours and hours upon. It had been stretched over him, then tucked in around him, the quilt, a bright, beautiful, handmade shroud.

Peyton stepped forward and pulled the hideous brown quilt back into place.

Is this, Rachel wondered, *what she'll use to cover me when I'm dead?*

HE'D FELT HIS HAND SWEATING WHILE he listened to Rachel's telephone ring on. Six rings, seven, the phone company told you to wait until ten, but that seemed forever. As though no one would take ten rings to answer a phone, but he was on eleven or twelve when the guy—what was his name?—picked up on it.

"Hello?" Something so stiff in the way he said it.

"This is Drew. I'm Rachel's son. You remember."

The silence was even stiffer.

Drew had gone on awkwardly, fully expecting the guy to hang up on him at any moment. When he'd managed to tell about the car and the girl disappearing, he began to figure out that this was a man who had never hung up on anyone in his entire life.

"Look," he heard himself saying, "I love my mother and I know she's been pretty freaked out about me, and that I gave her cause and all that, but this is big-time shit. I mean, that Peyton"—he'd hesitated over the name, because it wasn't the name she'd used at Benedict House, she had called herself Paula something there—"that Peyton is, well, dangerous. Crazy. No shit, crazy all the way."

The guy was still there, still listening. He went on to tell him about what it was like when Peyton was teaching psychodrama, only he even played it down because he didn't think the guy would really believe the truth. He finished that part with, "But, like, she tormented my mother at one point, trying to get her to leave town, never see me again, see? I mean, wouldn't you? Leave, I mean?" He felt he had fairly well stated the case in his mother's favor. While he was explaining it, he did see how it might have seemed from his mom's point of view, too, because hadn't he, Drew, been more than a little swayed by this Paula/Peyton person? For a while, anyway. There wasn't anything he'd put past Paula or Peyton or whatever the fuck her name was.

He knew he had to clinch things, though, because the guy hadn't really made up his mind. "Look, just think about this. You said you loved my mother and wanted to marry her. If you do marry my mother— and I understand, she's freaked out right now and maybe right this minute you can't see that happening —but if you do . . ." He took a deep breath. "Then I'll be your son, too." And he waited, wondering why he'd suddenly thought someone might want him as a son, and he realized while he was waiting that he wanted Zachary to say yes not just to helping Rachel but to him, to him, as well.

And it was crazy, man, because all these years, all this time, everyone had been on him about how deprived he must feel without a dad, and the fact was he'd never felt it. It hadn't seemed weird at all. He'd never felt that anything was missing, or at least he'd never had strong yearnings for some guy to take him out with a rifle to shoot some birds or whatever it was that fathers were responsible for doing. Oh, sure, when that girl's dad, his girlfriend who died in the accident, started taking him out and doing things, all pal-like, that'd been okay, but he hadn't needed it, hadn't needed it ever, it was just okay, that was all. It was even hard for him to get jerked up into feeling any kind of rage for Rob, like at Benedict House, because he didn't feel rage for Rob, he felt nothing, zilch, just a stone-cold empty place there in the Father slot. It was Rachel he hated, because it was also Rachel he loved. He had feelings for Rachel, strong ones, mixed-up ones, but feelings, man, they were there. And right now he had feelings, too. About this guy. He had laid himself on the line, he felt. Exposed himself to possible pain. *Get ready shithead*, he told himself. *Here comes another load.*

But when Zachary answered him there was something quirky and all curled-up in his voice, something that told Drew he'd been thinking about a son a lot, thinking about something he, also, hadn't had. "I'll be right there," he told Drew. And he asked to speak to the cop in charge, the one who looked like Santa.

IT DIDN'T MATTER THAT THE QUILT WAS NOW covering the photographs, it didn't matter because Rachel now had images of Drew fixed firmly in her mind. Not the awful images she'd allowed to overtake the good ones, but the good ones back again, the good ones she ought to have been remembering right along, before she fled Kingsville, right along.

She remembered once when Drew was eleven or twelve. He'd gone to the indoor pool at the university with some other children whose father was on the faculty there. Suddenly Rachel had a pang of fear—as though the others wouldn't take good care of him, as though she ought not to have let him go.

She had raced down the streets to the enormous building that housed the pool. The roof was open, and she could hear the echoing laughter and cries.

Instead of being reassured by these, her fear had deepened. Suppose her boy, her Drew, was already struggling beneath the surface of the water? Suppose his cry of help went unheard in all that rowdy play? Suppose, suppose, suppose . . .

Rachel had been panting as she pushed the door to the building open and began searching the surface of the water. The pool was huge, and Drew was nowhere.

Then she heard a sound, like a whip pushing through the air, and she looked up at the diving board on the far side, the high board, not unlike the board Olympic divers use, in fact, probably exactly like it, that height, with that amount of spring.

Drew was up there. He was unaware of her, unaware of anything except his own presence and power. She could still, if she thought to, see the way he looked that day—his muscles gleaming from the water and his hair slicked back. There were several people watching him, but he didn't seem aware of them at all. He was so alive, so happy, and she, Rachel, was so proud, so proud to be his mother, to have produced him, brought him into the world.

She'd left without his having seen her and she'd walked home euphoric. She never told him about that day, about what she'd feared and how at odds it was with what she found.

Is everything like that? If I think back, will all the bad—all of it—be washed away?

"Did you come to my house in Kingsville?" Rachel

asked, but Peyton only laughed. "I want to know," Rachel said. "Did you come there? The day of the letter about Drew, did you?" She was thinking of the blood in the sink. Thinking that not Drew, but Peyton, crazy Peyton, had put the blood in the bathroom sink.

"Stupid Rachel. Didn't even see that the stamp wasn't canceled on the letter, did you, Rachel? Didn't even notice. Well, of course I was there. I had to be there to put the letter in your box."

"And the sink?"

Peyton didn't say, but Rachel knew now. Knew.

A few hours ago, every bad thing that had ever happened regarding Drew, every argument, every terrible word, had been uppermost in Rachel's mind. It had been that way back then, in Kingsville, hard on the heels of whatever Drew's then current problem was. And of course there were problems, plenty of them, one after the next after the next. It wasn't easy raising a boy on your own, she told herself now, in an effort to assuage the pain that she felt when she thought of how wrong she'd been then, how wrong she'd been even now, thinking evil of Drew only until Peyton had revealed herself.

That's what I've been like right along, Rachel acknowledged. She always thought the worst and let the worst take over, like rust or mold or weeds or cancer, until it seemed as though nothing good, nothing whole, had ever passed between her and her son. This moment —seeing the error and the compounding of the error and the error again and anew—threatened to undo her.

And Peyton saw it, saw Rachel's moment of guilt and weakness and, perhaps, surrender.

But no! Rachel reached toward the quilt and tried to pull it back along its rod, deciding to goad Peyton further with her happy memories of Drew.

Peyton tried to stop her, and in the scuffle, the quilt

remained where it had been, but a few photographs came skimming behind it to the floor.

Rachel dropped to her knees and grabbed at one, a picture of Drew in a gaucho outfit, Drew at maybe seven years of age. "I sewed that for him, Peyton. For Halloween. He won Best Costume that year. Ah, but I saw you had the newspaper clipping up there." She had seen something that looked like the yellowed photo she'd once cut from the Kingsville paper.

Jealousy flared in Peyton's eyes.

"Here's Drew on a pony!" Rachel continued, when Peyton came and kicked at Rachel's hand, hard.

The pain weakened Rachel momentarily. She lay still on the floor, rubbing her wounded hand with the good one. Through eyes clouded with tears she was able to see the last of the photos that had fallen:

Drew running down a long gravel drive, an enormous greyhound at his side. Drew's legs, both of them, off the ground, and the greyhound's legs, all four, also off the ground. Drew and the greyhound, their energy and their strength and their giddy knowledge of both suspended there for all time.

Rachel felt a surge of maternal pride. She caught hold of it as she might a sturdy root on the bank of a swift-flowing stream. *I will not let go*, she pledged.

SANTA TOLD HIM HE COULD WAIT RIGHT there. There wasn't any need to put him in the lockup. "The whole thing's screwy anyway," he admitted. Drew had picked some pretty powerful people to get himself mixed up with, too. Take the car, for instance. The car had belonged to a big Galveston developer, and when they called him, he, like Drew, had started talking about this long-haired girl.

Turned out the girl was his daughter, Gwendolyn, and he'd reported the car stolen just to give her a little grief. Turnabout, he called it.

The other bigwig, it turned out, as the officer who looked like Santa rambled on, was Rachel's boyfriend, Zachary. A big-time publisher in Austin. Put out almost every book on Texas that was ever worth reading.

"Historical stuff, a lot of it," the cop went on, proud to have been reading that sort of thing.

But all Drew cared about was getting out of there. He kept looking at the clock and wondering how long Zachary would take to get there and whether or not he'd change his mind.

It was fully morning by now. Anything might have happened, anything. Drew tried not to think that, but he couldn't help it, the thought kept coming back.

Finally Zachary came with a lawyer, a tall, thin-bearded man who pushed some papers forward and effected Drew's release. Drew watched through a plate-glass window in the wall and thought how simple it all was, like somebody buying something, a car, a house, a color TV.

The big moment came when Zachary came to the door behind the cop and he and Drew looked at each other, Drew knowing that he ought to smile, but unable to, and Zachary, well, not smiling either. They shook hands, and Drew said, "Thank you," and Zachary only nodded.

Outside, with the traffic on Interstate 35 all but drowning him out, Drew told him everything he knew about Peyton, about the psychodrama coaching, about her strange interest in him. "I don't know

what she wanted, man. She never, like, came on to
me, never wanted sex or anything, but something.
There was something there. She kept telling me I was
special and that I was just like her. It gave me the
creeps, but after a while, I figured if they'd hired her,
Benedict House, I mean, there must be something to
it. But the whole thing was how the parents had to
die for the children to be free. I thought, fine, symbolically, but symbolically, shit. She meant for real."
He looked at Zachary to see whether or not the man
believed him.

Zachary said, "Well, look. There's more to it than
that." Then he pointed at a car that was only just
rolling into the underground parking lot and he said
that the chief of police was a friend of his and how
Drew should come along and tell his friend all that he
knew.

When Drew finished, the chief said to Zachary,
"You mentioned Trump," and Zachary told him yes.
The chief said, "Okay," as if the Trump thing
cinched everything, and then he was on the phone for
a while. When he got off, he said to Zachary, "You
might have said something about that a little sooner."

Drew felt as if his head would split, not knowing
what that meant. This was his mother, after all, and
here they were, doing all this code stuff.

"That's what I'm thinking," Zachary said. "And
don't imagine that I'm not bothered by it."

"By what?" Drew asked. Both Zachary and the
chief looked sharply at him, knowing he was pissed
off but good. He almost apologized, but before he
could, Zachary came over and clapped an arm around
his shoulder.

"Drew," he said, "I'm a native Texan, and a history
buff, and a publisher, and—"

"—a walking encyclopedia," the chief cut in.
Zachary waved him quiet and went on.

YOUR PRECIOUS BOYFRIEND, RACHEL," PEY-
ton said, pronouncing the words as if they were laughable, a disgrace. "Your sweet Zachary, well, he's known
about me, hon!"

Rachel must have reacted visibly, because Peyton
laughed before she went on. "Oh, don't worry, I don't
mean he actually knew, but he suspected something, Rachel, and you know what? He's such a stick, so refined and
well mannered, Rachel, such a goddam stick, he did
nothing. He said nothing. I'll bet he didn't even try to talk
you out of going into business with me, did he?"

Rachel laid her cheek against the cool earth floor. *I
will not let go*.

"I didn't think so," Peyton said. "So in a sense, he's
the reason you're here."

Not let go.

Peyton stood and came over to where Rachel lay. She
bent over and looked at Rachel's face. "Did you hear
me, hon? Zachary's the reason you're here." And Peyton cocked her head to better enjoy the sight of the
meaning as it sunk in.

YOUR MOTHER," ZACHARY SAID TO
Drew, "accused me of being unfair, because try as I
might, I could just not warm up to that woman. In
fact, it was more than that. The first time I met Pey-

ton, I felt a kind of physical reaction, I felt the hair at my collar pinching, the way dogs must feel when they ruffle their fur at each other."

Drew knew what he meant. He remembered the first time he'd seen Peyton, he'd have sworn that he'd felt it too. He was over by the window, looking out at Corpus Christi Bay and thinking about the sailboats and how much he'd like to be on one of them when he'd felt just that pinch that Zachary was talking about. He'd turned and there she was, Peyton, or Paula as she was calling herself, that first time.

But there was more. It seemed to him now that the sun had dropped behind a cloud right then, too. Everything got darker, cooler, and it had been Peyton's doing.

"I felt," Zachary went on, "and I know this sounds like an exaggeration, but I felt that I was in the presence of someone evil. I'd never have told Rachel or anybody this, because I tried to brush it away, but then it got worse. Peyton looked at me and I could see in her eyes that she knew what I was feeling." He wiped his forehead. "After that, whenever your mother accused me of not liking Peyton, there wasn't very much I could say. I felt that if I told her what I felt, she'd suggest that I see a doctor. I felt that no matter what I said, I sounded like some gospel-toting preacher. Jonathan Edwards. Sinners in the hands of an angry God or what-have-you."

Drew was disappointed. He thought there would be more than just this feeling. But it turned out there *was* more after all.

"I avoided Peyton, and I tried to discourage your mother from going into business with her—this Patchwork thing. Still, since she was your mother's partner, there was no way I could totally stay out of her way. She had us over for drinks, for instance. I rather think she enjoyed having me over, knowing full well how I'd reacted to her.

"Anyway," he went on, "I remember going into one of the rooms and seeing a picture that she has in there—a black-and-white photograph that's been re-touched so that it looks—"

"I know," Drew said. "Like blood."

Zachary didn't ask how he knew, he just went on with the story. "The symbolism of that picture—blood on the girl's feet and blood coming out of the door—it's just so obvious. But the thing was, I'm maybe one of ten people in the city who would know that cabin, know that place, and Peyton knew that about me, I'm sure. It was the Trump cabin."

"Scene of one of Austin's biggest murders," the chief put in. "Unsolved, too." Zachary looked away. The chief's phone rang. The chief listened, said, "Yo," the way they do in old war movies, and then Zachary and Drew were in an elevator going down into the garage.

Drew wanted to hear the rest of the story, and Zachary told him to wait, that the cops they were riding out with would have to listen to it, too.

In the cop car, Zachary told the driver, "They're at the old Trump cabin. Do you know where that is?" They didn't, and Zachary directed them as they sped crosstown. He went on with the story, for the benefit of the cops, who he said were too young to know, and Drew, who had the right.

"The Trumps owned half the mountainside along 2222, which is the best way to the lake. That's where Peyton's money comes from, the sale of that land. She kept, I would guess, the cabin itself and a good bit of acreage around it.

"The Trump place—that cabin—is where all the bodies were found. Peyton's parents. Her grandparents, too. Peyton must have been thirteen or so then. Brothers and sisters, too, and they were all killed, wiped out.

"The parents had been tortured, not just killed, but tormented. It was a very grisly, very famous case, too."

"And unsolved," Drew said. "Except that you think that Peyton was the one who murdered them." It made him dizzy to think of it, how close his mother was to her, how many times she and his mom had been alone. How often he himself had been with her, too.

"Yes," Zachary admitted, "I do. After I looked at that picture I went back and looked up the photos that were plastered all over the papers. It happened back in 1971, and they were all still available in the library, not even on microfilm, but the newspapers themselves. Peyton even looks like them, the resemblance is there—" He broke off abruptly and Drew knew what he was doing, blaming himself for not saying anything then.

"Hey, look," Drew said. "It just seems like you should have known, but believe me, you didn't know, not for sure, back then."

Zachary looked up.

"I mean it," Drew said. Drew told him of other things that seemed to fit. He remembered books Peyton had had in her room, things she tried to get him to read. One was called *The Kids Next Door* and it was even subtitled something like *Sons and Daughters Who Kill Their Parents*, and others like *The Deadly Innocents*, and he couldn't remember what all.

From the looks of the landscape—the fact that the houses had gone from clustered to widely spaced to practically nonexistent—he figured they were almost there.

PEYTON TOOK A BURLAP SACK FROM ONE OF the corners and carried it to the wooden table, where she sat down. She emptied the contents and then called to Rachel, "Rachel, come here. I want to show you my scraps. After all, you showed me yours once, remember?" And she laughed.

Rachel was angered to think of how Peyton had duped her, duped her all along, duped her into showing her precious collection of fabric remnants, many of which had been Drew's. Then she remembered Peyton telling her she'd picked up "little-boy vibes" from one of the pieces, and she wanted to tear Peyton apart with her bare hands.

She stood up, and she didn't even try to dust the damp brown dirt from her face or her hands or her clothing. She went over to where Peyton sat. Without any hesitation at all, she grabbed the edge of the table and she flipped it back so that Peyton and the chair that Peyton was sitting in went backward too.

Except that Peyton rolled free and was on her feet in an instant. She came forward and slapped Rachel's face with all her might, her hands clasped together and swinging as if her arms held a golf club. She slapped one way and then the other, and then Rachel fell and Peyton grabbed her by the shoulder and pulled her upright and onto her feet.

While Rachel wobbled there, Peyton righted the chair and then pushed Rachel down into it. Rachel reached toward Peyton again and then tried to duck when she realized Peyton had locked her hands together again and was swinging forward with yet another blow.

Then it wasn't day anymore, wasn't the least bit light.

ONE OF THE COPS PICKED UP A MICRO-
phone and started talking into it. Drew turned and
through the rear window saw another cop car, un-
marked. A SWAT team, he figured; four guys in it,
and every one of them ready to gun Peyton down.

Except that the other car turned off, apparently
not a police car at all. The four guys were executives,
probably, on their way to some boost-sales meeting.

And meanwhile, this nut had his mom.

Even the chief had declined to go, sending Drew
and Zachary and two guys in uniform, both of whom
looked far too young to be doing his mom or anyone
any good.

Fuck.

Zachary was directing them, and Drew was
amazed to see the little T-bird come into view. Until
that moment, Drew had been afraid that maybe
Zachary had it wrong, that Peyton hadn't been a part
of this Trump thing, that they wouldn't be able to
find her in time, wouldn't be able to save his mom.
But the T-bird was there, and zigzagging off away
from it was the caliche road that Zachary said led to
the cabin.

Drew thought about the moonfaced girl out there
someplace. But that was crazier still. She'd have come
back to the road, hitched into town. The little bitch
probably watched the cops haul his ass away and
then, yeah, did just that. But what if she was out
there? What if the cops shot her by mistake?

Still, it was light outside, they could see. And anyway, the moonfaced girl would be long gone, long gone by now.

But what about her father's car? Didn't she care about the car or her father or, well, him?

To Drew's consternation, they drove past the drive and past the T-bird, which, he noted, had a Disabled sticker on its windshield now. The car looked white with road dust, as if it had been left there for a long long time.

"Why aren't we going up there?" Drew asked. Zachary laid a hand on his arm, as if he ought not be asking.

"Policy," one of the cops said.

"What do you mean, 'policy'?"

But he might as well not have spoken at all. The cops just drove on, one of them hanging on to the mike, though it had been a while since he'd last used it.

"She might be dead already," he said, knowing as he said it that it couldn't be true, but just wanting to make the cops up front squirm. They didn't bat an eye, and once he'd said it, Drew couldn't keep from thinking about it, mulling it over in his mind. Rachel dead.

No. He'd have to have felt it somehow if Rachel had died. She was his mother, after all. He'd have felt something, some sympathy pain, a spurt of it at least. But he hadn't with his dad. Hadn't with Rob. But this was Rachel. Rachel, with whom he'd had many a knockdown drag-out battle. Rachel, who'd bloodied his nose. Rachel, who'd stuck him in Benedict House and split, and Rachel, whom he'd wanted, time and time again, to pound with his fists. Rachel, who wouldn't be in this fucking mess right now if, maybe an hour ago, she'd listened to him, believed him, trusted.

He loved her anyway, that was what it came down to. Loved her despite all the shit.

Zachary had been looking at him and maybe he did know what Drew was thinking. He said, "I understand, son. I do," and gave him that shoulder clap.

Drew decided that Zachary was the kind of guy who would go to any lengths whatsoever to avoid a scene. And so what was he in the middle of? Not just a scene, but a whole high drama. Life and death. Publicity for sure. *Welcome to the family, Zach, old man. Sorry my mom didn't let you in on any of this before.* But shit. Didn't it make him care for Zachary one hell of a lot more?

He thought of a story he'd read a long time before, about a kid and a bunch of guys in a lifeboat. The kid was on watch while a shark cruised the boat all night long. In the morning the kid found out some other guy had been up too. The kid said, "I wish I'd known." Drew felt like he was the kid and Zachary was the guy, only they were both awake and in it together.

"Drew." It was one of the cops, holding out a little headset. "It's our hostage negotiator. He'd like a word with you."

AT FIRST SHE THOUGHT SHE HAD BEEN PARA-lyzed, but then she realized that her hands were tied. She jerked one and then the other and both had been fixed, at the wrist, to one of the struts of the chair.

Peyton had evidently propped her up in the chair while she was still unconscious.

The blow Peyton struck had given Rachel a headache, the sort that changed depending on the way she held her head. Tipped down, she discovered, was the worst: it felt as though the pain oozed forward, like syrup, even filling the sockets of her eyes. Tipped back and slightly to the side felt best. In that position, though, she found herself staring at the huge brown quilt.

Peyton seemed to enjoy that. "Any ideas, Rachel?" she asked, as if this were a parlor game. When Rachel didn't answer, Peyton laughed lightly, as if something clever had been said.

Rachel, meanwhile, wanted to take in the rest of the room, hoped, in fact, to spy some way that she might escape. The pain, though, when she tipped her head forward, made it seem unlikely.

She did catch sight of Peyton's quilting scraps.

"Shall I tell you what you're tied with?" Peyton asked, when she determined what Rachel had just noted. "Blue denim—from my father's overalls, hon. And there's another, a long red piece, the flannel. That was my mother's, uh, nightdress. She had a daydress, too, but she was wearing the, uh, nightdress when . . ." She paused, as if the phrasing were critical.

Rachel, meanwhile, focused on the cloth. Could she feel the denim, distinguish it from the flannel? Would that help to take away the pain? She concentrated, and for the brief moments that it took to do so, her headache went away.

What else could she think to do? What else? Could she resume her taunts, continue to make Peyton jealous? Or would that be especially dangerous now that she was trussed here, tied to the chair, helpless?

Do something, she decided. *Anything. Speak*.

"Peyton," Rachel said, as calmly as she could. "Drew brought a girl with him. A very pretty girl, with wonderful, wonderful hair."

Peyton said nothing.

"Oh, you think I'm making it up, but I'm not. A very beautiful girl, with hair that must come down to, I'd say, her waist. At least to there. Drew has always had girlfriends, even back when he was very very young." She strained to see the reaction her words were having. As far as she could tell, there'd been none. Then she thought of a way to really drive the taunt home. With a burst of inspiration, she said, "Very well-brought-up little girls. Girls who—" "Stop it." Peyton was on her feet and before Rachel in a flash.

Oh, please don't hit me, don't hit me again, Rachel thought. She tried, however, to look neutral or at least not afraid. Her eyes must have widened, however, because at that precise moment, she'd seen something, someone at the cabin window, and though she'd tried not to let Peyton notice, her reaction must have been plain, because Peyton turned swiftly and walked to the cabin door.

Peyton opened the door and listened, but everything was quiet outside. Even the windmill seemed to have stopped. She came back to the table, but let the door stay open wide.

There was daylight, but it wasn't bright. It seemed retarded by the enormity of the brown quilt on the far wall. Rachel hoped for sunlight, hoped, too, for a breeze. In response, the brown quilt seemed to sway— once, twice—but that was all. The windmill didn't turn and the leaves outside didn't rustle and, other than the token back-and-forth, the quilt fell dead still.

THE NEGOTIATOR'S NAME WAS JACK
Shaw. He'd been called at home, which was far
South Austin. "Putting my boots on right this very
minute," he told Drew, grunting for emphasis.
"There. Now as soon as I get in my car and head out
that way, we can continue this little interview of
ours."

Drew found himself wondering if the man used
"little" to reduce the effect of the situation. He wondered what Shaw would look like. He told Shaw
that, yes, it was true that he knew both women, and
that, yes, one of them was his mother.

"Okay," Shaw said. "Put my man back on."

Drew handed the mike back to the officer who had
given it to him. All Drew could hear, though the
channel was open, was the officer answering,
"Right," and "Yes, sir" and "Right" again. Drew
started mimicking him, repeating the replies in a silly
falsetto voice.

The other cop, the driver, turned all the way
around to look at Drew and said, "Ease up, son.
We've been through a lot of these situations and we
know what we're doing. Shaw especially."

"Yeah." Drew spat. "If he ever gets his ass out of
bed and over here."

The cops glanced at each other, but said nothing.
Zachary patted Drew's arm, urging him to lean back
again in the seat, but Drew jerked away. Finally
Drew realized there was nothing else for him to do

and he did lean back, but his breath continued to come hard, come in anger.

BOTH SHE AND PEYTON HEARD IT, THE RUS-tling behind the cabin.

"Raccoons," Peyton said, though she went to the door and looked out more than once. She seemed to be trying to decide whether or not to leave the door ajar.

But the air was much cooler out of doors. It was as if the cabin had gathered and compressed the air that was inside, making it close to unbreatheable. With the door open, the stale air had begun to leak out. It would seem even more unbearable if Peyton were to shut the door again.

But Peyton looked at Rachel as though she suspected that now it was fully light outside, Rachel might flee. *Fat chance*, Rachel felt like saying. What did Peyton think she was? Some sort of amazon? Someone like . . . a comic-book character ages and ages ago . . . Wonder Woman? Did Peyton think that Rachel was Wonder Woman?

Rachel heard herself laugh lightly at the thought. *My God, I'm hysterical.* She righted herself and stopped.

Peyton had given her a stern look. Now she walked over to an old treadle sewing machine against one of the cabin walls.

She pulled each of the drawers out in turn, as though looking for something. Then she stood and let her eyes fall closed. It seemed an invocation, but it was only some mnemonic method. Finally she remembered where whatever she sought might be.

Rachel, meanwhile, tried to occupy herself with

whatever would chase the pain in her head away. She
tried quilt patterns again, and that, too, made her laugh.
"Hand of Friendship," she told Peyton, "Hand of
Friendship has other names, ugly names, Bear's Claw
and Duck's Foot, and..." Her laughter resumed until
Peyton found what she'd been looking for and held it up
before her.

A child's dress, a terribly poor child's dress, a dress
made from a sack, a scratchy brown burlap. "It was
mine," Peyton said. "I was sent to school in this dress.
Imagine it," and she scraped the fabric against Rachel's
cheek.

"You would never have guessed, would you, Rachel?
No, never." She dropped the dress and began to sift
through the fabric scraps she'd earlier poured onto the
tabletop. "No, you associate me more with these." She
raised the pieces, let them sift through her fingers.
"Blue silk, red voile, or, here, even this muslin. This
finespun dotted swiss."

Had Rachel imagined it or did it seem that Peyton's
voice had cracked? A hint of remorse? A ray of hope?

"I'll miss you, Rachel," Peyton said. "I really will.
That's the hardest part, I think. I hadn't expected to...
to like you."

"Then why are you doing this?" Rachel asked, her
voice so frail, so thin. "Why?"

Peyton looked surprised. "To free Drew," she said, as
if she were repeating some well-known truth. "To free
Drew. Why else?"

A tear rolled down Rachel's cheek, and her nose felt
drippy, too. It was incredibly annoying not to be able to
lift her hand and wipe her nose and the tear, and she
sniffled, thinking all the while how remarkable it was to
concentrate on something like a runny nose or an un-
wiped tear when your death sentence had just been pro-
nounced.

And Peyton noticed her discomfort. Peyton took a small blue square and let Rachel blow her nose in it, much as a parent might. She dropped the square to the ground when Rachel had finished.

Rachel determined not to cry anymore. She wondered what time it was. She'd dressed so hurriedly, dressed for flight. God, it seemed a month ago. Had she her watch? Rachel couldn't remember and focused on trying to feel her wrist, trying to determine whether or not her watch was there upon it. It was a good distraction, one of the best that she'd contrived. She focused on it so completely that when Peyton spoke, it startled her.

"Typical hazy gray Austin morning," Peyton said companionably, as if they were sitting on the balcony of the Stephen F. Austin Hotel overlooking the morning traffic. Sipping thick black coffee and waiting for a croissant.

"The sun will burn it off," Rachel told her, thinking, *God, we are both crazy, both of us stark raving mad.*

THEY RENDEZVOUSED WITH SHAW IN the parking lot of a U-Totem. Shaw had called for someone who was supposed to be the staff psychiatrist, but Drew had nixed that, saying that he wouldn't even stay there if a shrink—any shrink— got involved. After all, wasn't that what Peyton had been at Benedict House, more or less? Uh-uh. He would keep his distance from any head-messing types.

Zachary took Shaw aside and mumbled with him and then they went inside the U-Totem and came out with a box of doughnuts and enough coffee to go around.

The five of them, Shaw and the two cops and Zachary and Drew, fell into silence, and the one who broke it was Shaw, talking to Drew. "So this nut who's got your mom, she was your teacher, right?"

"Right," Drew said.

"What'd she teach?"

"Psychodrama," he said.

"Psychodrama," Shaw repeated, and he looked over at Zachary, but Zachary didn't look back. Shaw continued, "All right, Drew. You tell us about psychodrama, okay? You tell us what went on there. And, wait a minute, where was this? What school?"

"Benedict House." He saw Shaw lift his eyebrows when he said it, but he knew he had to.

"In Corpus?" Shaw asked. And when Drew nodded yes, Shaw called the two cops who had driven Drew and Zachary out there over. "Get on the phone to Corpus. Benedict House. Start building a dossier on this—what was her full name, son?"

PEYTON SWEPT THE FABRIC SWATCHES OFF the table in one motion. Rachel couldn't help but gasp. Didn't the pieces mean anything to her after all? Or was that just a symbol, a sort of obliteration of the past? *I carried mine with me,* Rachel thought proudly, thinking of how when she'd fled Kingsville, she'd carried her scrap bag—her history—along.

Then Rachel saw why the table had been brushed clean. Peyton had pulled the photos of Rob dying down from the wall and was setting them, as one might deal a game of solitaire, down in front of Rachel.

Rachel couldn't keep from looking at them, and Peyton laughed at this, but Rachel couldn't stop. She had tears in her eyes, though, and that blurred them somewhat. They weren't blurred in her memory, though.

She wondered how she'd known, looking at the snapshots, precisely the circumstances under which they'd been taken. How she'd known Rob had just seen Peyton, and how she'd known he was dying and then how she'd known he was dead.

She couldn't remember if she'd known how he'd died, and there hadn't been any blood, only in that final photograph, there'd been a kind of puffiness about his face and arms and a sort of foaminess around his mouth, as though saliva had built up there and now was seeping out.

Rachel shivered at the thought, but couldn't stop thinking it. Dared she ask Peyton? Peyton didn't seem to have a weapon, after all. No knife, no gun, not anything of the sort.

Those strips of cloth, Rachel supposed, could be used to strangle someone, but if Rob had been strangled, wouldn't the photographs show it, bruises or something?

How was she planning to do it? With her bare hands? Even with Peyton's strength, Rachel knew she couldn't have overpowered Rob or any reasonable-sized man with her bare hands.

And anyway, you would have to hate somebody an awful awful lot to kill with your bare hands.

SHAW AND DREW ARGUED ABOUT STRAT-
egy, but only briefly. "Look," Shaw told him, "the
decision is mine, pure and simple." His notion was
to advance upon the scene, announce his presence
and that of what he called his "assault team," and
then keep Peyton and Rachel in there as long as he
could.

Drew thought it was crazy.

And to his credit, so did Zachary.

But Shaw insisted it was not just theory, it had
been tested and proved time and time again. "The
longer people are together, the less chance there is of
any of 'em getting hurt."

Drew was about to say, *Listen, dickhead*, when
Zachary intervened. "Let me remind you," he said,
"that in this case the women have been together, so to
speak, ever since I've known Rachel. Peyton has been
pretending to be Rachel's friend."

"Exactly," said Drew, glad his obscenity had been
intercepted.

Zachary repeated the stuff about the Trump family
murders and how he was certain that Peyton had
been the one survivor—which to his mind meant the
murderer.

"Jesus," Shaw said. "Jesus God Almighty." He had
already sent one of the cops off in search of information about the Trumps, but then he turned to Zachary and he said, "Hey, listen. Do you remember how
those people were murdered?"

"Poisoned, I think." Zachary cast a worried glance

239

at Drew. He didn't seem to think it right that Drew should overhear this, though indeed he was of age. On the other hand, most poisons were slow-acting, which might mean that Rachel, even if already given whatever substance Peyton might use, could survive.

"Poisoned," Shaw said, as if mocking Zachary's assessment. "Jesus sweet..." He turned back to Drew, as though only considering what had been the very first thing Drew had told him. "Your father. Down in Galveston—" He broke off, as if there wasn't sufficient time for him to complete the thought. "Hank!" he called to the cop. "Get me Galveston. Hurry it up!" To Zachary and Drew he said, "Poison, yes, but if I remember it right, it was a real special kind. Real special, all right."

RACHEL HAD TO URINATE. WOULD PEYTON let her? Was there a bathroom? She looked around the cabin, but couldn't see one. There was just the one big room.

Peyton noticed Rachel looking from side to side, but didn't ask Rachel what she wanted. Rachel felt desolate. As if ignored by someone to whom she'd hoped to matter.

Then Peyton sighed and stood. She gathered up the photos and laid them aside. "I guess it's time," she told Rachel brightly, and she stepped outside.

Rachel listened, heard Peyton disappear in the direction of the car, and then sure enough, after an interval, heard the car door open, then shut again.

Peyton stood in the doorway with a large woven basket on one hip. The basket had a lid and a long strap, as a shoulder bag might. Framed there, Peyton looked like a model in the pages of *Vogue*.

The Indian Motif, Rachel found herself thinking, looking at Peyton's sandals, her gauzy dress, the bright raffia basket at her side. *She looks so sane,* Rachel thought. It was an alarming realization, that someone who looked as stylish as Peyton could walk around, be talked to, admired, and yet be crazy. She'd always thought that crazy people went uncombed and un-washed, but not Peyton. Model, indeed.

And, like a model still, after Peyton was examined for a sufficiently long period, she came forward, grace-fully, and laid the basket on the table where the scraps and the pictures of Rob had been.

For a brief moment, Rachel thought the basket held food. Breakfast. Perhaps the very croissants she'd thought of earlier.

Peyton flipped the lid up and peered inside, frown-ing, concentrating. Then she thrust both hands in quickly, and when she pulled them forth, she held a long brown snake, maybe just a little thicker than a garden hose.

Rachel watched in fear and fascination as Peyton shifted the bulk of the snake under her and behind her body. The long tail thrashed there irritably, then came to curl around Peyton's waist. The head of the snake Pey-ton trapped between a thumb and forefinger.

One hand was free now. She used it to lift the basket away, leaving the table bare again.

"I want you to meet Rachel," Peyton said very softly to the snake. Its eyes seemed to move or at least to blink. And its tongue flickered too. Peyton held it close to Rachel's face, so close that it seemed doubled in Ra-chel's vision.

"You'll be kind to Rachel, won't you? Won't you? For a while?" Then, "Good boy," and she used her free

hand to uncoil the snake's length from her waist so that
she could place it down on the table.

The snake wrapped itself around her arm instead,
around and around and around. It seemed to ripple as it
did so, its color changing from one brown to another
and another still. When it whirled, Rachel could see its
underside. The scales there gleamed, as if made of
ivory.

Patiently, Peyton began to unwrap it again, determined to have it rest on the table she had bared. But the
snake, with implicit power, like a fist clenching and un-
clenching, resisted.

THEY WERE AT THE FOOT OF THE CA-
liche driveway now. They had been joined by four
men dressed in camouflage who had driven up in a
plain gray van. Shaw talked to them briefly, drawing
on a sheet of foolscap. The men all crowded around
to take a look and then began examining the drawing
singly, passing it from one man to the next.

Drew wanted to see, but was afraid they would
jerk it away if he reached for it. He decided to spare
himself the possible embarrassment, though he hoped
against hope that Zachary would approach the group
and take the sheet, because he doubted they would do
anything to insult him.

He was about to suggest this to Zachary when he,
and the others, too, heard the sound of someone running, feet slapping muddy ground and coming toward them.

They all tensed. Drew stepped forward, and he
was the only one, the only one who dared to move,

because he knew who it had to be, it had to be the moonfaced girl. It meant she hadn't hitchhiked to safety, but instead had followed the drive where Peyton's car had turned and had holed up there. Maybe she knew he'd come back, or maybe she just hoped it. The moonfaced girl. Gwendolyn.

She seemed to be running with her eyes closed, running *at* them, not *to* them. She must have seen, though, because she came right toward Drew, fell in his arms, coughed and gagged and cried. And she kept trying to say something, but no one could understand, and he held the girl and rocked her and shooshed her until finally she was able to tell them she had seen Drew's mother, tied, in a cabin, with Peyton holding sway. Then she began to babble again, and it sounded like she was saying, "It's a snake, it's a snake, I saw it, saw it, but it's . . ." before she broke down and became incomprehensible.

Drew had to shoosh her and pat her and rock her for a long time before they could be sure about what she'd said. After this, the briefing continued. "Okay," Shaw said. "So there are two women in there, and, we think, a snake. We want you to shoot to kill," he joked. "You guess which one."

"A snake. Oh, shit," one of the guys in camo said.

"Hey, don't complain, Bubba," another joked. "At least this time we get to take somebody out."

"Hey, all right," a third added.

"Okay, now listen." Shaw had waited patiently while the men had bantered. "This one with the punk haircut, kind of crewcut up on top? According to all we have here, she is totally, but totally bananas. We have to get the other woman out of there first, because this snake might still be in there, see? And it may be that the crazy one is the only one who can control it."

"Are we talking rattler, Sarge?" one of the two men in uniform, the ones Drew and Zachary had driven out with, called out.

"We think so. We don't know for sure. The report on the Trumps said rattlesnake venom had killed them, and it would make sense, a rattler, up here." He gestured at the terrain. "Galveston medical hasn't reported back yet." He glanced at his watch "Probably too early for them," he muttered. "So just go up there quiet as you can and get positioned, okay?" He looked up at the sky and spoke to no one in particular. "All we need now is the goddam Channel 24 helicopter out here before our boys get set." Then he spoke to one of the officers in conventional uniforms. "Call Channel 24. Tell them if that chopper of theirs comes anywhere near this scene we'll blow them out of the fucking sky."

Drew stayed near Zachary, and he didn't quite know why. He asked, "Did you know about the snake thing?" He meant with the Trumps.

Zachary shook his head that he hadn't known, and for a moment Drew felt sorry for him, as if, until that moment, he'd gone unchallenged as the font of all necessary information. He had to keep in mind, though, that this wasn't any kind of silly competition, like a Trivial Pursuit game. This was, as far as his mom was concerned, life and death. Still, not knowing about the rattlesnake thing, that was a biggie, unless it was part of the information the police always claim to withhold so they can know when they're talking to the true killer and not just some asshole who confesses to things.

"Stay nearby, boy," Shaw told Drew. "You're my only negotiating point."

"That's nice to know," Drew said sarcastically. It

was out of his mouth before he had a chance to think about it, but Shaw didn't seem to mind.

Shaw and the other cops made Drew kind of more or less relax in that, however awful the situation, they acted like it was no big deal. They even joked around a lot, like that stuff about getting to blow someone away.

"This the weirdest one you been on?" Shaw asked a uniform, but out loud, so that everyone could hear. The uniform said it was. "Not me," Shaw said. "Weirdest one for me was a call we got about a guy who was throwing feces at people." He waited for the effect. "So we go in, and sure enough, here's this seven-foot guy, stark naked, just giggling and throwing feces out the window."

"Where was this?" a cop asked.

"Over on Duval."

"Whose feces was it?" the cop wanted to know. He used the word "feces" naturally, the way policemen say "vehicle" rather than "car."

"His own, man. He'd been saving it up. Anyway, we took him in, and when we get him to the jail, he tries to kill himself. Guess how?" Shaw waited. "I'll tell you how. He bites—get that, bites—his wrists open. Got an artery, too. Weirdest thing I ever saw in my life."

Everyone was quiet, thinking about it. Then one of the cops said, "Yeah, well, I had a guy over in Guadalupe. He had this storekeeper, you know? Anyway, when I came in there and started talking to the guy, he reaches in his pants and I thought, *Oh, no.* But he pulls out a bunch of Twinkies. Guy had stuffed like twenty Hostess Twinkies down his pants."

They all, Drew and Zachary included, laughed. Before they could start thinking that maybe this was

some kind of picnic, though, Shaw had the camouflage guys moving up the drive and he and the men in
uniform had moved away a bit, their expressions
sober now.

PEYTON MANAGED TO IMPOSE HER WILL UPON
the snake, peeling it away until finally she was able to
flop it onto the table, where it wound itself up in a way
that seemed to Rachel haughty and arrogant.

For a long time the snake just lay there in a heap.
After the initial shock, Rachel was able to retain a sem-
blance of calm by concentrating on the fact that she had
to go to the bathroom and couldn't. She felt much as she
had in grade school, waiting for recess. Or so she told
herself.

She knew the snake was not a rattler. Like anyone
living in Texas, Rachel had seen rattlers, often saw them
dead on the road, smashed by a car in the act of crossing. Recently, she'd seen one dead on the pavement in
front of a tract house under construction. No, this was
not the fearsome rattlesnake.

That fact raised in Rachel something like contempt
for Peyton. As if Peyton thought that she, Rachel, was
so easy to intimidate that she could dump a snake—any
old snake—onto a table top and expect Rachel to die of
fear.

Peyton watched Rachel, watched the thoughts as they
flickered in procession across her face.

Peyton walked around the table until she stood di-
rectly in front of the snake's head. She leaned forward,
flicking her fingers in the snake's direction. Its tail
flapped, then flapped again, and then, so suddenly that

it ought to have been accompanied by a loud, whooshing sound, the front of the snake rose up at least two feet, and, in the same swift motion, an enormous hood unfurled about its head.

A cobra.

Rachel felt a few drops of urine hot between her legs. She concentrated, concentrated, hoping those would not be followed by a gush.

Peyton, meanwhile, swayed in front of the cobra, and it swayed with her. It seemed they were dancing.

Rachel's bladder held, but the pressure was greater than Rachel had ever felt.

Peyton laughed and bent forward from the waist until her own head was but an inch in front of the cobra's. Then, unbelievably, she kissed the cobra on the flat of its head, and darted back. "The kiss of death," she breathed, as if the act had excited her tremendously. "My daddy taught me that. Of course, he didn't have a cobra, he'd just heard about it. My daddy's specialty was rattlers. It was the one good thing he taught me."

While she spoke, the snake seemed to search for her, search for the source of the sound.

Her face drew into a pout, and she looked down at her feet. The snake, meanwhile, stayed upright, poised to strike. It wove slowly back and forth, as if Peyton were still guiding its movement somehow. It was rhythmic and hypnotically regular. Rachel wondered if perhaps it was the snake that charmed the charmers rather than the reverse.

"He used to do it for money," Peyton said. "Imagine that. All this land he could have sold and that's what he'd do for money. Wouldn't listen to me. Said I was too young, and a girl to boot. And then one day he said maybe I wasn't too young at that, but he didn't mean my giving him advice, I can tell you that."

The snake withdrew its hood, dropped down into a heap again. Peyton didn't seem to notice.

"The filthy son of a bitch," Peyton said. "Smelled like a goat. Fucked like a billy, too. And they all knew. My sisters and my brothers, and my mama, too. Hell, I told my mama.

"One night they were drunk as coots. My daddy and my mama, and I'd even made sure the young ones got their fill, so that they were, every last one of them, tanked up, too.

"And I tied every one of them up, just the way I've tied you. And I waited until daybreak, when they were more or less sober. And I came in with my daddy's snakes and I said, 'Hey, look how good I learned how to do this. Look what I can do.'"

She reached down and clasped the cobra again at the point behind its head. She let its tail lash about and then she caught it, led its length along so that it coiled several times around her throat.

She laughed at the efffect the display was having upon Rachel. "They were just as wide-eyed as you," she said. "Really, you should see yourself." She held the snake's head up beside her own, and narrowed her eyes as if in imitation of it. Whether it was a trick of her imagination or not, Rachel thought that Peyton's features seemed more angular of a sudden, her hairline, the shape of her nose, the intensity in her eyes.

Peyton was delighted by Rachel's reactions, whatever they were. Once again, she laid the snake upon the table alone. This time the snake went willingly, even letting Peyton arrange its body in whatever way she wished.

But the snake's eyes were trained upon Rachel.

Rachel felt the press of her bladder again. At the same time, she had a sense of being unable to breathe. She gathered her courage and tried to clear her throat, hoping that Peyton, more than the snake, wouldn't notice.

The snake burst upright and unfurled its hood again, staring right at Rachel. Then, with an enormous dipping motion, it turned its back to her. Rachel gasped and even tried to stand though she was tied to the chair at the sight that was before her.

The pattern on the reverse side of the cobra's hood repeated the pattern on the wall, repeated the quilt pattern, the deepset oval eyes and the sad upturned grin. What was more, Rachel suddenly knew where else she'd seen it: on the mask that Peyton had been carrying, the mask she'd used to frighten Rachel at the store.

"Naja naja," Peyton chanted. "He turns his back to warn."

Rachel listened, knowing then that it was what Peyton had been doing, warning her, warning her away.

"Naja naja," Peyton went on, like the sound of rattles and drums. "Naja naja warns you, warns you stay away. Death awaits if you don't heed."

Were these the words of an ancient prayer or poem? Rachel didn't know. She watched as Peyton knelt on the ground where the snake, its back to Rachel, could see. Peyton leaned back and the snake withdrew its hood, lowered itself, and slithered across the table and onto Peyton's chest.

Despite herself, Rachel leaned forward to watch. Then the snake wound itself off Peyton's body and down to the floor.

Peyton grabbed the snake and tossed it unceremoniously back into the basket. "All right," she said to Rachel. "If there's one thing I can't have, it's you smelling up the place the way they did."

Rachel must have looked puzzled. Peyton explained that she was going to let Rachel go to the bathroom.

She untied Rachel's hands. "Did your daddy ever fuck you, Rachel?" she asked.

Rachel winced and said no.

"I didn't think so. They talk statistics and you'd think that, when they do, nearly everybody's daddy did, but when I ask anyone, they tell me no. What about your mama, Rachel? What do you think your mama would have done if your daddy was fucking you and your mama knew?"

Peyton's voice, Rachel noticed, had taken on a decided country cadence. For the first time since she'd met Peyton, she could clearly see the background she'd come out of. *Yesterday,* Rachel thought, *I would have said "risen above."* But what was worse? Murder would be worse than incest, wouldn't it? "I'm so sorry, Peyton," she said sincerely. "I'm sorry that I never knew and couldn't help and . . ." What? Peyton's was another world, unlike anything she, Rachel, had ever known.

Suddenly it seemed to Rachel that Drew's upbringing had, by comparison, been as wholesome and clean as any sitcom kid's had been.

"My daddy even used me in his act," Peyton went on. "Let the goddam rattlers climb between my legs. That was a big trick of his, his favorite part of the show. Make me lie down on the ground and lift my dress up and spread my legs and then out would come those rattlers of his and they'd be all over me. Long as you stay real still they won't bite.

"It's funny how a kid thinks, too. I used to worry about my underpants looking clean and even after my mama had washed them, I'd take them down to Bull Creek and do them again. As if the rattlers or the people would care."

She told Rachel how her father had placed signs on the highway announcing the snake show. Not too many cars, but enough, came up the long caliche drive.

Maybe word even got around. Then Peyton's eyes filled with tears. "You'd think after those damned rattlers, that dick of his wouldn't have made much difference. Isn't that what you'd think?"

"Why didn't you just run away?" Rachel asked. But hadn't she herself, and recently, thought of killing Drew? In defense of herself, but, really, wasn't that what Peyton had done too?

"Running wasn't enough," Peyton said. "I wanted them to suffer and I wanted them to die. I got strong, watching them die, Rachel. I can't tell you how good it felt. Their death was, I don't know, a kind of gift to my spirit, my self. I had, all of a sudden, this power!

"I had thought about it so many times, thought about it while the snakes were crawling all over me, and that particular night, I laid there and listened to my folks start breathing in a way that told me they were asleep.

"There were eight of them in all, and that's how many of my daddy's snakes I brought in. Eight, all at once.

"I wore the snakes on my body, Rachel, and I came into the house and I laid each rattler down like it was a present or something. I gave my daddy Striker, who was the meanest one, the one who'd strike at nothing, and, as a matter of fact, he did strike my daddy's arm before I got the next snake from around me and down near my mama. Good old Striker, didn't rattle, didn't do anything but bite.

"Daddy was so drunk, he was struck three times before he came to and knew what had hit him, but by then I had all the snakes down in place, and when the rest of them woke up, it was strike, strike, strike, the whole place hissing with the sound of them and one or two slithering across the floor and away.

"I don't know how long it was until they were all unconscious but I watched them as long as I could and then I had to go out in the woods and let myself be found, you know, 'Girl Escapes Murderer's Clutches,' or whatever they said about me, I don't recall.

"They thought it had been done by devil worshipers, I believe. Devil worshipers." She laughed. "It was this gift, this power, this coming-into-one's-self that I wanted Drew to know."

Rachel found herself wondering if Peyton's relationship with Drew had been sexual. Somehow, she didn't think so. Perhaps it was that in all the while she'd known Peyton she'd never known her to go out with a man. That hadn't seemed strange until now, possibly because Rachel herself had lived much the same way. Then, too, the new knowledge about Peyton's father also made it seem unlikely that Peyton would have anything physical to do with a man. Or perhaps it was simply that Rachel didn't want it to be so; didn't want her son to be involved with a woman like Peyton, who could eradicate even the tiny bit of sympathy Rachel had begun to feel.

Peyton handed Rachel a white bone-china chamber pot, and difficult though it was to poise herself in an ungainly stoop, Rachel managed somehow.

"Finished?" Peyton asked.

She had remained between Rachel and the cabin door. Now she told Rachel to turn around, and she grabbed Rachel's hands and jerked her wrists together, winding a strip of fabric around and around and around them.

Must do something, Rachel thought. *Must*. But even as she thought it, the press of the bindings told her she had thought it far too late. "My circulation," she said. "You're cutting off my circulation."

In response, Peyton merely shouldered Rachel back into the chair.

HE WOULD HAVE TO HURRY. AS HE'D
slipped off into the brush, he'd heard Shaw ask the
others, "Hey, where's the boy?" Well, if he was a
negotiating point, he was going to do just that, and a
lot sooner than those asshole cops had in mind. He'd
get away with it, too. Even if Shaw had been able to
radio the assault team, what were they going to do?
Shoot him down? And they couldn't very well intercept him, either. Not if they didn't want their presence to be known.

But they *were* trying to intercept. Shaw and Zachary and now the girl were in the car driving up the
caliche road, creeping right along, as though they expected to be able to see him off in the brush.

Christ, he was sure they'd hear him breathing, so
extreme had his burst of speed been.

He stood perfectly still and waited until they'd
gone by. There was a bend in the road up ahead, and
he knew they'd have to stop there. When they did, he
pounded forward, pounded on. He tried to breathe in
rhythm to his strides, but he found that his strides
came much faster than his breath could.

He wondered, though it didn't slow his progress
any, what his life would be like now were he to move
back in with Rachel and, hey, maybe even Zachary,
too. He'd have a mom and dad, like those old shows
on TV. *Leave It to Beaver*, that was one of them. He
was too old to be the Beav. He'd be Wally, and
Zachary would be Ward and Rachel could be whatever the name of Beaver's mother was.

Except that he was too old to be Wally, too, and he

was too old to be even himself and be living back with them. Still, maybe he could live close by, maybe see them once in a while. He and the girl, maybe, could set up together in an apartment or something.

He raised an arm, wiped the stinging sweat that was dripping down into his eyes. Went on.

Of course the girl's rich shit father wouldn't let her, probably. Gwendolyn. What an ugly goddam name. No wonder she hadn't told him what it was.

Maybe he could get the girl to stand up to that father of hers, say "Fuck you, daddy," and then they could get a place of their own. She liked Austin, she'd said so.

That would be better than picking up again with Rachel, even if he hadn't been too old for it. It seemed to him that every single time they'd have an argument he'd resolve not to have another one, and then, every single time, they would. As though neither of them—and it was not just him, it was Rachel, too—as though neither of them could be in the same room together for five fucking minutes without a fight breaking out.

That probably hadn't changed.

Except that he loved Rachel, he'd admitted it, he'd said it out loud. If you loved someone, you didn't fight with them all of the time, did you? Did you?

He had a pain in his side, a stitch, he remembered someone calling such a pain. He would have to stop. Have to stop. He leaned against a tree and rubbed at the spot where the pain was even though it didn't help. Then, when it was muted, he moved on. He was running tired now, he knew. He hadn't paced himself, had gone all out, and now he regretted it. Still, he'd had to get away from the cops, and it looked as if he had.

Then, boom: he saw the house. There was a clearing between the patch of woods where he stood and it. Were there guys in the trees, the guys in camo fatigues, with guns? He didn't know. He only knew that Peyton, crazy Peyton, Paula, whatever she was calling herself, was in there, and she had Rachel.

He remembered how weird Peyton had been. She used to come to the doorway of his room while she thought he was asleep and just stand there, the hall light silhouetting her, just stand there, watching him. That was how he'd recognized her shape, he'd seen it often enough, the outline of it. The oddest thing was, he didn't want to fuck her brains out, the way he might have some other girl, he just didn't, never even once. No fantasies, no nothing.

But her standing there like that. He'd asked around, kind of felt the other guys out, and she hadn't done that shit with anyone else.

But he was special. She kept telling him that throughout. He was special and she was going to free him, she was giving him some kind of gift, she said.

Once she came to his door with a kind of cape on. He pretended to be asleep as usual. She started reciting some kind of crazy prayer: *O spread your hooded watch for the safety of our slumbers*, something like that, he didn't remember the rest. Weird Paula.

Where were the guys Shaw had dispatched out here? Like, why couldn't they use gas? Just toss a couple canisters of tear gas in there and drive his mom and Peyton outside. Then they could grab Peyton and he could grab his mom.

Shaw didn't know what he was doing, that was what. Shaw didn't know and as a result his mother might die unless he, Drew, did something about it right now.

PEYTON KNELT AT RACHEL'S FEET AND RE-
moved her shoes. She'd brought a bowl of water that
smelled of camphor and she placed Rachel's filthy feet
in the bowl, splashing the water up along Rachel's
ankles.

The camphor was cool and Rachel was almost
tempted to let Peyton continue, but she knew she
couldn't, knew she had to act at once.

But even under the circumstances, it wasn't easy. She
remembered hearing about women who held back, even
when fighting a rapist or a murderer, and now she understood, because it was difficult for a normal person to
contemplate striking a blow with all of her might. But
she had to, she had to, she steeled herself and drew her
feet slightly back and then forced them upward, toes
pointed, as hard as she could.

She upset the bowl and caught Peyton square in the
jaw. She also managed to tip over the chair in which she
was sitting, and she just was able to tilt her head forward so that her shoulder hit the ground harder than the
rest of her. She lay there, feeling as though she'd at least
put Peyton out of commission. But suddenly Peyton was
hovering over her again.

Peyton knelt down next to her and stared with cold
ugly eyes. *If my hands were free*, Rachel thought, *I
would claw her face to ribbons, tear those eyes out with
my fingernails, stretch her mouth with my hands, pull
her hair and her nose and drum my fists down on her,
down down, hard as I can.*

But she *was* tied.

Peyton stood and even dared to step across Rachel as

she lay there contemplating her hatred and wondering how best to unleash it. Peyton, meanwhile, picked up the basket, removed its lid, and turned it onto its side. Slowly, rhythmically, the cobra emerged.

It propelled itself across the room toward Peyton, who had begun to move away from it. Now she froze, watching the snake with admiration. "Naja naja," she chanted, and lay down, prostrating herself before the snake.

The snake seemed to dance before her in response.

Rachel, behind the snake, stared at the clown's face on the back of its hood, the same face that decorated the quilt on the wall. She stretched her toes forward and groped with them, trying to keep from making any obvious movements and yet at the same time hoping to find something, anything, that might serve as a weapon or distraction or both.

The snake circled Peyton, and Peyton lifted her head and smiled at it. Then the cobra turned, moved toward Rachel, who was helpless on her side. Rachel closed her eyes, but found that was scarier still. She opened them again, horrified to note that even a movement that slight had drawn the snake to its full hooded height.

She tried not to blink lest the snake strike. Tried.

Peyton edged out of range. She picked up a handful of scraps and began to drop them, causing the cobra to poke toward each one as it fell. Brown snake swaying amid falling bits of bright green and red and blue and pink and orange falling like enormous flower petals.

Rachel felt she was slipping into something like delirium. It looked so pretty; the colors, the wafting fall, and the brown snake swaying, his clown face shifting ever so slightly, ever so—

A voice from outside. Drew's voice. "Hey, I'm here."

"He's here!" Peyton leaped to her feet. Then she grew

wary, as if it weren't Drew at all, but some impostor sent to trap her.

"Hey, listen," the voice continued, closer. "See if you remember this poem."

Peyton tensed. Even the cobra seemed to wait.

"'O spread your hooded watch . . .'" Drew began.

"'. . . for the safety of our slumbers,'" Peyton joined him, so that what Rachel heard seemed a chorus, from without and within.

Then Drew's voice stopped, while Peyton's went on excitedly, "And soothe,'"—she looked down at Rachel and whispered, as if confessing to something—"'the troubled longings that clamor in our breasts.'"

PEYTON CAME TO THE DOOR AND POSED there, arms stretched out on either side, touching the frame with her hands.

He felt a momentary revulsion, the same that Zachary had described and that he, earlier, had remembered. He would have to overcome it. To save his mom, he would have to. "I missed you," he said.

She cocked her head to one side, as if she found the statement curious or doubtful.

Easy, easy, don't do anything wrong, that might spook her. "Your hair," he said, touching his own. "You changed it."

She said nothing.

"I like it," he went on. "Doesn't look very Indian, though. Not the way that long pigtail thing did."

"You remember that about me," she said.

"Well, sure."

He was listening for the sound of a rifle being

cocked, something, anything, that would indicate Shaw's boys were on the job. He heard nothing, not one thing.

"My mom in there?" he asked.

Peyton nodded, yes.

"Is she ready?" he asked. He wasn't quite sure what that meant, but he figured that Peyton's answer would tell him if Rachel was dead or alive.

"Yes, yes, yes," she said, her eyes lighting up as though now, only now, did she really believe it was Drew.

"You told me I had to deal with her, remember? Put her away. Kill her, you know. Then, you said, I'd really be free."

"Yes." She let one hand fall to her side, and the other she extended toward him.

Then he knew. The rifles were up there, all right, up there and aimed, but they hadn't fired because she was in the doorway. They were afraid, and rightly so, of shooting into the house.

He had to get her out in the open, where they could take her.

"Come," she said, gesturing back toward the cabin. *Don't go in there*, that much he knew. "No, baby, you come," he said. He hooked his thumbs in his belt hooks and puffed out his chest. He felt like the biggest asshole in the world, but he still thought there was a chance it might work. "You come to me."

Peyton turned as if she were reentering the cabin, but she stopped once she was able to see inside. Then she focused again on Drew. "And if I do, will you come back with me? Will we watch Rachel die together?"

He swallowed. "Sure," he said, with as much swagger in his voice as he could manage.

"And once she's dead, Drew, anything is possible.

We can do anything, you'll see, and we will, too. We'll have money and time and we'll be free."

"That's right, baby. And all you've got to do is come to me."

THE COBRA SEEMED TO HAVE LOST INTEREST. It dropped again and began slithering down along her side.

She could feel the snake's motion through her clothing as it moved, glided, beside her. What she felt was not fear, but a sense of relief. It was the cobra in its hooded form that was to be feared. The cobra in repose was no threat at all.

Still, when the snake moved past the cuff of her jeans and brushed against the bare flesh of her ankle, Rachel jerked involuntarily.

And the snake bobbed up, swelled, and struck.

HE CASUALLY UNDID THE TOP BUTTON on his jeans. "Come on now," he said, "you know what you need." He wasn't even thinking about being an asshole anymore, about how this must look. All his concentration was on one thing: getting Peyton out into the open.

And the bad part was, he wasn't at all sure he'd taken the right tack. After all, she'd never made a move on him, never at any time. Maybe what she had was a misguided mother thing. Shit, what if that was it? She wanted to mother him, not fuck him at all.

Well, then, hadn't he just messed up everything?

Except that she looked down at his crotch and when she did that, he knew his first choice—his instinct—had been the right one.

He moved his hips a little bit, back and forth. "Come on, baby. Come on."

She stepped out into the clearing.

THE SNAKE BIT AND HELD AND SEEMED TO chew at the flesh above Rachel's ankle. At first there had been no pain and Rachel had only stared and watched as the soft pink inside of the serpent's mouth closed down upon her. As it thrashed and clung to her, however, there was pain, a series of pains like little shock waves starting at her skin and then extending down deep throughout her foot as a whole. Rachel kicked at the snake with her other leg, but the cobra hung on, thrashing, chewing, pouring its poison into her.

It seemed minutes before she was able to scream.

HE BOLTED FORWARD AT THE SOUND OF Rachel's voice. A shot had cracked through the air and stopped Peyton where she stood like a freeze-frame, arms spread, hair flying, mouth an anguished O.

She crumpled, and Drew leaped right over her through the cabin door.

There was his mother, on her side, arms tied behind her back. A huge brown snake was clinging to her leg. There was blood, blood running over her ankle and even, it seemed, smeared a little on the thrashing snake.

He grabbed the snake behind the head, and he squeezed for all he was worth. He squeezed even though the tail of the snake whipped about him, whipped his face and his arms and whipped his back.

He felt as though the fucking snake's innards ought to come squeezing out like toothpaste through its mouth, but that didn't happen.

The snake's mouth was open, all right, and he could see not just its bloody fangs but some little teeth, bloody too. The whipping got lighter, less furious, and Drew in a burst of inspiration put its head down on the floor and then closed the heel of his shoe right down on it and didn't let it go, didn't let it go, didn't let it . . .

"Drew?"

There was blood all over the floor and blood seeping through his shoe and there were snake guts everywhere.

He could smell all that now, all of a sudden, and the smell made him feel as if he'd puke.

Then he realized that the moonfaced girl was there. "Get out of here," he said softly. "Hey, really. Do."

His mom was on the floor, her hands untied now. They'd draped something over her leg. It looked like an old piece of patchwork, an antique. They'd tried to tear the big brown cobra quilt off the wall for her, but she'd gone completely nutso over that, or so Shaw said, anyway, while they were getting his mom more comfortable. She was very very still. They told her that to move could spread the venom faster.

Her eyes though had flitted around and around the room until they'd landed on him. *Eyes do talk*, he thought. Hers were talking then. He started to walk over to her and was startled to find that he barely could hobble.

Shaw gave him a man-to-man punch in the arm and said, "You'll be going with her, son. To take care of that foot." Drew looked down stupidly at his shoe and saw that it was torn and bloody. Had the cobra bitten him? He didn't know. If it had, he doubted that it had any more of its poison to spend. Against his will he remembered how the snake had clung to his mother.

Zachary was beside his mom, but she was looking past Zachary, looking, still looking, at him. Drew limped over to her. Shaw was saying something about how both his and his mom's were just extremity wounds, as if neither one of them had a problem in the world.

His mother's voice sounded hoarse. Somewhere in the back of his mind was a notion that her vocal cords were probably paralyzed from the bite. He could just make out what she was saying. It was a question; she was asking if he forgave her.

"For what?" he asked, to say that he did, but he knew they had a lot more to get out, about how it was a two-way street and she had some forgiving that he'd be having to ask for soon.

"Love you," she said, voice and eyes too.

"I love you," he answered, loud enough for everyone in the room to hear.

Then the helicopter from the hospital was landing and people outside were yelling up at it.

They loaded his mom first, and even before they did, they gave her something, antivenin, he thought. They took the patchwork thing off her legs and they slit her jeans and he thought he'd puke when he saw how swollen that leg of hers looked.

Then they yanked his shoe and took a look at his foot and gave him a shot of something.

Meanwhile, Peyton was trying to be heard. She was telling Rachel what a cobra bite would do. It wasn't like what happened to her folks, she said, because a rattler's bite was different. First Rachel would be short of breath, she said, and get all blue trying to suck in enough air and then, before she passed out from that, she'd get these tremors, these quakes. That was how it had worked on Rob.

One of the cops in uniform held up a cassette recorder. "I read her her rights," he boasted. "It's all right here on the tape. Don't matter to her, though. She just keeps right on."

Shaw waved Zachary over to the car and then he looked around and yelled, "Hey, Gwendolyn, come on. You get to go with us, too."

The moonfaced girl ran toward the cop car. Her hair looked just as Drew had imagined it would when she rode her daddy's oil well: long and fine and spun out in a stream of silk behind.

He watched her out of the window of the copter as it started up, up, on its way to Brackenridge Hospital. He saw his mother straining, watching too.

"Pretty," his mom said, and she tried for a smile.

The attendant told his mother not to talk. "We'll be touching down in a couple minutes," he said, "and there'll be plenty of time for a family reunion then." Plenty.

Drew asked how long it would take Shaw to get Zachary and the girl to the hospital. Half an hour, he said.

His mother paid attention to what the attendant had said and didn't talk the rest of the way except for one word which she wrestled with and finally was able to make clear: "Family."

He closed his eyes and tried to picture what a patchwork quilt named Family would look like and he saw the four figures all in a row. They'd be holding hands. A border, maybe, or separate squares. He didn't know. That was his mom's department. All he knew was who they'd be. Himself and Gwendolyn and his mom and Zachary. Family, yeah.

He told his mom that and he didn't even have to be looking at her to know that she had smiled.

ACKNOWLEDGMENTS

I WOULD LIKE TO THANK Suzie Arnold, Rosemary Bacak, Ron Bernstein, Bob Rafferty, Paula Tremblay, Judy Wederholt, and Lori Fritz Williams, all of whom were kind enough to read an early manuscript of this book, and bold enough to make what turned out to be super suggestions. I'm grateful too, in the same regard, to Barbara Grossman and Lee Seifman, my editor and her assistant, at Crown and to my agent, Ellen Levine. I also want to thank Jack D. Kelley and Mark Booher, who gave me technical advice (on police procedure, in the first case, and on the mysteries of the Kaypro II, in the second).